KT-481-936

THE
IMPORTANCE
OF BEING
ME

CAROLINE GRACE-CASSIDY

BLACK & WHITE PUBLISHING

First published 2017
by Black & White Publishing Ltd
29 Ocean Drive, Edinburgh EH6 6JL

1 3 5 7 9 10 8 6 4 2   17 18 19 20

ISBN: 978 1 78530 124 7

Copyright © Caroline Grace-Cassidy 2017

The right of Caroline Grace-Cassidy to be identified as the
author of this work has been asserted by her in accordance with the
Copyright, Designs and Patents Act 1988.

All rights reserved.
No part of this publication may be reproduced,
stored in a retrieval system, or transmitted in any form,
or by any means, electronic, mechanical, photocopying,
recording or otherwise, without permission
in writing from the publisher.

This novel is a work of fiction. The names, characters
and incidents portrayed in it are of the author's imagination.
Any resemblance to actual persons, living or dead,
events or localities is entirely coincidental.

A CIP catalogue record for this book is available from the British
Library.

Typeset by Iolaire, Newtonmore
Printed and bound by CPI Group (UK) Ltd, Croydon, CR0 4YY

For my sister, Samantha.
There is no better friend than a sister.

part

1

1

"What has she got that I haven't got anyway?" I lament.

"Botox!" Claire responds without missing a beat.

I had just put fork to mouth, taking a monumental bite from her home-made banoffee pie. Banana, toffee and biscuit making my acquaintance: very pleased to meet you, my saccharine-tasting comrades. As the flavours erupt in my mouth I shut my eyes briefly in wondrous appreciation. God, I bloody love cake! Cake and a cup of hot strong tea. Easily pleased these days.

On opening my peepers, I see Claire smirking and spinning herself around on her stylish chrome high stool. It's one of those modern-type stools that wouldn't look out of place in outer space. Trendy. In vogue. Round and round she goes, pushing herself off the marble kitchen island with every turn to gain traction, like a beautiful, yet obviously disturbed, type of woman-child. Then she halts. Regaining her focus on me, she gathers her dizzy head together. Palms of her hands resting over each ear, she raises her sienna

Leabharlanna Poiblí Chathair Bhaile Átha Cliath

Dublin City Public Libraries

eyebrows as high as she can, pulling her soft, freckled skin taut across her cheekbones. I actually have to cover my mouth with my whole hand before I choke. It's uncanny. She is the spitting image of ... *her*. The look is hysterical. I begin to shake with laughter. Claire's eyes are pulled up so high they are almost popping out of their sockets. This is the look of beauty. Hollywood says so. I think Hollywood needs its Hollyhead checked, passing this look off as beautiful. What am I saying? I can't blame the rich and famous of La La Land any more – it's the look of our generation, right? I'm weary with contempt at how hard it is for women to age gracefully. When did age become such a brutal thing? Such a taboo? Didn't it used to be a rite of passage? A time to finally just be yourself. A well-earned thing. My Granny Alice embraced it. To be honest, she couldn't wait for it. Alice always sang to me the importance of being yourself and embracing where you are in life.

"Don't look too far back, Courtney. You're not going that way."

Alice would always tell me that, before she was robbed of her brilliant mind by dementia in her sixties. She had been my go-to person for everything in my life. Alice would just listen and pick me up, place me high upon that pedestal she so fondly held me on. Alice had embraced getting older: the purple rinse, the comfortable Softspot shoes, the free bus travel, the OAP offers. Now it's a dying generation of women. Older ladies as we once knew them are a dying breed, but I want to be one. I want to see them still represented in society. I want that wheeled trolley that all your shopping fits into. No more carrying or paying for evil plastic bags. I want the OAP half-portion roast beef

4

and potatoes and two veg and a dessert. I want people to give me a seat on the bus if it's full. I will have earned that much. For what reason do none of us want to age any more? I know one thing for sure: I want to not care what the mirror shows me some day. Just like Granny Alice. I'm eagerly anticipating that feeling. That acceptance. That freedom.

Claire remains frozen in time. She pouts her lips now in a ludicrous way and I jerk my head downwards still chewing. I cannot laugh. I must not laugh. With this mouthful, it will not be pretty if I do. Plus Claire's kitchen is absolutely spotless and I don't want to be responsible for wrecking all that Herculean work. Looking firmly at my black-and-white triple-striped runners, I chew faster the large wedges of banana. Determined to get it down, I swallow carefully. A banoffee spit festival avoided.

"You are quite correct, Mrs Carney, take a gold star from Ryan Gosling's unrivalled backside." I laugh freely before I lick the white cream from the prongs on my fork, musing on Ryan Gosling's firm bottom all the time. I feel like doing my happy dance, but I remain seated.

"Oh that I could. Actors, yes ... but especially professional tennis players ... Give me a bit of 1990s Agassi! Totally delicious, with or without the wig!" She moans out the words seductively and licks her lips now.

"Claire!" I laugh at her boldness.

"What? Just because you have willingly entered the nunnery! I'm still a full-figured, too-hot-to-handle hot-blooded woman." She shimmies her shoulders at me then makes a peace sign, a little like a Spice Girl might have done. Geri mainly. She's showing her age, but I won't tell her that.

"Eh, a hot-blooded happily married woman!" I hiss quietly across at her.

"Actually, Courtney, as a very happily married woman of fifteen years no less, I rely heavily on my imagination to keep it that way, I will have you know! That's how I keep it mucky in the bedroom. Every time Andy Murray has that shirt over his head at Wimbledon, showing off that rippling torso, I blink my eyes several times and take imaginary photos for my mind's memory bank. Click. Click. Click. Martin still maintains he fancies me, but Jaysus, with the lights off maybe. We'd be lost without the ole Internet for some sexual . . . well . . . for want of a better word, stimulation."

I hold up my hand immediately and she stops dead.

"Thank you! TMI!" I shout at her and she laughs.

She blinks over and over and over now and says, "How is it we talk about the whole kit and caboodle but you never want to hear about my sex life?" Screws up her nose, freckles waltzing.

"It's just not me . . . I don't talk like that . . . It's private." I shiver for dramatic effect.

"I know you don't have one!"

"Well, since, as you rightly point out, I don't have a sex life, I have no gross bits to share." I shrug my shoulders.

"Sex isn't gross, Courtney! It's bloody marvellous!" She does that sexy move with her shoulders again while rolling her tongue around her bottom lip. I shake my head in full amusement at my friend and sip my tea. Everything there is to know about Claire Carney I already know: her electronic bedroom antics with Martin she can keep to herself, thank you very much.

"However, we really should stop teasing her behind her back at this stage, it's not very nice. I don't mind it when I'm with you, but later on I feel very uncomfortable with myself. Bitchiness was never something I did well or was comfortable with." I grimace at her, referring to her earlier impressive impersonation.

"Oh for God's sake, why ever not? She doesn't deserve not to be teased behind her back! She puts the bitch in bitchiness! Bloody cheek of her! Bloody plastic cow! Moo!" Claire rubs her strained eyes after all that blinking as she rotates the stool again.

"Ah, come on, Claire, mocking is catching." I appeal to her softer side.

"Moo!" she repeats, then adds as she spins round, "What a favour she did you, though, Courtney: you and I both know that to be the truth, the whole truth and nothing but the truth. Mar-need David, Courtney no-need David. Good riddance!" Claire says as she goes round and round again on her kitchen travels. Ignoring her now, I drink my tea and examine my nails. Much in need of a polish. What is it they say, a pop of colour? The most overused expression in the world. Claire eventually stops in front of me and shakes her index finger firmly from side to side before she pulls the thin gold butterfly clip from her short red hair. She recklessly uses her teeth to re-open the slide and then fixes it back in her side fringe, taking it all back off her face. Tidier. Everything about Claire Carney is tidy. If she were a Little Miss book she'd be a mixture of Little Miss Tidy, Little Miss Neat and, well, between you and me, Little Miss OCD.

"She really did, I know that much. Ah, look, we both know I hadn't needed David for years." I fiddle with my fork on the side of my ornate Chinese-letter-decorated dessert plate and sit back, but not before I dance my baby finger around the edges collecting abandoned cream. I suck. Holy moly but it's good. Claire makes the most amazing banoffee pie. Claire makes Mary Berry look like a junior *Bake Off* contestant. She is really that talented. I keep telling her she should open her own bakery shop. In fact, she would tell you I've been harassing her for years to get her finger out. Granted, she has been making cakes for occasions from home for a few years now – masterpieces, I think – but that's why I know she can open her own place. Claire gets loads of orders locally for birthdays, christenings, weddings, and she can make a work of art.

We bond often over our mutual love of cooking and eating. I'm the savoury to her sweet. Cooking is something I both love and need to do. It's my passion. When I'm making food, I'm relaxed and totally in the moment. It all stems back to when Granny Alice would cook for me: it wasn't just dinner she was making, it was something different, something magical. It was theatre. Alice would make me taste her food as she cooked and guess the ingredients. She would sing opera while she cooked and tasted and ooh-ed and ah-ed, adding a pinch of this here and scattering a smidgen of the other there. Her Italian-born mother lived on. Legend had it Alice's mother Virginia once cooked her seafood linguine for royalty, but that's as far as the story goes! We had so much gaiety over food. A shared passion. Plus in those days I was proper hungry, you know? I ate porridge for my breakfast, then a light lunch and a hearty dinner. No snacks. No sweets except home-made desserts on a Friday. When I'm eating the food I prepare myself now, I feel sunniness, vim and vigour. Food and I have a very special relationship.

But I'm losing my train of thought. That's what food does to me! What I should be telling you is who Claire and I are laughing about. It's the woman my husband of fourteen years left me for. Mar-nee. Mar-nee Maguire. No, the hyphen is not a spelling mistake, that's how Mar-nee spells her name. Mar-nee is a beautician. A beautiful beautician, or so the world is trying to brainwash us to believe. Like I said, if that look is beautiful, I am clinically blind. Hopefully I am not on my own in my antipathetic opinion. Mar-nee has had a lot of work done to her face and other body parts. To be perfectly honest, it's hard to tell where plastic Mar-nee starts and human Mar-nee ends. We surmise, of course. David tells me categorically she is all natural, but of course she absolutely is not. She's definitely had fillers, as well as copious amounts of Botox in her forehead and around her eyes. Her eyebrows are so high they nearly hit her hairline, giving her the expression of someone who has just seen their parents having sex. Not to mention those bee-stung lips: so awfully bee-stung they must have enraged a ten-frame Langstroth hive of expectant queen bees! Then there is her chest area: let's just say it arrives a long time before she does. Mar-nee also has all that fake hair, a gazillion curly extensions, the colour ever changing. So much hair that whenever I see her I can't help wondering if in a past life she was indeed a little MarMaid. Tall. And rake thin. Obviously. But here's the thing. Mar-nee is who she is. Not my cup of tea, but what is one person's nightmare is another person's dream come true. Claire says that Mar-nee stole my husband from me. I do not concur. I think that Mar-nee met a very unhappy man who was fixing her stubborn blocked beauty salon toilet and just got to know him. Then she fell in love with him. Then took her chance. Oh, I have no doubt she encouraged the affair and then pushed him to leave me, but hey, *c'est la vie*. He's the one with the balls: he should have used them!

Now, I know this might sound like I'm telling you a great big dirty lie to protect myself, to save face, but I promise you I'm not. When I found out that David was having this affair, I didn't care. At all. I swear. I'd been expecting it for years. In a way, I think I'd been hoping for it. Subconsciously pushing him towards it. For example, when I was going through a self-help phase and reading *The Secret*, I asked the universe to make David happy. Subconsciously I knew what I was asking for: the problem was that I knew I couldn't make him happy because, you see, he couldn't make me happy.

Sometimes in my head, late at night or early in the morning over his slurpy Crunchy Nut breakfasts, I would dream up scenarios where David would meet another woman and move out. Leave me be. It's terrible, I know, but I'm telling you because it's the truth. And listen, I'm no dummy: I'd had all the usual affair clues in the months leading up to it. David was no Oscar-winning Al Pacino. He couldn't have dumbed down the signs even if he had bothered to try. He smelled different, and by different I mean he started to wear copious amounts of spray deodorant to work, soon followed by actual aftershave. I don't think he had even owned a bottle of aftershave since we were on our two-week honeymoon in Majorca, when I gifted him a bottle of Fahrenheit in the duty free on the way out there.

He also began to dress...well, again, differently. David's normal look was black jeans, a black shirt and black shoes. That was all he ever wore as far back as I can remember. His homage to his idol Johnny Cash, he used to joke. As the affair garnered momentum, he began to wear strange clothes. At first it was just a faded denim jacket, then this very out-of-character, swimming-cap-type white beanie hat. He came home one day with a huge Brown Thomas designer store bag. He had shuffled in the back door (no one uses the back door in our house except to put recycling in the green bin or to throw seeds out to the birds) and he was unlike himself. Shifty. Jumpy. Cagey. He'd ignored me diligently stirring the cream sauce for my seafood linguine at the cooker and walked swiftly past. For a second, a split second, I wondered had he bought me a gift. As I removed the herbs from my sizzling sauce, I'd heard him moving about upstairs. About twenty minutes later, he came back down and shouted into the kitchen from the hallway that he had to go out for a few hours, that the beautician's shop he was fixing the plumbing in was squealing again. (David called people who complained about his workmanship 'squealers'. We had a lot of them.) A heavy penny dropped in my mind. I turned off the heat, ruining my linguine, and a sniff of further destruction to come had filled my head.

Creeping out of the kitchen into the front room and pulling back my heavy silver curtains just a smidgen, I'd peered out the window. There he was, my husband, looking at his reflection in the wing mirror of his white *David Downey Plumbers 24/7* work van. In shock, I'd dropped the curtain, and when I'd grabbed it and pulled it back again my mouth fell open.

"What the actual hell?" I'd whispered into the curtain. He was dressed in sky-blue second-skin skinny jeans and a leather motorbike jacket zipped to his chin, with blazing white runners – those big ones kids wear. He was fixing his hair with his fingertips so it stood on end. He'd looked like one half of Jedward or, should I say, Dadward. Or should I say just plain awkward.

"Maybe, just maybe, be careful what you've wished for, Courtney," I'd whispered to no one as I watched him pull himself up into his van, check his face one more time in his rear-view mirror, scrub his teeth with his index finger and reverse out of the driveway. Slowly I'd dropped the curtain, walked back into my small kitchen and scraped the sauce into a Tupperware. Then I'd opened the fridge and pulled out a bottle of cold beer. Twisting the cap off, I'd leaned against the back door and drunk the bottle back in a few gulps. Relief had flooded through every part of my body. It was hard to put into words how I'd felt, but bizarrely the main word, I think, was hopeful. Hopeful that he was going to leave me. Or hopeful that now I knew he was having an affair I'd cop on and fight hard to get him back. Hopeful that my life was going to change, one way or the other.

And then I had said nothing. Done nothing. Questioned nothing. The blinkers were well and truly in place. Even when he'd arrived home that same night, hours later, flush-faced, whistling nervously and in the most incredible mood. I simply blocked it out of my mind as I got on with day-to-day living. In my own head, I couldn't figure out what to do. Over the next few weeks, as I let it sink in, I'd observed him as he treated his mobile phone like a suitcase with a soon-to-be-detonated bomb in it. He watched that phone like Jason Bourne. Occasionally, just to rile him, I'd ask him could I use his phone, pretending I couldn't find mine. He'd turn a whiter shade of pale.

"W-w-w-why? W-h-h-what?" he'd stammer.

"It's dead."

"I'm expecting a very important call now ..."

Occasionally he'd pretend a call had come in and it was an emergency job, but he'd forget to turn off the phone or even put it on silent and it would ring out as he was pretending to be on it! He made no attempt to have sex with me, but in fairness I didn't blame him. It wasn't anything new. Getting me going was like trying to jump-start a rusty old farmyard tractor. My sex drive had packed its suitcase and moved out years ago.

"So long, Courtney," it had waved back at me. "Nothing left for me here, pet."

Not David's fault, I must admit. He had tried and tried. Offered different solutions. Came home with books and DVDs and various colourful vibrating toys that I'd refused to even try. He was patient and gentle when we did have sex, but he knew what it was. Fake sex. A exercise in timing and fake moans on my part. He never complained. He never took it personally. Maybe he should have. Maybe I should have. Maybe I should have communicated that to him.

As the affair grew legs, weeks went by with David

avoiding being in the same room as me as much as he could. He worked very long hours. Squealers were coming in out of the woodwork. He even went so far as to get Mar-nee's friends to call the house and tell me about their leaking showers, leaking toilets and exploding boilers. Every time I'd ask for a number to call them back, but they'd mutter that they had David's mobile and would call him on that. Then he would call minutes later and moan that he had an emergency job to go to, so not to wait up for him. Of course I could have easily confronted him, asked where all this extra money was, but I didn't, because I couldn't make myself want to stop him. I didn't want him to end it and I still needed time to clear my head out.

However, four months later, when he did eventually tell me he was having, as he put it, "more than just a sordid affair" and that they were head over heels in love and he was leaving me and moving into her luxury apartment ... then I'd cried. I'd let this happen. They were a horrible mixture of tears: relief, sadness and absolute guilt. Relief for me. Sadness that I had failed at my marriage. Absolute guilt for our beloved only child, fourteen-year-old complete daddy's girl, Susan. Believe me when I say I was heartbroken for my beautiful Susan and what we had not been able to do for her. Keep her family unit together. Give her a so-called "normal upbringing". Put her needs before our own.

But I did not care at all about me being dumped, unwanted. It was peculiar. I didn't care that I couldn't keep my man. That my husband had rejected me for a younger model. I didn't care I was going to be divorced. I didn't care I was going to be alone. I still don't. I promise.

This worried me more. Why didn't I want a partner, a lover? Was I frigid? A horrible word, I know – a word, by the way, that David had never, ever thrown at me on any of the occasions I refused to have sex with him, although he easily could have. I fretted at the relief I felt at being on my own. Was that normal?

Like I said, there was Susan to consider and I cared deeply for her feelings, but the marriage really had run its course ten times around the block and back again. I'm not proud of the fact that's how I felt when my vows disintegrated, but I'd known for years that our marriage was dead. It should never have been brought to life in the first place. Had it not been for my ticking time bomb of a biological clock the day I turned a mere twenty-one years old, there would never have been a wedding at all. From that day on, I craved a child. No one understands this because I was so young, just starting out in life. When I met David at twenty-two, I knew exactly where I wanted my life to go. Marriage and kids. Marriage and kids. Marriage and kids. I take full responsibility for my actions. Yes, I was naive and needy and, by God, I learned my lesson. David was never the right partner for me. I married him for all the wrong reasons. Basically, I married David to have a child.

Anyway, this is all old news. It's over a year down the line now but myself and Claire are still slightly obsessed with the pair of them. Occasionally, like today, I feel a terrible guilt that we talk about David and Mar-nee behind their backs and say not-so-nice things about them as a couple. As human beings go, neither is really that bad. They both adore Susan, that's for sure. Mar-nee has no biological children of her own. Claire keeps tapping her finger at me when I say that and adding, "Yet." David and I are very much on speaking terms. Civil. Co-parenting. So we have to be okay with each other for Susan's sake. David is … How can I put this in our very PC world? Easily led. A follower. I rarely have one-to-one dealings with Mar-nee. When I see her, we nod at one another, exchange pleasantries. That's as far as it goes.

Claire goes on. "I know but when I saw them in Aldi on Thursday night and him in those distressed, tangerine drainpipe trousers, studded belt and poured into that three-sizes-too-small khaki bubble bomber jacket, I almost lost a dribble. This close."

Claire extends her hand and draws her index finger and thumb as close to each other as she can without them touching, and crosses her legs tightly. Claire has a tendency to pee when she laughs too much. Little Miss Dribble. Then she flaps her hands as though she is a bird trying to take flight. Sometimes Claire's abundance of energy exhausts me. Only sometimes, though.

"Oh, oh, oh, and his hair? I forgot to tell you about his hair! Dear Lord above, it's a kind of deep charcoal bluey-black now, but it's styled and flicked over one eye and I swear to you, Courtney, he walked into the trolley bay … twice!"

Claire wraps her hand over her mouth as she can see I'm not comfortable any more. I sigh. I can't help myself, but I'm about to keep this conversation alive.

"Why is she making him dress like that? Last month his hair was peroxide blond! All her doing. You know, I actually feel sorry for him, because if it wasn't for the fact that he publicly humiliated me and then ceremoniously dumped me for one of the Housewives of, literally, Orange County, I'd probably still be his wife. Every cloud." I curl my lip.

"You'd imagine being a beautician she'd be losing clients due to her fluorescent orangeness, right?" Claire has not forgiven Mar-nee for having an affair with a married man, nor has she forgiven David for having an affair while a married man. In Claire's world that is just not a forgivable offence. Period. Claire argues that he should have left me first.

I go on my familiar rant. "Like I always say, Claire, I'd probably still be absolutely cringing every time he pulled back the bed sheets and patted my side. Lying there in his faded-grey, shabby, ancient underpants. Me crying inside for my long-lost sex drive. I'd be going through the motions or else I'd probably be coming up with bigger and more bizarre excuses as to why I couldn't have sex. I must have had thrush at least 199 times during our last years of marriage. I said gross things about my vagina that no woman should have to say. I had a period every four days, for crying out loud! I'd still be bored to tears at his innumerable stories about the round of golf he played, dissecting it hole by hole as I ran away into the arms of a long-haired Mills & Boon man in my head. I'd probably still be making David just as miserable as I was and, no matter what you say, he didn't deserve to be miserable. He's not a bad man." I mean that sincerely.

"Do you like long-haired guys?" Claire is on it immediately. She has been trying to set me up with people on Tinder just so she can see what's going in there. Claire refers to it as "'in Tinder" instead of "on Tinder". It amuses me, like it's some hidden world. Tinder, however, scares the crap out of me.

"No. I do not. And I do not want a Michael Bolton look-a-like arriving at my office tomorrow morning, okay?"

"Michael Bolton hasn't had long hair in years."

I tilt my head to one side and glare at her. The glare says "back off".

"So I have to hear about your imaginary thrush and upset vagina, but you don't want me to talk about my married sex life. Is that right?" She laughs.

"Stop!" I hit my forehead with my hand. "Stop … Sorry, that just came out. Can we please just change the subject?" The remaining banoffee pie reminds me I simply can't leave it sitting there a second longer. Well, I could but I won't. Picking up my fork again, I dig in. Claire nods as she swirls her latte, gathering the leftover white foam from the side of her tall glass. Yes, Claire has one of those amazing latte-making machines. Claire's kitchen has it all. Every modern appliance. Grey slate floor, grey units with shiny chrome handles, utensils and pots and pans hung so low you need to duck your head, and an oven you could live in, it's that big. It's one of those kitchens from every glossy interior magazine that makes you say immediately, "Oh God, I need a new kitchen!" Claire's kitchen would not look out of place in an actual restaurant. Don't get me wrong. Like I said, I absolutely love cooking myself and I'm a bit obsessed with good food, but I've an old hob of an oven, a cracked microwave, ancient copper-bottomed pots and pans, and that's about it.

"A bit too sweet, this batch?" Claire nods her head at my dessert plate.

I run my tongue around my mouth, the back of my teeth especially. If I say so myself, I'm getting quite good at this testing lark.

"A tad too sugary maybe, love," I tell her truthfully as I feel grains still undissolved. She pulls a page off her pad and makes a note. I watch the freckles on her nose move around as she concentrates and pulls her concentrating face.

We have been friends since our college days. We both studied Drama & Theatre Studies in the Samuel Beckett Centre at Trinity College, Dublin. It was an instant connection. We were both only children, and the ease we felt in each other's company was wonderful. As we finished college and moved on, we both fought over the same auditions. Tough wasn't the word for those years. I worked really hard, but "nearly" just became a word I couldn't hear any more. My interest in acting began to wane and romance took over.

Claire was in the same club as me as far as her love life was concerned. She had met her boyfriend, Martin Carney, when she was only fourteen and they had become engaged at nineteen. Other people thought it was weird and that she was mad. I didn't. We both got married the same year. She was my bridesmaid. I was hers. Claire's decision in holy matrimony was a lot wiser than mine. Her EuroMillions numbers came up. Mine was a scratch-card that got soaked in the rain.

"I honestly still don't know how you stayed together for so long." Claire puts down the pen now, lifts her glass and props her chin on it, her elbows resting on the marble island.

"Nope, me neither. Stupid really. It wasn't David's

19

fault. I was twenty-two years old and on a mission, and hey, I got my Susan so ..." I trail off.

"We aren't discussing Susan today. That was the deal. It's us time." Claire's voice is soft but firm; she knows the trouble I'm having with Susan only too well. Poor Claire has to listen to it day in and day out. She's unbelievably understanding and supportive. I'm sure she has a very strong opinion on Susan's behaviour, but she simply sits on the fence most of the time and just listens to me ranting.

"You're right, and I suppose you're right too about me wasting all my best years. David and I were no toffee-and-biscuit combination, that's for sure," I say, licking my lips.

"Eh, I never said that, and you aren't exactly washed up, Courtney. You are only thirty-eight years old, a total ride-bag and people still say you look like Kate Winslet! Which you do! If I wasn't happily married, and you were gay and I was gay, well hey! We'd be a best-friends gay sandwich!" Claire is joking, but she is always telling me how beautiful I am. Bless her.

"Speaking of sambos, would you like a soft white roll with chicken and coleslaw?" she asks.

I shake my head and at the same time a tiny bit of leftover banana falls from my fork to the worktop. Claire is on it like a hawk; before I can blink, she has whipped out her blue J-cloth and it's gone. I snort out a laugh.

"Do you actually have a secret pocket that you keep cleaning cloths in?" I ask her in all seriousness.

"Funny, aren't you? If I am going to try and set up a business from my kitchen, like you and Martin keep banging on about, I have to keep it immaculate. When ...

20

If I decide to register as a business from home, the health board could call in at any time. I need to be in the habit of keeping it spotless."

Her eyes dart around the pristine kitchen. The blue cloth mysteriously vanishes again.

"You sure I can't tempt you to join me eating a sandwich? I abhor eating white carbs alone," she half jokes.

I shake my head again. "I'd still prefer you bought premises and set up a bakery with a real window where real people can see your cakes." It's more Martin pushing for the at-home business than me.

My phone rings out on the worktop and we both look at the caller ID: it's my uncle Tom. Claire makes a vomit sound as I press decline and put it back in my pocket.

"But it's all online now – you can see them all on there. I'll have my own website," she says.

"Not the same," I say with a light shrug of my shoulders. "Picture it: you're walking across Sandymount Green and suddenly you think you can smell baking. You sniff the air, à la Scooby Doo and his imaginary scent line. You know that sweet, fluffy scent … baking shortbread or vanilla essence. Like when you walk around Marks & Spencer and you're physically drawn to the baked-cookies counter. Then as you keep walking you stop outside the most amazing window: cakes of every size, shape and colour. Icing that looks so artistic it should be in a gallery. You push open the door and go in, and that smell … oh, you buy it all then! You can't smell a website, Claire." I have risen dramatically from my stool, arms outstretched for effect.

"Just as well you knocked the acting on the head and

21

decided to find holiday homes for people instead," she tells me as she claps very slowly.

I know deep down that an actual bakery would be a dream come true for her. But it's not really my business, it's her business, *their* business, so I move on. Change the subject.

"But actually, hang on, seriously … When people say to me I look like Kate Winslet, why do they always have to jump in with the follow-up: 'When she was in *Titanic*, mind you'. Never when she was in *The Reader* or *The Holiday* or *Revolutionary Road*. I'm a very specific Kate Winslet." I twist the fork to lick any remaining banoffee off the back of it now. The health board wouldn't like this.

"Because, you jammy cow, you don't look thirty-eight at all, you look thirty if a day! A younger Kate, and you have that incredible body shape that every woman wants. I'd kill for your figure. I am, as always, very seriously considering a gastric band." Her eyes narrow in disapproval at me licking her fork as she pulls at her stomach area.

"Have you got your eyes tested yet?" I laugh at her absurd comment before putting the fork back down. I am full! Why am I still licking cream off a fork? "Plus, I swear to God if you mention that gastric band again I'm making you put money in a swear box! I'm making a gastric-band box!" I mean it.

"But it would be the answer to all my problems!" She jumps off the stool now and runs her hands up and down her body. "Then I'd lipo the rest off. Here, here, here, here and here." It's like she's doing the dance to the "Birdie Song". She pulls at every part of her body.

"You don't want to be skinny, Claire," I say for the

millionth time. "Your head would be too big."

She answers me for the millionth time. "Oh yes I do, Courtney. Oh yes I bloody well do. Stick thin. I want the lollipop-head look. I want to one day stand beside Posh Spice and have people comment on how much weight she's put on! It's the bloody cakes. During the week when I don't have you here to feed and taste, I eat them all myself. I had an order for two lemon cheesecakes for the women's bridge club yesterday, but of course I made three, didn't I? Did I come up with a good business plan and do a buy-two-get-one-free deal for them? My big fat arse I didn't – I sat down in front of *Loose Women* and devoured the whole extra cake with a hot pot of tea!" She pretends to wail as she sits down again.

"Big deal, Claire, who are you trying to impress anyway? Martin loves you for who you are. He has loved you since you were fourteen years old, for God's sake." I hate when she is down on herself and how she looks.

"It's not about Martin, it's about me. I despise being fat. I lust after beautiful clothes, Courtney. Fashion. I'd give anything to walk into River Island and buy off the peg."

"We have been through this a million times, though. I've gone to Weight Watchers with you how many times now?" I point at her accusingly.

"Eleven."

"Eleven. Exactly. And you have quit after the second weigh-in every time."

"I don't like the leaders, that's why! They are so patronising and I just want to eat every time I see their smug faces!" She wails some more. "I can't even watch the

Kardashians any more. Khloe's gone and ruined it for me. She was the only reason I watched: to see how she coped with all those skinny sisters!"

"Khloe got fit ... and plastic, but that's another day's argument. You want to get fit, that's different, but don't keep torturing yourself about size ten River Island jeans, Claire. I, on the other hand, am the single loser – I should be the one out there, like you say, inside the Tinder machine!" I tell her, waving my hands, magician-style, in front of her.

Her face is suddenly serious. "I don't think you have ever understood just how beautiful you are, Courtney." Claire isn't laughing now. Her shining green eyes glare at me and I know she's trying to push me to get out there and date again. It's just I have no interest. Zero interest in meeting a new man, or men. No interest in ever meeting another man ever again. I'm happy with my living situation – just Susan and me and a job that I'm happy in that keeps food on our table and pays my bills. I never had the boy obsession. Teenage lust skipped right on past me. There wasn't a band I goofed over or an actor I thought I was in love with. Hearts were never scrawled across my school books or school bag. I never hearted anyone all through my school years. In fact, I never had a boyfriend until David. There had been kisses behind bike sheds during games of spin the bottle, the odd slow dance at Friday-night discos at the local GAA hall and even a few boys asking me out, but I was just never interested. I loved cooking for me and Alice and babysitting for my neighbours at weekends. Boys just weren't my thing.

"If you weren't my best friend, I'd hate you. I'd give

you filthy looks in the street. You always look amazing and hardly ever try. Me, I never look amazing and I always bloomin' well try. Try to hide every flabby inch on my ever-expanding torso." Claire pats her stomach now. Then pretends to use it as a punchbag. "G-g-g-gas ... G-g-g-gastric ..." She holds her fleshy tummy between her two hands.

"Stop," I say softly. I know only too well how much Claire struggles with her weight and it's a daily battle of self-destruction, starvation and bingeing. Claire has done every diet known to man. She's lived off apples and water, cayenne pepper and honey, chicken and salad, fish and peas, water and oranges. It's always some new craze, except juice detox. That's never going to happen.

A bang comes from upstairs and Claire pulls herself off the stool by the heavy marble worktop with a long, guttural sigh.

"How is he? Any better?" I raise my eyes to the white drywall ceiling to enquire about her man-flu victim of a husband upstairs. She rolls her sea-green eyes.

"God, Courtney, he's absolutely wrecking my head. You'd swear he had the worst flu since swine flu mated with the Zika virus. I'm up and down those stairs like a yo-yo. It's times like these I'm glad we don't have kids, otherwise every day would be like this!" She winks at me. There is no reason why Martin and Claire don't have children other than the fact that Martin did not want children in his life. When Claire told me this very matter-of-factly one night in the early days over my home-made margherita pizza, I was immediately alarmed. Not because Martin didn't want children, that was totally Martin's decision, but because

25

Claire had often talked about kids and she seemed to be putting on a brave front of sorts. We had been in my kitchen in Dun Laoghaire not long after I moved in with David, the Christmas before both of our weddings.

"You seriously make the most incredible pizza ever!" Claire had said as she pulled at the slice in her hand, the stringy cheese coming with her. "You are feeding my addiction! If pizza was a man I'd be having an affair!" she'd muttered through her full mouth, her then long red hair tied in a side ponytail.

"I think I have finally mastered the perfect pizza. It's getting the thin base just right so it doesn't crumble in your mouth and remains firm, with a bite to it. I use a really good-quality olive oil and a little over the recommended two hundred millilitres of warm water."

I'd sprinkled more freshly grated Parmesan over the top as she casually said, "So, Martin and I have finally agreed that children are not on the cards for us." She'd looked down at her phone and used her wetted finger to pick up loose shavings of cheese, avoiding my eye.

"Oh...oh. Can I ask why?" I'd held the grated Parmesan bowl steady in my hand.

"It's just what we both want. I'm going to get the coil fitted before the wedding." She'd lifted her wine glass, swirled the red liquid and taken a long drink.

"Right." I'd put the Parmesan back in the middle of the table.

"We just think that we can do more things you know? Martin really wants to travel...He wants to see India, and the world, really." She'd removed a cherry tomato from the pizza and popped it into her mouth.

"Can't you have children and travel too?" I'd gently probed while pretending to busy myself uncorking a bottle of red.

"No ... no ... Because you see, we need to be able to live freely, go wherever we want at the drop of a hat. We do not want to be tied down."

I hadn't liked how her voice had sounded. It wasn't like her normal voice. It was rehearsed. But I hadn't questioned their joint decision any further, and it's something that has nagged at me ever since. Troubled me. I'm not sure why I said nothing else. I just got a feeling that was the way she wanted it. She was telling me, not asking me. Her mind was made up.

I won't lie, it puzzled me no end in the early days, especially after we all got married, when I was a self-confessed how-can-I-get-pregnant-quicker Nazi. Claire would listen to me talk about ovulation sticks and seemed slightly distant. When the four of us would go for a "fun" night out, I'd only drink bottled water because I was trying to get pregnant, and she'd tell me to live a little. When I wouldn't eat any of Claire's baking as I was off dairy – one of those old wives' tales said it aided fertility – she'd say, "This is why I do not want to have a baby." When I was obsessed with getting more vitamin B into my body and lived only on dull, dark leafy vegetables, she'd be eating chocolate donuts and lasagnes and white crusty rolls filled with hot chicken and butter. I was a bona fide pain in the arse. Sometimes I'd look at Claire and wonder how on earth she didn't want to be a mother. I couldn't for the life of me understand that about her. The want and physical need inside me was that strong. Looking back, it doesn't seem so hard to understand how watching me would put any woman off ever wanting to get pregnant. I wasn't much fun to be around. And especially now that I am the very proud owner of a moody, stroppy, sullen soon-to-be sixteen-year-old daughter, most days I get it. Kids are hard work, worth every ounce of labour, and everything thereafter, and I adore and worship the very ground my daughter walks upon, but still and all, hard bloody work.

"It's the second time this month he's been taken down with it. I told him to get the flu jab in school, but he laughed at me. You know, Martin, Mr Health and Fitness. He is sorry now. He just seems to be picking up every virus going around in that school." Claire pulls me back as she rests her hand on the slim gold handle of the kitchen door.

"He needs to boost up his immune system. Is he taking Vitamin C and zinc?" I ask.

"Martin? Martin Carney taking a tablet? How long have you known my husband, Courtney?" Claire does a double take and checks a watch that isn't on her wrist.

"Will he still never go to see a doctor? He still never takes tablets?" I shake my head, astounded.

"Never! Imagine, Martin has never been to the doctor in his whole life." Claire lowers her voice slightly.

"Not even as a kid?" I follow suit, lowering my voice, although I don't know why.

"Nope. Martin's mum – Mrs Carney Senior, as she likes to refer to herself – used home remedies for everything. Sure, he has me making poultices and putting them on his head. Here we go, what does he want me to do now? Boil his jocks in whiskey and rub them over his face perhaps?" She opens the door with a creak. I burst out laughing, and before she leaves the kitchen she pulls a book off the red laminated cookbook shelf. She pretends to lick the book cover. Then she holds it out to me. It's a biography of TV chef Jamie Oliver.

"Get out, you lunatic!" I say, laughing at her as she slips the book neatly back into its place.

The smell of cinnamon is making me hungry again. Maybe that why I'm *Titanic* Kate? A bit more meat on her bones back then. I run my hands down my thighs. Bit more meat on mine since the affair I know, that's for sure, but I think I look the better for it. Most people who are victims of spousal affairs can't eat, can't sleep, write wonderful, tragic poetry, or so I hear. Not me. I ate like a horse, and slept like a lamb, having my big double bed all to myself. Purposely I lay across my bed instead of down it, just because I could. I watched box set after box set of my own glorious girly choosing. I felt free. The single me relished the independence I had. I cooked food that I loved but that David always hated, in abundance. Lamb, for example. I roasted lamb shoulders with rosemary and garlic. I fried up lamb and chickpea curries. I did spring lamb kebabs with sun-dried tomatoes, yellow peppers and red onions. At night I made leftover lamb and mozzarella hot toasties and ate them in bed. I did it all. I ate it all. I loved it all, though admittedly I'd say there are fewer lambs left in the country, I ate that many.

By the way, to get back to Claire's rather flattering comparison, I'm very happy to be compared to Kate Winslet. I think it's the highest of compliments. I suppose I do have similar features. I have pale skin, large lips and big, wide, blue eyes with wavy, unruly long blonde hair.

29

Unlike the Oscar winner, however, mine was a short-lived acting career. My want for the norm was, looking back, quite bizarre. I thought I'd never get up that aisle and get my legs up in those stirrups. Poor David never really stood a chance. My body had an overwhelming urge to procreate.

No one really understands this primal need I had, I don't think. It took over my body. That's the only way I can explain it to you. It was a need like no other. An itch that I just couldn't get relief from no matter how hard I scratched. It was common for me to approach strangers with new babies in the street and try to sniff them (the babies, not the strangers!). I was obsessed.

Getting auditions was never a problem for me, but landing a job was. Possibly my Winsletty look was getting me through the door. I trod the boards in various theatres and had a part-time job with an events company, but I thought about having babies every single day. When I met David at a charity auction I was working at, and he told me over a bidding war on a Pro Golf lesson that he was single with a steady job and his own business, that was all I needed to know. Pathetic, right? I wholeheartedly agree. Courtney Downey the Venus flytrap. I was only twenty-two and very innocent for our times, probably because of how I was brought up, and it didn't seem to matter that David and I had absolutely nothing in common.

I lift Claire's glass, my empty teacup, cutlery and my practically clean plate and take them over to the sink to wash. It's odd, I guess, to most people that at the age of thirty-eight I have never been in love. Well, I am completely and utterly in love with Susan, that is true love,

30

but you get what I mean. Never have I felt those fireworks shoot up my stomach or had my knees turn to jelly. Those proverbial fireworks are still waiting to explode. I would have said it's all bullshit and that it doesn't exist, except when I see Claire with Martin, and then I know it truly does exist. Claire is head over heels, shooting stars, jellied knees, and extravagantly, pyrotechnically in love with her husband.

I really like Martin Carney. He's one of the most personable people you could ever meet. His personality is larger than life. He commands a room or a dinner-party table. Educated, great-humoured and confident. I wouldn't say we are very close friends, but we get on just fine. David used to say Martin was unreadable, but since the split Martin has always looked out for me and Susan. He will offer to do things for me around the house: things I think he considers are Man Things. I never take him up on the offers, as I can do all the Man Things myself, but I appreciate the thought. He is a careers guidance officer in the local secondary school and the kids absolutely adore him. Best advice-giver is whispered a lot on the grounds of St Jude's. Martin always dresses to impress the students. He wears a uniform of a crisp white shirt, polka-dot dickie bows, colourful waistcoats and black trousers, and his black patent-leather shoes are always exceptionally shiny. Martin is as immaculate as his good wife.

Claire comes back in, carrying a brown furry covered hot water bottle, a *Father Ted*-captioned cup and a blue bowl and crosses her kitchen to the sink beside me. "Just thinking there actually, Mrs Ex-Downey – please go back to your own name – I couldn't be Martin's friend if he ever left me, although Martin has a functioning brain, unlike ditzy David." I take the items from her hands and she bends down and opens the oven, looks in and makes a few humming sounds. Again I smell cinnamon. And familiarity.

"Another twenty minutes should do these, I think." She closes the oven by flicking her foot and catching the half-open oven door with the heel of her flip-flop. Claire is dressed in a pair of loose three-quarter length khaki combats, a white flowing man's dress shirt and the aforementioned flip-flops. Her cropped red hair requires no maintenance really, apart from a grip to keep her side fringe from falling over her left eye. She is make-up free, apart from her signature black-kohl cat's-eye flick at the sides of her green eyes. She's so striking. I never see her weight like she does. We stand side by side. Both exactly five feet six inches.

"How is he, Nurse Carney?" I ask her hurriedly in an American accent, as one might ask a nurse in the ER. She grins as she watches me squeeze lemon-scented washing-up liquid into the sink. She turns the tap on for me and leans against the worktop, facing me. Claire has one of these jet-spray-type taps I still cannot work without drenching the whole area. I swirl it to whip up some bubbles. She whips out the magic blue cloth and mops up my mess. Not answering me, she appears to be deep in concentrated thought. I repeat my question.

"How is he, Nurse Carney?"

"He's a bit out of it actually ... odd ... like the fever still has a hold, but he refuses to take any paracetamol so he's just going to have to suffer and sweat it out of himself.

But I've never seen him so subdued. He said his head is literally pumping off his shoulders, so I guess that's why." She looks me in the eye, and now she seems happy that she has worked out why Martin is acting so strangely, so she continues, a little more humour now in her voice.

"Current demands are simple: flat 7UP and another hot water bottle, although he's already on fire. No request for boiled jocks in whiskey, I am happy to report. I'm going to change the sheets when you head off to the shops, they are soaking wet. Get him to have a cool wash." She turns back to the complicated running tap and expertly turns it off. We both mull this over as I wash the dishes, leaving them to drip dry on her two-tier dish rack and we return to sit at the island in the centre of her kitchen.

This Sunday afternoon pretty much sums up my life right now. Susan spends the weekends with her dad, so I relax at Claire and Martin's, sampling her cakes and giving my humble culinary opinions while she makes notes. Occasionally, like today, we slag off David and Mar-nee. I know it's not very nice, but it is a distraction from the decision I have to make by the end of the month. The decision that is hanging over my every waking moment. Today is the sixteenth of May. The aforementioned decision needs to be made, and on my boss Lar Kilroy's desk by ten o'clock on the thirty-first of May. It's the offer of a lifetime where my career is concerned and I've worked really hard for it, but my life isn't only mine. I have a precious daughter to consider.

To make matters worse there is a new girl in town, or in our office anyway: Yvonne Connolly, all bouncy black blow-out hair, blinding suits and chalk-white teeth, who also happens to be brilliant at her job. I should know: I trained her. Never expected she would be so good so soon. She is just waiting for me to turn this job down and her name is all over it. I've worked too hard to let that happen but I have to listen to my daughter too, don't I? At the end of the day, I'm a mother first and foremost. But I really want it. For the first time in years, I'm actually excited about something for me.

2

After my banoffee-and-bitching session with Claire, and with my well-worked-out-to-the-rounded-cent, budgeted weekly shopping crammed into the boot of my tiny white Peugeot, I take a leisurely drive home. These days I have to go compare. I buy milk and bread in one supermarket, my meat and chicken in another, and my cleaning products in yet another. It will be five o'clock before David drops Susan home. David's timekeeping now that he's with Mar-nee is perfection. She has made several positive David improvements, I have to give her that much.

David was actually late for his own wedding. I'd had to circle the church five times waiting for him to turn up. Granny Alice had grunted and gritted her teeth beside me in the bridal car, holding my clammy hand tightly in hers. Uncle Tom had cruelly laughed in the front, saying, "Knew that fella was a complete knob. Looks like yer still on the shelf, Courtney." Eventually David turned up, oblivious to the small panic he had created. He'd been watching the Masters by all accounts and lost track of time. Go figure.

Claire and Martin's house overlooks the sea on Sandymount Strand so I take the coastal route home to my house in Dun Laoghaire. As I drive I allow my mind to drift slightly. I try to organise my weekly schedule in my head, but as always my mind floats straight to my pubescent daughter, Susan. The reason Claire did not want to discuss Susan today is that mother and daughter are going through a real rough patch. Dangerous ground is being trod upon. Susan is no longer overly fond of me, her mammy, or, as she calls me in her American accent, her mom. These days I am sworn enemy number one and I do not like this phase in our relationship. I do not like it one bit. Obviously all I want is for her to be happy, but I honestly don't know if she is or not. There is so little connection and communication between us right now. We used to have a brilliant relationship before the spilt. But now I'm constantly on her back, according to her, and it's true. I am. If you see her Snapchats, you will see me literally behind her back, sneaking up on her, despairing of her every move being Snapchatted to God knows who. Nothing in my house is private. Every inch of it has been Snapchatted to the world, from my toilet to my messy wardrobe. It's almost like Susan can't live without telling people she is living.

Walking into the kitchen. "I'm walking into the kitchen."

Opening the fridge door. "No nice food in the fridge again."

Standing in the middle of the kitchen. "Kitchen floor needs mopping."

In the back garden. "Mom's empty wine bottles need the bottle bank."

Opening the press. "Down to the last teabag."

Dull. Dull. Dull. I cannot see the point in it. Susan lives in a world of social media. It consumes her life. Her every waking moment. The world's top surgeons couldn't remove that iPhone from her hand if they tried. It is now an extension of her arm. Honestly, it riles me every time I try to talk to her and it keeps beeping and beeping and beeping and beeping and beeping some more and I don't know why I get so utterly mad. Yes, it is 2017, it's what they all do. I know that.

"It's two zero one seven, Courtney, it's what they all do," David tells me all the time when I call him to complain and ask him to talk to her. I ask him whether we're monitoring it closely enough. Just because it's what they all do, does that make it right? How safe is it all really?

"Chillax. It's just a bit of harmless fun," is his repetitive answer. I don't think David had ever heard the word "chillax" until he met Mar-nee Maguire. Now he uses it in almost every sentence to me, and we have to talk a lot. You see, we never went to court, David and me. I know. I might live to regret that decision. We just decided it was best for Susan if we could manage our affairs in private and slip easily into our new lives with as little upheaval as possible, so we agreed to co-parent. Thankfully the break-up was all very quiet and low-key, as we had Susan's best interests at heart the whole way through. The night we told her was horrendous, though.

As the traffic lights turn amber, I brake slowly, press the clutch, wiggle the gear stick to be sure I'm in neutral, and pull up the handbrake. An older couple pushing a double buggy wisely make sure I've fully stopped before they trust the green man. They both look exhausted. I think back.

We were sitting down to dinner in our kitchen and every bite stuck in my throat. I'd made our family Friday-night favourite on a Monday. My much-loved grilled chicken breast, sweet garden pea, red onion and wild mushroom risotto with Avoca's pink lemonade. "Second-helpings Friday" as David used to call it. Susan's suspicions were immediately aroused as she stood by me, my eyes watering, chopping spring onions. Susan was fourteen but very clued in. She knew we were fighting about stuff and heard all the badly hushed conversations, but I was so careful to shield her as best I could. Occasionally she would say, "I know you and Dad hate each other, Mom." I would tell her not to be so silly, that I certainly did not hate Dad at all. Eventually it was me who broke my little girl's heart.

"Susan, Daddy and I have decided we cannot be married to each other any more. Daddy is going to move out." Harsh words, no sugar coating for her: just the truth. Don't get me wrong, I didn't just blurt this out; I had been on every break-up advice website from Dublin to Toronto. Truth was the only way. Truth, the whole truth, and nothing but the truth.

"I fell in love with someone else, sweetheart, it's not all Mammy's fault," David had stupidly spat out after we had absolutely decided not to tell her that bit. I'd gripped my glass so tight I'm amazed it didn't shatter into a metaphor for our broken family life. Susan had just looked at us both. Her bright eyes were glazed, but she was composed. Her risotto was largely untouched.

"Who did you fall in love with, Daddy?" she'd asked carefully. My heart had lurched into my throat.

"A lovely lady called Mar-nee, beautiful, sweet, sweet Mar-nee Maguire, and I know you will really like her, sweetheart. I'm going to be staying with her, but she's so lovely and she'd love to have you come stay too – she has a spare box room that just has salon supplies in it right now and says you can do it up as you wish. I thought the three of us could go to IKEA and—"

I'd slammed my hands down on the table and immediately regretted it. The upside-down glass ketchup bottle had toppled over. I had been trying to get the sauce at the end of the bottle out. Susan had yelped.

"Sorry … sorry. Please, David, now isn't the right time to discuss Mar-nee. We need to talk about Susan and her feelings," I'd implored.

"Calm down, Courtney, eh? Chillax." David had folded his arms defensively. The first "chillax" had been thrown my way. I had tried to compose myself beside this bloody idiot.

"I am really calm, David, I just want us to focus on Susan and how she is feeling right now." I'd grabbed a bobble on my wrist and tied my long hair up in a topknot for something to do with my hands. The kitchen clock had ticked so loudly all three of us looked up at it. The small hand counted down our last meal as a family. No one had eaten. No one had spoken until at last Susan pushed back her chair, scraping it off the tiled floor (normally a no-no), coughed and then said quietly, "It's grand, whatevs … I knew anyway." She had slid the screen of her iPhone across, illuminating her drawn face, then held the phone out at arm's length and made a sad face into the screen.

"So … Mom and Dad hate each other, Dad taking off." She actually Snapchatted our breakup. They were our daughter's final public words on the matter of her parents' marital break-up and her father moving in with his new, younger girlfriend.

Now, I push my foot down hard on the clutch and move into first, pressing the accelerator softly. When David had finally moved out, Susan had stood by his plumbing van sobbing and sobbing. The neighbours, taking for ever to put out their brown bins, watched it all. No doubt David had told them all our private business already. When he drove away I'd cuddled my shaking little girl, but something had changed in her. I'd felt it instantly. She seemed stiff, aloof, far away. I'd held her as tightly as I could and made soothing sounds and told her how much I loved her and said over and over again, "Everything is going to be all right, love."

"I'm going on the iPad in my room," was all she had said back to me as she'd ducked out of my embrace, and she pretty much stayed in her room on that iPad for the next year and a half. For some bizarre reason, I felt that she blamed me.

Our routine is that Susan stays with me during the week and David and Mar-nee at weekends. Holidays are shared out equally. The first Christmas was the hardest. Our first one as a broken unit. What we'd agreed was that David has her for Christmas Eve each year and Christmas Day Susan spends with me. But the problem is Susan wants to spend more time with her dad and Mar-nee. I'm not stupid – I know why. They are very lenient on her and the time she spends on the phone and iPad. David thinks social media is all fine and just a part of growing up nowadays. A bit of fun. Chillax, Courtney. But I don't find it fun. Not one single bit. I don't get a single laugh out of it. We used to laugh all the time, me and Susan, before the split. God knows who she's laughing with now in her Snapchat world. We laughed so hard I have the lines to prove it. I'd slap my knee, throw my head back and freely guffaw with her.

I relax my feet, look up and risk a wry smile in the rearview mirror. Avert my eyes quickly. Crow's Feet Winslet. Listen, I can be against Botox but I can still have a moan about ageing.

Susan and I were so close. Like, ridiculously close. Cooking was something we did together every evening: she'd be my helper. When she was much smaller we would play cookery school. Susan would be the head chef and I played her commis chef. I was teaching her to cook and she was having so much fun, covered in flour and other messy ingredients. At weekends we went horse riding to a local school and we'd take the hacks around the area together. David worked Saturdays and Sundays on call-outs most of the time so I would drive her to parties or we'd go to Dundrum and browse the shops, sipping smoothies and enjoying one another's company.

When she hit thirteen, the change occurred. Perhaps a coincidence, I will never know, but it was just after David insisted we get her an iPhone for Christmas. Now we rarely do anything together, never mind laugh. Well, Mar-nee makes her laugh all the time, she tells me.

I stare up into the mirror again, lick my index finger to

wipe some running liquid eyeliner from under my ice-blue eyes. I used to be the person who Susan said saw the good in everything and was so lovely. Courtney Downey, her mum, her glass was always half full. Courtney Downey, her mum, she's great craic. Courtney Downey, her mum, always up for a laugh. "Mum, I love the way we are best friends!" She'd hug me closely.

"Mothers aren't supposed to be best friends with their daughters," Claire used to say, and I used to disagree with her.

"Why not?"

"Well, because you need to point out all the shit they are doing wrong ... No one wants a BFF like that," she'd answered truthfully.

"I do that too!" I'd argued.

"You don't, Courtney ... You never tell Susan anything negative."

"What's that supposed to mean?" I had got stroppy and defensive.

"I'm not meaning anything ... I'm just saying if you treat her as a best friend, she has no boundaries, right?"

I ponder this old conversation now as I turn to look at the calm summer evening tide. Holding the button down on my electric window, I inhale the seaweed and salted air. I'm sure Claire was right, of course. What I hate most of all now is I'm so regularly angry with Susan. It's just not me. That's not the type of person I am. Sometimes when I am deep in an argument with her I don't understand who I have become. I'm not someone I like. I forget to be grateful for all the blessings I have. Her. Our health. My job. Having my only other blood relative, my maternal grandmother, Alice, still with me on this big green earth.

Slipping the car into fourth gear, I drive on up the free open road. The truth hurts me deeper than I let myself feel. That truth is that for the last year Susan has preferred Mar-nee to me. Pathetic to think, pathetic to admit, but it cuts like a knife.

"She just gets me, Mom, she's just more on my wavelength," Susan had almost shouted at me only last night when I asked her to put down the phone and stop FaceTiming Mar-nee and get into bed. She'd corrected me and told me they were Snapchatting before she threw the phone onto her cluttered dressing table and then asked again to spend one night mid-week in Mar-nee's luxury apartment. Purposely I'd ignored the request and asked her, "Where are Sophie and Emily? Why are you always talking to Mar-nee on that thing?" I was referring to the two girls on our road who still call for Susan though she seemed to have completely dropped them. I realised I sounded like a dinosaur when I referred to Snapchat as "that thing".

"They are so immature, Mom. Like, I never hang out with them any more. Plus Sophie doesn't even have a Snapchat and Em's mother is always watching every move she makes." Susan shuddered.

"Immature as they might be, they have been your friends since you were six years old!"

"People move on, Mom." Susan had dragged her dark ponytail from her bobble and run the pink Tangle Teezer through it.

"People, not fifteen-year-old girls." I had picked up five dirty glasses from her dressing table and stood at her door.

"Sophie still goes horse riding with her mom and Emily just wants to walk around the estate all day looking for John Murphy from number six. John looks like such a loser on his skateboard, I can't cope . . . literally!" She facepalmed herself.

"I don't think you are being very kind, Susan." I'd clinked the dirty glasses off one another.

"Maybe you just don't get me, Mom." She'd picked up a tub of some kind of expensive salon moisturiser and twisted the lid off.

"Aren't you a bit young to be using so many products on your skin?" I'd exclaimed.

"It's never too early to start looking after your skin, Mom! I mean, you really don't take proper care of your skin. Like, Mar-nee can't understand how you never tone?" She hadn't meant to be hurtful, I know that. She must have seen the look on my face. "I-I-I-I-I mean you are super pretty, Mom. You have good skin . . . for your age . . . You know you could get rid of the bags under your eyes with Bag 'N' Vanish – it's the latest top-of-the-range eye-care machine Mar-nee has – and a little dab of Botox at the sides of your eyes. There's a lot we could do with you!" She'd jumped off the bed and approached me. With her index fingers raised, she'd brought them up to the sides of my eyes and pulled back my skin. Looking really pleased with herself, she'd said, "There! See! Come look in the mirror, Mom." She was delighted with herself. I, however, was offended and I simply couldn't play along. I'd removed her hands slowly.

"Thanks, Susan, but I'm happy to grow old gracefully," I'd said, trying to keep the hurt out of my voice. I know she hadn't meant to upset me.

"Just so you know, no one else is!" She'd padded away in her bare feet.

"I hope you aren't ever considering messing with your beautiful face when you're older?" My voice had gone an octave too high.

"I'd do it now if I could. Kylie Jenner had her lips done at sixteen; Kris, that's her mom, is *so* cool and she's, like, absolutely ancient but looks shamazing," Susan had informed me.

"Kylie Jenner looks ridiculous," I'd said, and meant it. The poor child. What will she look like in twenty years' time?

"Oh please!" She'd pulled back the yellow and white daisy-print duvet cover.

"You really think she looks pretty?" I'd asked, bemused.

"I think Kylie Jenner is the most beautiful girl in the world, Mom. Everyone does." She'd slid under the covers, pulling the duvet up over her chin, and I wanted to cry.

"Good night, Susan." I'd flicked off the light, completely disheartened. All this image obsessiveness really worries me. Susan. Susan. Susan. My heart's desire. The one true love of my life. My nine-pound, eight-ounce bundle of absolute joy. My swinging-pig-tailed, soother-sucking two-year-old. My clingy junior infant. My delightful Communion girl. My ten-year-old cooking buddy. My only child. Now, my moody soon-to-be sixteen-year-old. College not too far away. I can't get her to go anywhere with me any more without a bribe, but Susan and Mar-nee go shopping together. I don't know what age Mar-nee actually is, it's hard to tell through the stretched skin and chemical desperation, but she actually dresses like Susan:

45

green bomber jackets, denim shirts, dark leggings and Timberland boots.

"Please, Mom … Before you go downstairs, please … You didn't answer my question. Please let me crash at Mar-nee and Dad's one night during the week?" she'd begged.

"No. No way. It's not on, Susan, you already spend every weekend there. That's the deal. You live with me during the week. I'm not having this argument again, love." I'd shut the door quietly behind me. I had tried to be understanding. Had tried to hide my hurt. Again.

Turning the corner, I head towards our suburban house: 16 Clover Green Hill. It was actually left to David when his mother passed, so he already lived there mortgage-free when I met him. To be honest with you, it's never really felt like my home. David very kindly lets Susan and I remain there: less disruption for her. I pay him some rent – a very small amount, it has to be said. He has to pay half of Mar-nee's colossal luxury-apartment-complex mortgage since her tenant moved out to make way for him, so he gives us very little. He pays for Susan's phone bill and the medical insurance and that's about it. I can manage. I have a really good job. I don't want anything from David other than for him to be a great dad to Susan. And he is, I have to give him that. No, he's not a great disciplinarian, but he loves the very bones of that girl. Our agreement, the verbal one, is that Susan and I can stay there until Susan is eighteen and then we re-discuss the living arrangements. Claire is beyond maddened by this. She is always pointing out that I have no legal leg to stand on. Claire doesn't trust David one iota any more.

"So what if he and Mar-nee decide to have a baby and they want to move into Dun Laoghaire? For all we know, under all that botulinum toxin she could be twenty-five! Use your brain, Courtney!"

But what can I do? Other affordable property options aren't really waving me down in the street. I can't afford to buy a house now, or ever, and it is Susan's home. Granny Alice's house in Inchicore is rented out by my uncle Tom to students to pay for her nursing home. Anyway, David would never kick us out. Planning has never been one of my greatest gifts, or saving for that matter.

I don't really remember my own family home. My parents both died within ten months of each other when I was six years old, and I only have one or two very vague memories. Playing on a makeshift tyre swing with a thick blue rope attached to the tree in the back garden, which my dad made for me, and my mam spooning chocolate sauce over my square-shaped ice cream. I remember how I had to wait for seconds before it hardened, then I'd crack it with my spoon.

My dad was killed in a motorbike accident on his way to work in the local garage and my mother, who had been ill for many years with MS, passed ten months later. My beloved maternal granny, Alice Bedford, took me in and gave me the most beguiling life. Alice's only son, Tom, was a lot older and had married and moved out before I ever moved in. Alice and I lived very happily in her two-up two-down in Inchicore. She worked as a cook (no women were called chefs in those days) in Dublin in a small local café, Rosie's. They did wholesome, old-fashioned foods for the building-site workers and the bus drivers around.

47

Corned beef and cabbage. Ham and boiled potatoes and thick gravy. Hot meat sandwiches on thick cuts of white bread, saturated in real butter. Warm food. Filling food. But at home in our little haven in Inchicore, she made fabulous modern Italian cuisine, inspired by her mother's heritage. Her secret recipe for seafood linguine was simply out of this world! Alice's Seafood Surprise, she called it. Never would she let me peek at how it was made; instead, she'd make me taste and guess. It was a game I loved. I never got it exactly right, and to this day I still make that Seafood Surprise dish, but it never tastes as good as Alice's. I'm still missing something, and now I'll never know what that special ingredient was.

She managed to make these dishes somehow. Woodcock's, the local fishmonger, would sell her scraps at the end of the day as they were cleaning down, the ends of what fish hadn't sold, and still she could make that master-piece. Expensive cuts of meat were also hard to afford, but Granny could make the most mouth-watering pasta carbonara with the original recipe, which uses guanciale, or pig's cheek. I would help her make home-made pasta. She would let me whisk together the flour and eggs as she stood over me, adding a pinch of salt and a tablespoon of olive oil. Her mauve padded housecoat, as she called it, protected her good clothes. Then I would cling-film our dough and while it sat for thirty minutes we'd put on old records and have a little dance. Although we had a television, we rarely put it on.

Tom never called to see us. If Alice was sad about this, I honestly don't know. She never mentioned him. How we loved to dance to her old-time favourites, Bing Crosby and Doris Day. The good sideboard would be pushed down so we had more room to twirl. It was innocent and wonderful.

Her old rolling pin was so heavy only she could roll out the dough. I looked over her shoulder and saw how Granny would dance the pasta from one hand to the other and I always marvelled at how it never split. Using her sharp knife she speedily cut it all into strips and then sent me off to wash up for dinner. I always remember being starving for the feast that would await me. As a chef, she was way ahead of her time.

Anyway, where was I? Oh yes, Mar-nee and Susan. Well yeah, they get on like a house on fire. Mar-nee and Susan Snapchat each other all day every day. It's mind-blowing. You will have guessed by now that I hate Snapchat. Granted, I don't really know what it is, but I hate it all the more for that. I hate the whole iPad, iPhone, Internet-reliant world Susan now inhabits. I detest how it's stolen my daughter from me. Yes, I could probably confiscate the devices, use the not-under-my-roof line, but that's just not me. Susan isn't a silly girl; in fact, she is very clever. This is what surprises me most! The last thing I want to do is to treat her like she is stupid. It's what they all do now, I get that, but all I'm trying to do is make her see for herself what an absolute waste it is to spend so much time on it. I'm no dictator, but I am a parent and I worry. Now that I'm mainly a single parent in the actual "parenting" department, my life is harder.

I pull into the driveway just as David texts to say he has just dropped her back. I see him and Mar-nee in their little yellow sports Mazda parked across the road, waiting for me to pull in, to make sure she isn't in the house alone. My mouth involuntarily lifts in a wry smile as I see David's ridiculous hairstyle. I raise my hand. Mar-nee drives off, overly revving the engine. However, I'm relieved to see David isn't attempting to drive with that limited vision. Claire is quite right: there is no way David can possibly see properly.

Getting out of the car still chucking to myself, I'm relieved the dreaded weekly shopping is done. Tonight I'm going to make us a vegetarian tagliatelle carbonara with chanterelle mushrooms, red onions and my home-made creamy sauce, and I have a date with the lover of all lovers. He who never disappoints me. He who fills me full of confidence. He who can do no wrong. He who goes by the name of Senor Pinot Grigio. Bliss. I pop the boot and start to unpack the bags.

Tonight I really need to sit Susan down and talk about the big decision we need to make. Another conversation that is not going to go my way. She wants nothing to do with my new offer. Slowly, slowly catchy monkey.

Susan opens the red front door, phone in front of her face, telling all her followers that she is opening the door for me. Snap. Chat. No hello for Mummy. Her Timberland boots with the open yellow laces crunch down our short gravel driveway.

"Hi love! Can I get some help here please if you have a minute?" I ask with a big smile, a runaway cucumber balanced under my chin.

"Mom is on my back again. Later, guys!" She pouts her overly glossed lips and raises two fingers to her iPhone. Her long nails are painted a luminous green.

50

"I'm not on the warpath, love, I'm just looking for some help." I take a deep breath and keep the huge smile plastered across my face. Her face is so heavily made up I have to bite my tongue. Right now she'd pass for eighteen.

"Okay, well for starters I didn't say you were on the warpath, I said you were on my back," she replies, giving me what I call her If-I-Have-To half hug.

"How were Daddy and Mar-nee?" I ask, ignoring her defensiveness and holding her close. Beaming. Beaming. Beaming. I'm a modern woman. I live my life my way. Ha! I want to be better at getting her. "Did you do much over the weekend? You never called me last night."

"Both full of awesomeness, as always. Nah, we just chilled, did some face packs and watched YouTube videos ... Sorry, I forgot." She grunts, pulling away from my embrace and twisting her dark hair around and around her baby finger. We both watch the curl spring up.

"Wonderful. I hope you gave them both my love. Grab a bag, will you? And, love, I need to talk to you seriously this evening about Mr Kilroy's summer job offer. I think it will be so exciting for the both of us." I throw that little chestnut in at the end. Her face does something I'm a little unfamiliar with for an instant: it lights up. Could it be an actual smile? My heart skips a beat. Has she changed her mind? Oh glory be.

"So Mom ... Mar-nee is getting me these amazeballs henna tattoo transfers for my birthday that last, like, a year!" She releases the hair on the other side and it springs up too. My last comment clearly went completely unheard.

Oh Mar-nee. Why are you so stupid? I bite my tongue.

It hurts. Not as much as Mar-nee trying to win over my child with ridiculous gifts. Semi-permanent tattoos on a fifteen-year-old?

What Susan doesn't know is that I'm planning her sixteenth birthday. I'm throwing her a surprise party in our local GAA club next Saturday night. I've had it booked it for months and I've managed to invite most of her pals on the quiet. A surprise party. Martin has been brilliant helping me at the school. He went to her classroom and took her out for a turn working in the mobile library while her teacher Ms Butler gave out the surprise invites to the selected few. I've booked a local band that I think she loves, we are having mini vegetarian burgers and sweet potato fries, and Claire is making a huge iPad-shaped chocolate-biscuit cake. I've bought her vouchers for all her favourite shops: Superdry, Claire's, H&M. I haven't invited David and Mar-nee. Yet. I just don't trust either of them not to let it slip. Of course I will invite them, but not until closer to the event. They are due to have Susan on the Sunday anyway for a birthday lunch, so I know they will be here. A small but intimate party, I hope.

Susan grabs a plastic shopping bag and I follow her into the house. Our small hallway leads down to the kitchen. Opening the fridge, I start to put away the weekly shopping. Susan is a vegetarian now. That's fine with me. She was a great meat eater until she found out Mar-nee was a vegetarian. We used to make the most amazing home-made beef burgers, stuffed with spring onions and coriander, and cook them on our gas barbeque all year round. We would pan fry Angus steaks for minutes and eat them juicy and rare on our laps with granary bread and glasses of freezing-cold milk while we watched *The X Factor*. I watch now as she puts the unopened bag in-between her feet on the blue tiled kitchen floor and starts taking pictures of it.

"Come on, Susan, the frozen yogurt is in there." I make room in the freezer.

"One sec!" She snaps again and again, then speedily scrolls through the pictures and snaps again. What could possibly be so beguiling about a seventy-five-cent plastic bag holding frozen yogurt and frozen peas?

"Instagram." She answers my unspoken question.

She is incredibly pretty. Tall, like David, and of slim build, with jet-black shoulder-length hair and a blunt fringe. She calls them bangs. Her ice-blue eyes, identical to mine, compliment her rosebud lips and she now has perfectly straight teeth after five years of braces. But this evening it's hard to see her beautiful skin under the heavy foundation. I won't mention that, though. She is growing up, and I do get that; it's just she's also changing completely from the little girl I knew, and it's hard. I have to adjust. I miss the old Susan so badly.

"Just come on," I say, nodding to the bag. "Please, love." Smiling.

In the fridge, an old red chilli pepper is curled up, staring at me, begging to be put to rest. Removing it, I close the fridge and move to the wall, stepping on the silver pedal of the bin and dumping it in.

My phone beeps and I rummage in my leather jacket pocket for it. It's a text from the nursing home telling me Granny is still refusing to eat any dinner. Her sunken eyes and mouth this morning told me that life is ebbing away from her. "Fight it," I want to shout at her. But she is ninety-one years old. She has done all her fighting. I will drop by and try to feed her some porridge before I go into the office in the morning, like I do every morning. Her son, my uncle Tom, is there with her most evenings, so I try not to bump into him. He is her next of kin. He never took to me. Nor I to him. In fact, we never saw him all the time I was growing up. He never came by. He never called her. Her never took her for a lunch, or a drink, or to his house on the Northside. Christmases came and went without so much as a card. Funny how he's stuck to her side now, in her last days, isn't it? My thoughts are interrupted.

"So, Mar-nee has got this, like, amazing cerise-pink glow-in-the-dark nail polish and she said she'll do mine, plus my toe-toes, obvs … It will look so cool tomorrow cos we have yoga for gym cos we all need to chillax and stuff … So can I stay over there tonight, Mom, please?" She still hasn't unpacked the bag.

I shake my head and she drops her jaw and sighs heavily at me. I ignore her and she sighs again, louder this time.

"Sorry, Susan, but no. Absolutely not. It's a school night," I say calmly. Not this argument again. Surely Mar-nee mustn't be encouraging her to ask me this.

"So? She can drop me to school on her new moped on her way to the salon. Please, Mom, please?" She stands on her Timberland-clad tippy-toes, her hands clenched together.

"No. And I told your dad, Susan, you are not allowed on the back of Mar-nee's moped." I clench my teeth.

"Okay, I will walk then, get some of that fresh air and outdoor exercise you are so, like, totally obsessed with."

54

She is hopping from foot to foot now. A Mar-nee type rain dance, it seems.

"Look, love … I got us all the ingredients for your favourite carbonara. I thought we could cook together, eat dinner, have that chat about our summer and watch old episodes of *Dance Moms*? Snuggle up on the couch like we used to do?" I narrow my eyes at her before I take the bag up myself and take out the now dripping frozen items.

"I'm so over *Dance Moms*, Mom. I'll be so bored tonight!" She spits the words at me, the whites of her eyeballs rolling like a mad woman. And here it comes. My rebuttal. The words escape my mouth before I can swallow them back down and think of something better to say. Something less confrontational.

"Okay then, you can clean that bombsite of a room of yours. I can't even open your drawers to put fresh clothes into them and all our cups seem to have moved in permanently under your bed!" I know my voice is raised slightly now and I curl my toes up tight in my Adidas to stop myself and gather control.

"It's my room! You shouldn't even be going in there! Respect my privacy!" she stabs back, leaning against the kitchen table.

"Really? So how do all your clean clothes and uniform get in there then?" I try to lower my voice.

"I'd prefer to wash my own clothes. You never wash them properly anyway." She rubs her Timberland boot along the blue kitchen tiles.

"And just what is that supposed to mean, Susan?" I ask impatiently.

"Like, you are supposed to use fabric softener too. It's

55

as important how the clothes smell as it is how clean they are! This is two zero one seven, Mom!" She stares up at me. Is she wearing false eyelashes?

"Is that so?" I look closer at her eyes. If I hear that it is 2017 in that way once more this year, I will scream.

"It is." She steps away from the table.

"Well okay, I will buy fabric softener and you can start washing and ironing your own clothes. You *are* nearly sixteen." I turn back to the fridge.

"Thank you! I'd love that, I've, like, only been asking you for months if I can do all my own washing and ironing and cooking, but you still seem to think I'm a baby."

I push the old half-full milk to the side, add my new litre beside it and shut the fridge. Crumpling the plastic bag up in my hand, I say, "I love cooking for you, Susan." I am aware how weak I sound.

"I know you do, Mom, but I like different food to you now," she answers in a clipped tone.

"I make all vegetarian stuff!" I'm incredulous.

"Right, I know, but I'm leaning more towards veganism now—"

"Oh please don't be so absolutely ridiculous!" I slap my hand off the worktop. It's a much more aggressive action than I'd anticipated and I curse myself inwardly.

"See, here you go again. It's your way or the highway . . ."

"Susan, you are too thin already. Why on earth do you want to limit what foods you can eat?" I extend both my hands out wide, palms bouncing up towards the ceiling.

"Because I love animals, Mom!" Her eyes blaze at me.

"I love them too, Susan, but I think by not eating meat you are honouring that. I just don't see—"

"Mar-nee saw a PETA video and she told me about it. If you saw it, Mom, you would never eat any animal products again." Her eyes well up.

"Mar-nee shouldn't be telling you the things she sees, pet, it's too upsetting for a girl of your age. Mar-nee is an adult. You are growing; you need to be careful what you cut out of your diet," I tell her, trying to sound in control.

"You can't shelter me from the cruelty that is forced upon animals. You can't make me want to eat something that causes defenceless animals pain!" she shouts.

"Does it hurt a chicken to lay an egg? I don't think so!" I shout back. I've lost it. I've lost the argument at the mere mention that Mar-nee is, again, behind all this. I have failed at mothering my teenager once more.

"Why are you always so mean to me?"

"How am I always mean to you?" I'm kind of incredulous, but I hold it together. "I'm not mean, love, I just want you to be healthy and I want you here with me, that's all. This is your home. Here with me. You are my baby and I love you," I tell her in a soft voice as I step closer to her, my arms outstretched.

"Don't crowd me, Mom!" she screams, and turns on her boots and leaves the kitchen. I stand still, my mouth open. The kitchen clock ticks on. Time waits for no man. Or woman. I take a deep breath in through my nose. Hold it. Her bedroom door slams shut. I exhale slowly, but a lone tear trickles down my face. Moving to the kitchen table, I pull out a chair and sit down. How did we go from zero to a hundred in ten minutes? I drop my face into my hands. I'm weary of these arguments now, the frequency of them. Softly, I cry, feeling dreadfully sorry for myself.

When I dry my face, I realise I now carry tissues in my back pocket because one of us cries so often.

"Hormones! I bet your periods are synchronised!" Claire keeps saying. But I know it isn't that.

Pulling myself up, I unpack the rest of the shopping and put my wine glass in the freezer to chill. The lump in my throat remains. I'm incredibly hurt. This probably sounds all "poor me, poor me", I realise, but I've dedicated my life to Susan and when we aren't getting on I can't really function properly. I can't understand why she doesn't want to be with me. It's baffling to me. Claire also tells me it's a phase and it will pass, but it's getting tougher and tougher. What is the point in shouting up after her to come back down? What is the point in telling her I love her so, so very much and that is why I want her with me? What is the point in telling her I'm so deeply wounded she doesn't want to be with me? You see, I've said it all before. A thousand times this past year. She doesn't care. I hear "Hey guys!" from upstairs and I know she's lost to the world of her Internet friends.

With a heavy heart, I decide to begin prepping my sauce. After removing all the items I need to cook from the fridge, I switch the radio on. Talk radio fills the empty air. A discussion about something in American politics I can't really concentrate on. I click on the gas and the blue flames flicker to life. Dragging a bobble from my wrist, I tie my blonde hair up in a loose bun on top of my head, and wash my hands. Drizzling some olive oil in the pan, I leave it to heat while I crack the eggs a bit too firmly and beat them a bit too vigorously. Washing and dicing the mushrooms, I feel my heartbeat slowing down as I slide them into the bubbling oil. Speedily, I grate the Parmesan, add it to the whisked eggs and pour in the full-fat cream, beating it all with a fork. Cooking helps me as I try to block out the reality. It remains unspoken, but for how much longer? I know, in my heart, soon-to-be sixteen Susan wants to go and live with David and Mar-nee.

3

"Does it feel like a good decision-making day?" Lar Kilroy slides his black horn-rimmed glasses back up his nose with his baby finger and holds open the glass door of our office block for me. I balance our two coffees, my laptop bag slung over my left shoulder. He licks his index finger now and holds it up in the air as though detecting the direction of the wind.

"I have until Monday the thirty-first, stop crowding me, man," I tell him with a wink.

Lar grins at me as he takes his coffee. We stroll side by side to the lift and he jabs at the silver button. Lar is married, with a grown-up daughter in Dubai, and has just turned fifty-five years old. He is slightly overweight and he is the sweetest man in the world. I say "slightly" overweight now, as he has recently copped on and stopped eating sweets all day at his desk, swapping the giant Malteasers bags for Brazil nuts and chopped carrots and hummus. I may have had something to do with that. Mrs Kilroy is constantly sending me text messages to thank me. She is also hilarious and they have a very special marriage.

"Yvonne is all packed, all ready to go!"

He knows how to push my buttons. I don't rise to his bait.

"Meeting at eleven in regards to the latest Nerja swap and their subsequent relocation there," he says, grinning and giving me the thumbs-up. "Debbie and Harry Desmond and their two adorable school-going girls, eleven and fifteen, can't remember their names now, they've escaped me . . ."

"Yes, and, well, they are lovely people I know, but re-evaluating their decision in my own head, I want to wish them good luck with that," I say, thinking of how silent Susan was on the drop-off to school this morning, refusing to even come up and see her great-granny.

"She hates me." She had pursed her lips and stared into the iPhone.

"Don't be so insensitive. She is ill, Susan!" I had looked at her in disbelief.

Leaving her in the car, I'd gone up to visit Alice and fed her a couple of spoons of my home-made porridge and fresh blueberries. The ward smelled of faeces and disinfectant. I wished I could take her home. I couldn't. She needs twenty-four-hour care. She had taken three very small spoonfuls onto her desert-like tongue and smacked her toothless gums around the food. It had looked painful for her to swallow it. Then she'd closed her eyes. I'd held her frail, blue-veined hand and rubbed my thumbs across them. I will go back later, after Tom leaves. Knowing as I do, in my heart of hearts, that she wants to slip away

61

quietly, I need to respect that. Alice Bedford was never one for making a fuss.

"What do you mean? You've worked so closely with them," Lar asks.

"I mean it, Lar, God bless them. I hope it all works out for them and they aren't just filling the dreadful nothingness between mother and daughters. Those girls could turn at any given second," I say.

"What? What does that mean? Of course it will work out! You are the queen of relocating families. That's why I need you so much in St Ives! If it weren't for all the work you've done over the past few years, Court, we'd be out of business. I'd never have thought this could be a new venture. You've taken us to a new level! It was really you who came up with the business idea. All I ever did was holiday swaps; now we are dealing in life swaps!" Lar is visibly excited as the lift doors part and we step in and do a 180-degree turn. Lar loves abbreviated names, and even though I keep telling him I was actually christened Courtney, he insists on calling me Court. I kind of like it. I don't know why – maybe because it's so personal. Father-figureish. Paternal. Maybe I'm searching inwardly for a token father to replace the one I missed out on. Sigmund Freud would be delighted with me!

"Well, who could have seen Airbnb becoming so successful so damn fast! A relocation business was the obvious next step for you. And sorry, I'm having Susan issues. We'd another huge fight, then she refused to come out of her room all night. I had to take her dinner up to her, which was left untouched, and then she was mono-syllabic at breakfast this morning and on the school run.

She stayed in the car while I went to feed Granny again, refused to come up and see her. I'm weary of it all." I heave out the words.

"You are too soft on her. A good talking-to is what she needs. She is the kid, she shouldn't dictate how you both live: that's your job!" he reiterates for the hundredth time.

"Yeah, because that's really how we are right now: communicators! Dr Phil would have to dedicate two shows to us." I throw my eyes to heaven, or the white square panels on the ceiling of the lift, I should say.

We are pinged to our floor. Stepping out, I sink into the newly fitted soft beige and black carpet. It's a mark of the man that Lar is that the bigger the business grows, the more home comforts he gives to the staff.

"I want this place to be better than The Google. If you want to lie around on beanbags, I will buy them," he says at every staff meeting. No one here wants beanbags. Teabags, maybe. I like my job, don't get me wrong. I like earning money and being able to pay my bills, but it ain't no vacation. His new offer, however . . .

"Morning, Maria." I lean across our receptionist's dark mahogany desk as she's on a call and I grab my post. Maria nods at me and smiles, her headset bobbing as she readjusts the mouthpiece, pushes buttons in front of her and transfers a call.

See, Exchange, Experience doesn't have a huge office space. It's on the top two floors of an old glass building on Hatch Street. It has five members of staff and we facilitate people who want to swap homes for a short period of time. So if you live in a small country town in Germany and you want to experience living in the bright lights of busy mid-town Manhattan, we find you a like-minded New Yorker and through us you agree to switch your private homes for a week, or two, or three … sometimes even up to three months. Lar started up the business in the late '90s, when it was pretty revolutionary. But by the time I came on board, the business was already in decline. Nowadays people can set up a B&B in their own home and travel all over cheaply to Airbnbs. A few years ago I got really worried that Lar would finally go out of business for good. Simply put, See, Exchange, Experience was out of date. So I proposed to Lar a development of the business: a new branch for people who want to relocate.

I've been with Lar for seven years now. Oh, the acting career I craved and studied for, you might be wondering about that. Well, after I delivered my Susan I did go back out and audition, but I never landed a single gig. My heart was at home with her. Claire had thrown in the towel by that stage too and was working in a restaurant as front of house. She was great at the job, as she was so outgoing the customers all loved her. Claire had declared the Irish acting world Fattists and boycotted movies and theatres for years after. In fairness to David, he never put pressure on me to go back to work, but I knew I wanted to do something else outside the home after bringing up our daughter for nine years. When Susan was in third class, I saw an advertisement in a recruitment shop window off Grafton Street advertising for a part-time data-inputting post in See, Exchange, Experience and I thought it looked interesting. So I went in.

"I'll see you at the meeting at eleven, Court." Lar drags my thoughts back to the present and moves off down the

64

corridor, shuffling in his brown shoes towards his own office. I do the same. My private office is small but airy. I have a neat white glossed desk, iMac and a glass coffee table with a low-slung couch for clients. My sky-blue walls are covered with exotic pictures of faraway places, palm trees, golden sandy beaches, towering recognisable landmark buildings and all sorts of travel paraphernalia. One wall is decorated top to bottom in multi-coloured postcards that my clients have sent me over the years: my one request to them all. Sitting at my desk, I sip my black coffee and wake up my iMac. I just seemed to understand the business naturally. It's not that complicated. Double tapping my NERJA SWAP / RELOCATION DEBBIE & HARRY DESMOND file, it opens quickly. I remember the family well. One of their daughters is the same age as Susan and it's funny how you keep people who are at similar stages in their lives at the front of your head. When I was pregnant, I saw pregnant women everywhere. I noticed every pram and buggy. I heard every baby's cry in a restaurant. The Desmonds, tanned and happy, had popped into the office the day they landed to see me post-holiday-swap and the first thing that struck me was how different their fifteen-year-old daughter, Zoe, was to mine. Zoe just looked her age and had a Harry Potter book under her arm. She was polite and sweet and her interaction with her mother was so lovely. To me, Susan looked years older and acted years older. What was her hurry to grow up so fast? I wish I knew and I dearly wish I could change it! The younger one had worn the cutest pair of Peppa Pig glasses and I had become even more nostalgic for Susan's childhood.

Their move to Nerja is all sailing along nicely. I have already enrolled the Desmond girls in an English-speaking school in Calle de Frigiliana and they will begin the new term in September. They actually did a holiday swap with us first, and the thing is, I knew on swap they wouldn't want, as I call it, "comeback". I knew that once they'd experienced the beauty of Nerja, with its quaint, relaxed way of living, outdoor life and cobbled streets, their pretty but cramped Dublin terraced cottage would seem too small.

They had swapped with an English gentleman who was looking to trade his apartment overlooking the Mediterranean for three weeks to come to Dublin to search out his family tree. Ideally he was looking for a small house near the city centre, which is pretty hard to find – but the Desmonds had it. But when the Desmonds decided to move out there permanently, he didn't want to sell up in Nerja, so I found the family a villa just off Plaza Tutti Frutti. Harry is a computer analyst and works mainly from home. Debbie works in a local shop. I have made them both acutely aware that Nerja doesn't boast huge employment opportunities, but the cost of living is lower and Harry feels he can make it work. When See, Exchange, Experience was still just a holiday-swap company, lots of clients relocated, but all I ever gave them was free advice. It was my idea to turn it into a branch of the business. See, Exchange, Experience are now opening their very first office in Cornwall. We had so many clients wanting to swap homes with someone in Cornwall, and wanting to move there afterwards, that it makes sense to have a permanent base there. Ideally we can turn the

Airbnb clients to our advantage. Lar has a list as long as his arm of families who want to relocate.

Therein lies my big dilemma. Lar has offered me the managerial position in the new office, which is currently having its finishing touches done. He is aware of my situation, so his offer is initially for June, July and August while Susan is off school on her summer holidays to get the business up and running, but with a view to eventually relocating and managing the business in St Ives full-time if I want. With the job comes a large, brand-spanking-new apartment above the office that we can live in rent-free. I'd absolutely love to do it. When he first approached me with the offer I felt excitement like I haven't done in years. I'd called Claire immediately.

"Sounds like a no-brainer to me, Courtney, grab it with both hands! Cornwall? St Ives? It's your dream location! You are obsessed with Cornwall! This is all meant to be!" My friend had squealed with excitement. "Plus they shoot *Poldark* down there, don't they? I'll be over for a glimpse of Aidan Turner's naked torso!"

"It's not that easy though, is it?" I knew that Susan wouldn't be keen.

"Oh Courtney, when do you ever do anything for yourself any more? What has Alice always drilled into you? The importance of being you! Don't lose *you*. Susan will love it if she gives it a chance. She is nearly sixteen; you need to start thinking about what Courtney wants now too."

"Granny Alice was the ultimate independent woman," I'd said. "She did what made her happy and she always told me to do the same. She said unless you are happy in

67

your own skin you can't make anyone else happy. I know she was right, I know the importance of being me, it's just Susan is a part of me too, so I'm still working out how to make both of us happy. It's not easy."

But Claire was so right about one thing: Cornwall. I fell in love with Cornwall the very first day I started work in the basement office of North Great Georges Street as Lar's data inputter. Over the years I've actually lost track of the amount of holiday swaps I've done between Cornwall and the rest of the world. You see, apart from my honeymoon I had never been outside Ireland and Lar had this huge glossy poster on his office wall that said "Visit Cornwall". It was of St Ives, that year's winner of a showcase of national awards, including best family holiday destination by *Coast* magazine and one of the ten best European beach destinations compiled by TripAdvisor. St Ives to me looked like a subtropical oasis – on Lar's poster the beaches were golden, the vegetation was lush and the light piercingly bright. Some days I would stand and stare at that poster for ages, transfixed. I found it extremely therapeutic. It was no wonder to me when I began to research the area that the town had been attracting artists for decades, who came to capture its undeniable natural beauty. It's just the most beautiful place in the world and still hugely popular for swaps. After Lar promoted me from data inputter, the first place I went to organise a swap was to St Ives with the Woodcock family. They wanted to take two weeks in Blackpool during the Illuminations, and we matched a family in Bispham, Blackpool, who really wanted to attend a nephew's wedding in St Ives. It all worked out great.

David and Susan had been excited for me at the time.

I had flown over and taken the twenty-minute train ride on the popular branch line from St Erth to St Ives. I was in awe of the colourful fishing boats coming into harbour as the train snaked around the golden bays to the town. Kicking off my shoes before I checked into my hotel, I'd strolled along the white sand at Porthminster beach as I looked out for the Godrevy lighthouse, the inspiration for Virginia Woolf's famous novel *To the Lighthouse*, which I'd studied at Trinity. I'd stayed at the Blue Hayes hotel and the trip had been a huge success.

I peel the plastic lid off my fruit bowl and search out the pineapple, chasing it between the melon and the red grapes. Chewing the sweet fruit, I lean my head back on the chair. Now, things aren't that black and white. When I sat Susan down to discuss the possibilities of us going only for the summer (I didn't say a word about us relocating there one day) she'd freaked out. Thrown a wobbler. She had plans for the summer, she'd told me. When I dared to ask her what exactly those plans were, she informatively told me, "Wait and see." I told her I'd need a little more information than that. I won't bore you with the rest of the argument. Suffice to say it ended with a slamming door and a "Hey guys!" Claire and I had discussed it at length again when we were in Wong's Chinese restaurant in town on a Friday night, getting very tipsy.

"Have you accepted the job yet? Have you? And if not, well why the hell not?" Claire had asked me as she spooned her sweet and sour chicken onto her egg fried rice.

"Obviously I have tried to talk to Susan, who doesn't want to know, and I have Granny Alice to think of too. I'd have to say goodbye to her for good, I imagine. Breaks my heart to see Tom the vulture hovering over her!" I'd almost bawled at the thought when I'd answered Claire. My chilli and garlic prawns had sizzled over their little candle, untouched.

"Eat!" Claire had waved her fork at my empty plate as she chewed. Then she'd said, "Not necessarily, love ... I know obviously it's a possibility, but no one knows what tomorrow will bring, do they? I think you would be absolutely bonkers to turn it down. Agreed, Tom is a total vulture. Like, did he ever visit his mother until recently?" she'd asked and I shook my head.

"It's not just me, though, is it? Like I say, there is so much else to consider," I'd sniffed.

"I know." She'd pushed the bottle of Merlot to one side and taken my hands across the table. "Thing is, Courtney, I know I sound like a broken record, but sometimes you also have to think about yourself." Squeezing my hands tightly, she'd gone on. "Your amazing, wonderful granny would want you to take this opportunity. Listen to your heart and you will hear that. Susan will be going off to college soon . . ."

I'd raised my eyebrows at this doubtful statement.

"Or whatever she does in two years, but I know one thing, Courtney – and this is hard to say, believe me – but in a few short years you will be alone, and I'm so scared that David's going to take that house back from you. You see, rents in Dublin now, they are pretty unmanageable." The waitress had poured more wine into our glasses and we'd thanked her and drained them.

My phone rings out and I jump, back in the present moment.

"Good morning, See, Exchange, Experience, Courtney Downey speaking." I put down my plastic fork.

"Hello, my name is Tony Becker. Is this Courtney Downey?" a strange voice asks.

"Em…Well, yes…Like I said, I'm Courtney Downey. How may I help you?" I wade my finger around the juice of the fruit bowl. The accent is undoubtedly Cornwall.

"Right, Courtney Downey, I need a pair of hands here with all the paperwork. The suits at the town hall are on my back about these late-night opening hours on Thursday and Friday you're after and I need someone out here to help. I'm the builder, this is not my domain, I've enough on my plate. Up to my absolute eyes I am in getting this all finished: the electrics have been a bloody nightmare, I've lost Andy and I'm running out of time. Plus who's picking this furniture for the upstairs apartment? Brian Fogg needs to know."

"Eh, sorry, who is this?" I'm crunching up my forehead now, my high ponytail swaying from side to side.

"Tony…Are you listening to me, Courtney Downey?"

I do not like his tone of voice. "Yes, Tony Becker. I am. I am listening. But I have no idea who you are." I deliver the words slowly.

He imitates me, tenfold: "I … am … the … building … contractor … for … the … St Ives … Cornwall … See … Exchange … Experience … office … and … upstairs … apartment … Mr … Lar … Kilroy … told … me … to … speak … to … you."

"Can you please talk normally?" I say, riled now.

"He didn't mention it then, I gather?" He coughs loudly down the line and I have to hold the receiver away from my ear.

71

"No, he didn't, Tony," I say calmly when I hold the phone back.

"Oh for F's sake. Look, can you put me on to a person who works there who can fly over to St Ives and help me out down here with paperwork and furnishings. Neither are my department. I've a new project on a house restoration to get started in Land's End, not to mention my other very demanding business . . . I haven't got time for this."

What a hostile man. *Stop raising your voice at me, Tony,* I say in my head.

"Well, thank you for this, Tony. If I can take your number I will go and talk to Mr Kilroy as soon as he is free and call you straight back."

"Yeah, yeah that's what y'all say, forget it!" He slams the phone down.

I stab Lar's extension with my very un-Mar-nee short, unpolished, slightly chewed-on nail.

"Yo!" he answers like an elderly rapper.

"Who the hell is Tony Becker? He's literally just this second shouted abuse down the phone at me!"

There is radio silence.

"Are you there, Lar? Hello? Hello?" I do that ridiculously pointless move of hitting the buttons over and over. My office door opens. Lar stands there in his black stocking feet. He always removes his scuffed brown shoes in his office.

"But you didn't hang up. I didn't hear that hang-up tone," I say to him, confused.

"No, I just gently laid the phone on my desk and slipped out the door. Damn, I forgot my coffee." His little finger pushes the heavy glasses back up his nose.

"Ask Maria to bring it down," I say to him impatiently.

"Ah no, that's not fair on Ria, it's not her job to run around after me with my coffee. Give us half of yours, will ya?" He lifts a cup from beside my water bottle and I dutifully pour half of mine into it and hand it to him. He sits. "Tony is our building contractor. He's from St Ives and he knows Cornwall like the back of his hand. He needs another head over there, though: that's why I'm trying to push you for an answer. If you really can't go for the summer, I need to ask Yvonne. There are certain aspects of the paperwork, some part of the planning permission he needs help with before he can move on and finish the job. Plus the little apartment up above needs a woman's touch." Lar raises his coffee to his lips.

"It's not that easy. I tried to talk to Susan again this morning." I shake my mouse and minimise my Nerja relocation file. Why is life so bloody complicated?

"Aren't you the parent and isn't she only almost sixteen?" He sips and makes a face of complete bafflement.

"Yes, I do know all this, thank you, Lar, but almost sixteen-year-old girls are very different to how they were in your day. They have much...fuller lives." I hear myself and it sounds completely ludicrous.

"Any chance of a sachet of sugar?" He spies my slim sugar sachets for clients with our logo emblazoned on them.

"Absolutely not!" I reprimand him.

"Tastes of nothing without a bit of sugar." He slowly raises his eyes to the ceiling. "Here's the truth, though: you are living in your ex-husband's house paying him rent, even though the property is mortgage free—"

73

I interrupt him. "Mar-nee has a huge mortgage on her place, he needs—"

He interrupts me straight back. "I'm not finished, I'm offering you the chance of a lifetime—"

"So you keep telling me."

"So you keep telling me." We interrupt each other with the same sentence.

"Knock, knock." She doesn't knock. She just says the words and walks right in.

"Are you okay, Yvonne?" Immediately she gets my back up. I don't really know why. She hasn't actually ever done anything to me I can prove, but I just know she thinks she's better than me. Call it woman's intuition.

"I thought this meeting was at eleven." She slides her slender five-foot nine-inch frame into the spare chair beside Lar.

"How's Lar?" She pats his knee.

"Lar is good, thank you, Vonne," he replies kindly.

She is dressed in her usual power suit, white shirt and feck-off high heels. Red soles. You know the ones. Her long, jet-black hair is perfectly pulled into a low ponytail. I'm immediately conscious of my high messy ponytail. Her features are sharp yet she gets away with it and you would definitely call her very attractive. David used to say she was slightly scary in a really sexy way: Cruella de Vil meets Anne Hathaway.

"It's not the official Monday-morning meeting, Yvonne," I say as I stare at my slightly crumpled pink cardigan, cream nylon skirt and brown flat knee-high boots.

"Has Susan decided if you can go to the Cornwall office for the summer?" she asks in a patronising way.

74

"I'm not discussing that right now, Yvonne, I'm on the Desmonds' Nerja relocation, and we have that police officer in his Manhattan apartment in the heart of Greenwich Village looking for an apartment swap in Ennis, Co. Clare. Can you start on this? He's logged all his details and pictures; he just needs a follow-up call."

Piss off, Yvonne is what I'm thinking though. Right now I hate her and her easy, uncomplicated single life.

"Sorry, no can do. I'm off to meet Anna McDonough, the Tuscany swap woman, in about ten minutes to finalise her three weeks there. I need to check she has made all those changes to her priceless glass-ornament collection in Dalkey that we agreed on and that the cooker hood is fixed."

Lar leans in to her. "Oh great, yes, I meant to remind you of that last night. I viewed those pictures she put up myself. Make sure they are all removed and in storage and that cooker hood is fixed. Did you get her to re-sign? Clause ten is—"

"I'm on it, Lar." She smiles at him before adding, "I don't really need reminding. I'm not the one with lots of outside stuff going on. You can save all your reminders into a Google calendar, Courtney, you know that, right, hun?"

When people call me "hun" it reminds me of my age. I force a smile and say, "Right, hun."

"Anyway, I will be back for the meeting at eleven. I'm also planning on working late tonight so if anyone needs an extra pair of hands just holler." She rises like a goddess.

Why would anyone want to work late when it's unnecessary? She makes us all look bad – and I guess I have

75

just answered my own question. When she leaves, I pull at my nose, sniff loudly and make a noise. Lar knows I'm agitated.

"Listen, I want you in Cornwall, but it will be her if you can't go. What else can I say?" He shrugs his shoulders.

"Nothing, it's fine. I have to run myself. I'm meeting Mary O'Hare," I tell him.

He stiffens. "She's back?"

"Yes, she's back, and she's going to Denmark, to a luxury apartment for a week. It's not a direct swap, she's on swap points." I throw my eyes to heaven. You earn swap points when another member of our company stays in your home and you don't stay at theirs, then you can use them to travel when it suits you.

"Where is left for her to actually see? She must have seen the entire big bad world at this stage!" He drains his coffee cup. "And how I have a blade of hair left on my head with her is beyond me."

"You are bald, Lar," I tell him, deadpan.

"I am?" He looks totally shocked and runs his hand over his smooth head. We both laugh. This is our in-joke. Mary O'Hare was one of Lar's first clients. She was the first client he had who was willing to swap her sprawling mansion on Killiney Hill in Dublin with a family from a modest apartment in San Francisco, and from that swap on Mary continued to trade and went off to see the world. Sometimes she stays with her sister in Brighton and lets out her place, thus earning herself lots of swap points. However, she seems to think that she can call us all 24/7 to tell us the sights she is seeing, what she had for dinner, how her toilet isn't flushing, how her chicken was raw

76

in the middle. We are always here if things aren't going smoothly, but she takes our services a bit too far. This meeting today is so I can gently tell her, again, that she can't call us morning, noon and night.

My phone rings out and I reach for it.

"It's me again. Listen, if you can come over for a day next week I think I can sort the rest. Ideally I need ya to come Wednesday as the regular town-hall lady is having her hip replacement done and Marina, her stand-in, is so much nicer. I'm taking her to the Ploughboy for a drink later, in fact. I'll have you in and out in a couple of hours. We can see Brian Fogg in his furniture shop. If you need I can collect you from the airport and drop you back?" He talks so fast.

"Who is this?" I can't help myself.

"Are you actually bloody serious?" His voice is raised and very high-pitched. I start to shake with laughter.

"Oh, Tony Becker, sorry Tony, of course I know who you are. I've a lot on my plate here too, Tony. Can I go on Wednesday? Hmm . . ." I make sounds, sucky sounds, like I'm really thinking this over, clicking my tongue off the roof of my mouth over and over again. Then I focus on the framed picture of Susan on my desk. I took it last summer when we went to Doolin in Co. Clare for the weekend. She is standing in front of the Aillwee caves holding an ice cream with a chocolate flake. For the first time, I really look at it. It's her eyes. I lift the picture up in its Newbridge silver frame and pull it closer to my face. Her eyes look miserable. The cone is dripping, untouched. As I recall now, she threw it in the bin after. Then the whole trip comes flooding back: me buying her attention, buying

77

her smiles, trying so hard to make her happy. Nothing I did pleased her. She sulked and pouted and grunted at me. Every time I looked at her, she was on the phone. When I finally did get her to talk it was because we were going home a day earlier than I had originally planned. Enough was enough. Right now, I think of the joy on my daughter's face if I tell her she can have a sleepover with Mar-nee and David mid-week. It might just help us.

"Yes. Yes I can. I just checked my very busy diary there. But I will prioritise you, Mr Becker, and I'll see you on Wednesday so." I lean back in my ergonomic office chair and Mr Kilroy gives me a silent two-thumbs-up.

"Nice one. If you like I can book you a room at the Carbis Bay hotel. I get a discount. Email me your flight details; Lar has my email. See ya then, Courtney Downey." He rings off. I put the receiver down slowly.

"You're going to Cornwall?" Mr Kilroy slowly places a finger and thumb on each of the handles of his heavy-rimmed glasses and slowly takes them off.

"I'm going to Cornwall, Lar," I say, and I do my happy dance. He lays his glasses down on my white gloss desk and we clumsily high five.

4

"Still suffering like us Hillary Clinton supporters, I see?"
I ask Claire, nodding to Martin's red Mini, parked in
the driveway during school hours of a Monday, as she
very slowly opens the hall door to me. Claire and I were
very anti-Trump. Even more so now: President Trump
frightens us. Juice detoxes and the Trump: our greatest
current fears. Immediately I regret my words.

"Have I got news for you! I ... What ... what the hell is
wrong?" I gasp as I take her in properly. Claire's face is
paler than usual, freckles almost lost in the pallor of her
skin tone. Her side fringe, greasy, falls across her left eye. I
notice she is barefoot. Claire is never without either shoes
or flip-flops, always saying to anyone who is, "You'll get a
cold in your kidneys!"

She steps away from the barely half-open door and I
squeeze myself inside. Raising her index finger, she places
it over her pale lips. My normally immaculate friend has
chocolate sauce down the front of her cream V-neck

T-shirt and down the front of her blue linen trousers. I follow her down into the kitchen and she closes the door quietly. The kitchen is a total bombsite. A pile of cakes and sponges and buns and chopped fruit and whisked cream adorns the marble island and every available worktop. Dirty utensils and whisks and cutlery are strewn around everywhere. The smell of burning jam is overwhelming.

"What the hell is going on, Claire? What's happened?" I move to her, very concerned, as she stands in the middle of the kitchen, but first I go over and pull a bubbling pot from the stove and extinguish the gas.

She doesn't answer immediately but seconds later says, "Oh, Courtney...Martin is really sick." She stares at me with red-rimmed eyes.

"What do you mean, really sick?" I gulp out as I slowly peel off my cardigan. I'm suddenly perspiring through the thin pink cotton. I have trouble swallowing. "What? Where is he?" I am shaking now.

"Upstairs." Her green eyes are filled with water. Tears stream down her freckled cheeks, running into one another.

"What? What's wrong with him? Claire?" I put my hands on her shoulders to drag her focus back to me. Her eyes seem dead. Lifeless. She looks like a zombie. "Claire?"

"He's been sleeping with other people ... mainly men, Courtney...ones riddled with sexually transmitted diseases apparently." She gags. I'm sure she's going to vomit so I grab the small silver pedal bin and hold it open in front of her. She pushes it away. She swallows hard, with an audible gulp. I drop the bin and it clatters off the dark wooden floor. I can't get any words out. I can't process her words. They are all jumbled up in my head, but it sounds like she just said that Martin has been sleeping with men. Martin Carney isn't gay. What is wrong with her?

"But ... but ... but Martin isn't gay, Claire," I stutter.

She shakes her head and roughly pulls her fringe out of her eyes. Her hand remains on top of her head, clutching a clump of hair.

"No, he's not, Courtney. He is, however, very much a bisexual man." She lets go of her hair now and it stands on end, as though she's just got an awful fright. I know you won't believe this, but I start to laugh. I can't help it. It is completely ludicrous. Claire leans against the marble island in the kitchen and I spy a half-open bottle of red wine and a full glass.

"Are you drunk, Claire?" I ask, my laugh disintegrating at her expression. She just stares at me as though I'm completely nuts.

"A little. Yeah." She nods. It's only then I notice her red-stained teeth and lips. "This is far from funny, Courtney. I know you laugh in tense situations, but please ..." She trails off.

"I'm sorry. Jesus, you know I'm sorry, of course it's not funny, it's my nervous reaction, you know that ... I'm sorry. All right, so are you telling me Martin has been sleeping with other men and he has some weird disease?" My head is completely muddled as I move to the wine.

She pulls a face of disgust and shivers.

"I only left here Sunday evening," I say. "Martin was in bed with the flu, you were heading up to change his sheets, he wouldn't see a doctor ..." I list all the stupid facts until she butts in.

"Ha! Of course he wouldn't, he'd only want to have sex with him!"

"Claire!" I put both my hands over my ears.

"Or her," she adds. "You know what, Courtney? I don't have a problem with bisexuals. I voted yes for gay marriage, I have many gay and lesbian friends, I probably have bisexual friends: I don't nose into what people do in their private life unless, of course, that person happens to be my husband!"

"When did he tell you this? How did you find out? Why didn't you call me?" All very reasonable questions, I think, as I hand her the full glass of red and pour a little drop into another glass for myself. I'm driving but this is medicinal. Shock. I only came over to ask her if I could borrow her fancy luggage for my trip to Cornwall on Wednesday. I knew she'd be delighted I was going. I wasn't expecting this.

"I was too embarrassed." She gulps the red liquid. "I tried all day to call you, but every time I went to press the call button I couldn't do it. I mean ... I didn't have the words." She drinks.

"You are in shock," I tell her.

"It's more than shock, Courtney. I want to kill him." She manages to keep her tone level.

"So what exactly did he say to you?" I taste the bitter liquid.

Claire pulls out the high stool and hauls herself up. There is no spinning on it today. I notice the soles of her feet are black with dirt.

"Oh, where do I start? Where do I start, Courtney? I can't really get my head around all this." She heaves her chest up and takes a long, deep breath in through her nose.

"Just go slowly and tell me in your own time." I pull myself up onto my stool now, facing her. She exhales slowly through a tiny opening in her mouth.

"When you left, I finished my batch of cinnamon cookies and went up to change Martin's sheets. He was in the bathroom, so I made a start. I pulled off the duvet and a small brown plastic bottle fell onto the floor. When I picked it up, I saw it was a bottle of tablets. I read his name on them. He came out and just looked at me standing there, holding it. Martin, with a bottle of pills: he who has never taken a prescription tablet in his life. I asked him what they were. He told me they were antibiotics and that he had been to a doctor last week, on the advice of an ex-lover."

She looks up at me, her green eyes dull and frightened. With a shaking hand, she picks up her wine again and caresses it, both her hands wrapped around the glass for dear life.

"Oh my God ... Go on," I almost whisper.

"I was confused. And 'ex-lover'? Who? Anna-Rose McCarthy, seventeen years ago? I actually asked him that. He shook his head and then his face just crumpled, Courtney. He fell apart in front of me. He fell to his knees and told me he's been living a lie." She puts down the glass shakily and drags her hand over her mouth now, pulling the skin downwards. Then she goes on. "He said he was bisexual and had been sleeping with men, mainly on Friday nights when I was out with you ... in gay saunas ... and that some guy had come to the school and informed him that he had syphilis and gonorrhoea and that Martin needed to be tested too."

"Flipping hell." I draw out every vowel.

"I ... I ... I did notice this greenish-yellow stuff in his boxer shorts when I was washing them, but I didn't say anything as I didn't want to embarrass him. And he was always complaining that his testicles were painful ... Oh, Courtney, maybe I just didn't want to know. Seems he went for the bloods and he got a call to say he was negative for syphilis but positive for gonorrhoea and that he needed to inform previous sexual partners and start treatment straight away. That's when he took to the bed. Like, he does also legit have the flu; those aren't symptoms of the STD. He's still waiting on one more test ..."

She can see I'm not following her on this part.

"Don't you understand? So yes, he has got the flu, but he's also got a serious sexually transmitted disease, maybe another ... and you do know what that means, don't you?"

"What, Claire? Tell me," I ask, my mouth open.

"It means, Courtney, that whatever he has, you can be pretty damn sure I have it too. And do you know what my GP said when she came to the house to take my bloods this morning and I told her what was going on? She said, 'It's not a crime to be bisexual.' I said, 'It fucking is when you're married to me!'" Her lip quivers and her breath goes against her, then the tears roll hard and fast again.

"This all happened so quickly. How ... Like, how? What the hell?" My head is swimming.

"He could have HIV – we could both have HIV ..." She sobs.

"Jesus Christ," is all I can manage.

"I'll get my bloods back this week." She drains the glass.

I say nothing. It's like someone has hit me over the head

with a brick. My thinking is completely muzzy. She looks at my panicked expression.

"Yeah." She forces a wink. "Lucky me, hey?"

"What are you going to do?" I ask her. It's just so hard for me to take in. I always knew Claire was a bit more into Martin than he was into her, but I never for a second doubted he loved her.

"He's taking the antibiotics so that should help with the gonorrhoea, but he's still got the flu. He wants to talk tonight ..." She has to compose herself, get her breath back. I just slowly nod. "I will talk to him, but I have to be brutally honest, Courtney, I don't know if I can handle any of this. I'm sick to the pit of my stomach. I haven't eaten. I haven't slept."

I exhale the longest breath and shake my head. I am still lost for words. I just don't know what to say, but I have to say something.

"Does he still want to be married to you?" I ask.

"He does. He says he loves me, more than anything, but that he's always been bisexual and just hid it from me. He's asked me to accept him."

"And you never had any suspicions?" I have to ask.

"None." She sniffs and wipes her nose with the back of her hand. I pull a tissue out of my back pocket, then think again and hand her the rest of the packet.

"I don't know what to say," I whisper.

"No idea ... Although I guess it won't be that much of a shock to other people. I mean, look at me, Courtney. What man would actually fancy me? Perhaps I've just been his beard all these years." She looks up at me.

"Stop ... Don't do this to yourself," I say, with a massive

lump in my throat as I reach across for her tears and wipe them away. She blows her nose.

"I know people used to think that about me and Martin, Courtney, even when we were kids dating. Martin was so attractive and into fitness. I know people thought it was strange he picked me. I was never up to his standard. 'What does yer man see in the fat chick?' I heard that more than once when I was waiting on the sidelines cheering him on at basketball."

The floorboards creak and we both jerk our heads up. Suddenly it's like there's a stranger upstairs.

"I'd better go. This is your private business, Claire, I really shouldn't be here right now. But you know where I am if you need me."

She nods.

"Claire … How do you feel about Martin? Do you still want to be with him?"

"I think I need time to think before I can answer that one, love, okay?" she says, giving me a brave smile.

I give her a huge, bone-squeezing hug, take up my bag and move towards the door. She follows, passes me in the hallway and opens the front door for me. I step out into the welcome warm May air.

"And the worst part of all of this is that I gave up ever having children to have him." Claire looks around the garden as if seeing it for the first time.

"Oh Claire, I'm so sorry." I shut my eyes tight for a second, and when I open them, she has already closed the door.

5

"Final call for Aer Lingus flight EI552 to Newquay, now boarding at Gate 4C," the airport tannoy announces.

"Oh come on!" I throw my hands up in the impossibly slow-moving "Grab and Fly Coffee" drinks queue I've been standing in for about fifteen minutes. I move away, empty-handed, towards my gate. I am not good without my morning cup of coffee. Like, seriously. Usually Hajra, the nurse at Granny Alice's home, gives me a strong cup, but she wasn't on this morning, plus Tom was there early today for some reason, so I just left without, planning my coffee at the airport. I'll get one on the plane, I suppose.

Airports are beginning to become places I no longer like. I used to adore them. Probably because Granny Alice and I never left Ireland, and when I did get to an airport on my first holiday, on my honeymoon, aged twenty, to Majorca, it felt like the most exciting place on earth. Now, between the length of time it takes to get through security and the horrible, ominous vibe airports have hanging over them, I'm not as keen any more.

Moving towards the gate area, I catch a glimpse of myself in the long airport mirrors. The look is what you might call "business dress": at least that's what I'm hoping. My long blonde hair is GHD-straightened and sleek, pulled back into an Yvonne-style low ponytail. I'm wearing black patent shoes with a small, sensible kitten heel. The suit is tapered, with three-quarter-length black trousers and a smart suit jacket, teamed with a plain white T-shirt. As I step carefully onto the moving escalator, I hold onto the black handle of my small case tightly, standing on the right-hand side so others can freely pass me. I let a slow breath out and try to get my head together. So much is swimming around in it.

It took me two large glasses of red wine and several drops of Rescue Remedy to get to sleep last night, and the night before. Susan, as I'd correctly guessed, had been overjoyed when I told her that I was going to Cornwall on a work overnighter and that she would be staying with Dad in Mar-nee's apartment on Wednesday night. She'd actually squealed and hugged me. They were the first words we had spoken since our row on Sunday afternoon in the kitchen.

People push past me, running, panting, stressed. I inhale again. It's not like my nerves aren't on absolute edge already. Why I didn't cancel this trip, I do not know. Claire needs me, Granny needs me, and I'm leaving Susan in Mar-nee's dangerous hands.

I didn't see Claire yesterday. I called and texted, but she just said she was okay and that she had talked to Martin. I didn't get any more details, but we are going for dinner on Friday night so I will hear the rest then. I still can't get my head around all this. She thinks she will have her blood work back today, so I will check in with her later. I wonder how Martin feels, knowing I know all this too. How could he do that to her? I get his sexuality isn't a choice. That's not my issue. It's his blatant dishonesty and cheating. I hope I won't regret this trip. I get feelings like this a lot – I'm a big believer in "things happen for a reason".

"Excuse me!" A man with a briefcase slams it into my thigh as he passes by and I let out a scream. It bloody hurt. He runs on. No "I'm terribly sorry, are you okay?" or "Apologies, I'm in a dreadful hurry." Nothing. Nada. He reminds me instantly of my uncle Tom. Rude. Uncaring. I rub my leg and step off the travelator. I limp for a second before my body adjusts to the pain, then I just get on with it. I bruise like a peach, so this should be a good one.

At Gate 4C, people are already boarding, so I hand over my boarding pass to the male cabin-crew member and make my way down the black tunnel towards the aircraft. I struggle to get a space for my case in the holding area as it's already quite full, but I bash it in somehow.

As I settle into my window seat and click my seatbelt shut, I open my bag and take out the paperwork. Simple enough: we need the town hall to sign off on the office opening and closing hours we are planning. Lar and I thought it might be a really good idea to have late-night opening on Thursdays and Fridays to take advantage of tourist families who might be out for walks together to wander in. It is this issue the council needs to talk to us about.

The new office was a post office building many moons

ago, by all accounts. I haven't seen it yet. Then there's the matter of furnishing the apartment – maybe *my* apartment – above it. The thought makes my stomach lurch in excitement. Things like this don't happen to me.

"Ladies and gentlemen, I'm afraid there will be no hot drinks served on board today – we have a technical issue with our water boiler," the male cabin-crew member who took my boarding pass now announces.

Ah, come on. What are the chances? Politely, I watch as he demonstrates the safety procedures and I order a sparkling water and a chocolate croissant when the trolley comes round.

No one sits in the middle seat, so it's a comfortable journey over and before I know it Newquay is laid out below me like a patchwork quilt of greenery. I quickly put away all the paperwork and, with my nose pressed up to the thick glass of the small oval window, I admire the blinding blue of the sea. It's good to be back. This Tony Becker man is collecting me. I think back to the phone call we had last night before I left the office.

"It's a one-hour-and-fifteen-minute flight, so I'll land in Newquay at half past three in the afternoon." I read the details out to him as I managed my booking, checking in online, then printing off my boarding pass.

"Sound." He seemed to be scribbling something down. *That's sensible,* I thought. *One of these perfectionists, I bet.*

"So I'll see you then, Tony. We can go straight to the town hall. I'll check into my hotel after we finish all that needs to be done. Go see the new office, and was it a Brian Fogg's furniture place, did you say? I'm happy to grab a taxi outside after we go there so I won't need you." I folded the boarding pass in half and slipped it into my large diary.

"Huh ...? Yup, sound," he replied.

"All right, thanks, Tony."

"Yeah ... yup, sound ..." He'd hung up as he was still talking.

There's a niggly feeling I have that I'm not going to like this guy. He doesn't exactly seem personable. At least his work is nearly done, and if I do take the job for the summer I'll have no reason to talk to him again.

The seatbelt sign is switched on now and the pilot informs us we are about to land. Putting all the drama from home to the back of my mind, I bounce slightly as we hit the clouds coming down and tell myself to concentrate on the next twenty-four hours. The calm blue sea waves up at me and I'm beginning to feel excitement now at the fact I'm going to see Cornwall and St Ives again, and that I might be able to spend a glorious summer here on my own with Susan.

The landing is smooth and we disembark via the rear of the aircraft. Newquay airport, I remember clearly from my last visit, is like a small metal shed. It's located on the north Cornish coast and was a former tactical nuclear bomber base, but the most brilliant thing about it is how small and easy to navigate it is. My type of airport. I compare it with the chaotic mess that was Dublin airport on my way out and I breathe a Cornwall sigh of relaxation.

A twenty-four-minute commute is next, so Tony and I can discuss the paperwork on the trip up to St Ives.

Nipping into the ladies', I give my hair a brush and redo my ponytail, and I also smear some tinted pink gloss on my lips. I make my way to arrivals, which seems very quiet, and look around for a man standing on his own holding a card with either my name or the company name. There are no men on their own. There is a Chinese lady eating a Cornetto, a stressed-looking family and a young guy holding a fairly withered-looking bouquet of red roses. I lean against the rail and set my case between my legs, then check my phone for both the time and messages. It's nearly a quarter to four: maybe he was giving me time to get through to this side. I'd literally murder a coffee and there is a Starbucks right down the end of the hall, but I'm afraid to move in case he arrives and we miss one another. I text Susan, so she'll get it soon after school. And then I wait, and I wait, and there is no sign of anyone coming to pick me up.

Eventually, at twenty past four, I call his mobile. It goes directly to voicemail. I'm very conscious that the town hall probably closes at five o'clock, so I leave a message.

"Tony, it's Courtney Downey. I'm assuming you aren't coming to pick me up as arranged, so I'm going to take a taxi to the town hall immediately. I will wait there for you."

End call. What a total and utter arsehole. I wouldn't mind, but he was the one who suggested he collect me in the first place. My phone rings out. I wonder what his pathetic excuse will be, but it's not him, it's Celine, the party organiser for Susan's celebration in the GAA club. She is just looking for final numbers, which I give her. Only three place cards for the vegetarian burgers: Mar-nee, David and the birthday girl herself. God, I really hope Susan is going to enjoy this party.

Outside it's turned cloudy, but the air is incredibly warm and scented. Deciding to hang on for another few minutes, I lean up against the white "Welcome to Newquay" airport wall, then I check my phone one last time before I take the first taxi in the queue and give the address of the town hall. It's located just off the main shopping area, on Fore Street.

I hardly take in the breathtakingly beautiful rugged scenery as we travel; all the time I'm checking my phone from any news from poor Claire. What is she going to do now? How could Martin have been so cruel, so careless? What he's done is unforgivable. The worst part about it all is I know Claire will be heartbroken for life: that's how much she loved Martin. Nothing I can say or do for my wonderful friend will help her, and that breaks my heart too.

The taxi man starts to make pleasantries with me, so I put my phone away. We discuss the next few days' forecast and he recommends places to eat. It's a very interesting discussion, as he tells me he was once a chef.

"Many moons ago, dear, family business t'was. I got out!" His right arm comfortably leans out the open window. His accent is wonderful to my ears and I tell him this.

"Well, the West Country accent is full of dropped Hs and the TV world would have you think we all speak like Worzel Gummidge, but we don't. I love our history in language. Unique sounds, yes, but I also love the words and sayings we still have from back in the fourteenth century, like 'stank'. We love to use that word. If you've been for a tough walk, you will be heard saying, 'That was a good old stank now, wasn't it?' Unique."

I nod as I read his ID badge, which is pinned to a picture of three smiling young boys. His sons, no doubt.

"That's fascinating. But the cheffing … the restaurant business, is it hard work, Steve?" I'm looking for confirmation, not really asking a question.

"Tis hard hours, yes, but I loved it. I grew up in St Ives, you know, and although we are celebrated for our Cornish pasties, we also have some incredible fine dining. My grandmother had a restaurant close to the waterfront in the old fishing quarter. It's a fish restaurant called Meloria's nowadays, lobsters and crabs caught from the nearby quay. My youngest brother runs it, in fact. No easy task keeping the business a success, with the variety of seafood places here, but he's a determined-enough lad." The back of his head sprouts tufts of grey hair. I focus on his ID picture again. Steve has a long grey goatee beard and eyes that laugh.

"I could live on seafood," I tell him. "My greatest dish is a seafood linguine. My granny used to make it." The windows in the back are also rolled down and the seaweed scent fills the big taxi.

"Meloria's is somewhere you should eat at then, love – does sea bass, scallops, oysters, and it's overlooking the 'arbour. Jessica, one of the chefs, does the best seafood linguine. Keep my brother's pockets lined, too! Would be very nice of you." He chuckles.

He pulls up to the town hall, and when he stops, I put away my notebook and pay my fare. Steve jumps out and opens the door for me. Ha! Good to see chivalry is not totally dead.

"There ya go, it's that building right there." Steve points, then shakes my hand warmly.

"Thanks, Steve," I say, and turn.

"Hang on," he says, and I face him again. "Has anyone ever told you that you look a lot like Kate Winslet" – I wait – "in *Titanic*?"

"Yeah, I get that a bit." I laugh.

The town hall is a small, whitewashed building with a large green door. There are some local kids playing with spinners on the little red brick wall that surrounds it. It's situated at the very end of Fore Street, and I see visitors strolling up the cobbled street as I make my way inside.

"At bloody last!"

A man jumps up. A larger-than-life man. So all-consuming is his presence, I feel a bit weak at the knees. My brain goes underwater for a few seconds. He's about six foot three, a tower of a man, burly, and absolutely, completely and utterly drop-dead gorgeous. This man would not look out of place on the big screen. I was not expecting this. Tony Becker is sex on legs.

"Excuse me?" I finally shake the water from my brain and drop my suitcase. The cool, air-conditioned foyer is empty apart from the two of us.

"Courtney Downey, I'm presuming?" he booms at me. I feel about two feet tall beside him.

"Y-y-y-yes ... You are Tony?" I manage as I look up at him. My mouth feels so dry. I suck both my cheeks to drain some saliva.

"Yeah, I am, and you were supposed to be here an hour ago. I checked your flight. It was in on time; as a matter of fact, with the winds you landed six minutes ahead of schedule." He stuffs his hands deep into his jeans pockets. I see the silver buckle on his belt and a flash of flesh. My head bobs up and down until I rest on his face again. I'm a total mess. What is going on here?

"Well, you were supposed to collect me from the airport!" I blurt. Because I feel all sorts of uncomfortable, I'm bloody mad now.

"Eh, no, I wasn't actually. I distinctly remember you saying on the phone you would take a taxi and that you didn't need me." He stares down at me.

"I did not!" I slap my side in annoyance, then wince because I've just hit my fresh bruise.

"You did too." He slaps his.

"I didn't though!" I shake my head wildly.

"Appears you did!" He snorts and makes what I perceive to be pretend growling noises at me.

"Oh my God, you are so annoying…" I huff.

"Oh my God, so are you!" He imitates me with a smirk on his face. "Tell me, have you ever been arrested or charged with a crime?"

Before I can retaliate I hear, "Tony, are you both ready?"

An attractive woman in high wedges, a long red dress and a large circular donut bun in her hair approaches us.

"Ready, Marina, really sorry to have kept you. Bit of a mix-up here." His tone lightens and he spreads a great big smile onto his handsome-as-hell face. He's so like a film star. Dark hair, cut so short, almost shaved, with a little spiky re-growth. The darkest eyes and fullest eyebrows I have ever seen. For sure, Claire Carney would be blinking in rapid succession, storing this man in her memory bank. Or would she? Poor Claire. Her horrendous situation hits me in the stomach again.

Tony taps my shoulder. "You still with us?"

This is all a bit disconcerting. I'm still livid with him, but I compose myself, turn off my phone and enter the meeting room.

6

"Well, that was easy enough after all," Tony says to me now as we walk outside. The clouds have lifted, leaving clear blue skies above, and the direct heat of the sun on my face is wonderful. A wonderful smell of freshly brewing coffee hits my nostrils. I breathe it in. I'd presumed Marina would offer coffee, and I've have taken her hand off. Instead she had mineral waters and saffron buns.

"Yes, thank you for your help," I say, now absolutely roasting and removing my suit jacket. "It was really important we got those late-night closing hours on a Thursday and Friday agreed on," I say, businesslike. Tony sits on the small wall and crosses his long legs one over the other. Looking up at him, he reminds me of the giant from Jack and the Beanstalk. I feel like little Jack beside him: that's how powerful Tony's physical presence is. Sitting beside him, but not too close, I move my suitcase in between us both with my legs. I'd love a gum or a mint. I'm guessing my breath isn't that fresh. I'm regretting the garlic potatoes and tofu I made for our dinner last night, partly because it was very bland and unsatisfying and partly because I must stink right now. Normally it never bothers me that I cook with so much garlic.

"Can I drop you off at the hotel so you can drop off your case?" he asks, smirking at me now.

"No, it's fine, I will hold onto it for now. I'll get a taxi when we are finished all the business at hand. Thank you, though," I answer. If I don't get a coffee soon I will cry. He nods and shifts on the wall as he takes out his phone, scrolling through something.

"I know a good taxi guy I can speed-dial for you later, so." Then he pauses. "I never usually make mistakes like that. I'm so sure you told me you were getting a taxi from the airport."

Then I recall the conversation. He seemed preoccupied, writing something down, and I was in the process of checking in online.

"I think perhaps we were both at fault. I said I'd take a taxi back to my hotel when we had done all the business, if I remember correctly." I'm acutely aware of my appearance every time he looks at me and I don't know why. I'm wondering now, is my liquid eyeliner running? Is he noticing my three chins?

"Aha," he says, still scrolling through his phone. "I was sitting at the kitchen table trying to finish my crossword that afternoon, so I might not have been paying attention." He smiles widely. He has perfectly straight teeth.

"Your crossword?" I can't help but laugh.

"I take it very seriously, like to keep my brain active, ya know. Look, Courtney Downey, I'm sorry for the mix-up.

Allow me to drive you to the hotel when we're finished?" His wide eyes make his appeal for him.

"Thank you, that would be great, if you are sure."

He doesn't move, just continues to stare at me, and it's intense, and I feel a bit flushed and uncomfortable.

"Will I be waiting here until you get your car and then you never come back?" I raise my eyebrows in jest.

"You are a funny one … Don't you think veneers are the funniest things you have ever seen in your whole entire life?" he asks, tapping his teeth with his baby finger.

"No … What, do you have them?" I lean in to take a look.

"I do not! I literally can't look at them. I'm just instantly reminded of Jim Carrey in *The Mask* and it sends me into hysterics!" He laughs again at himself.

"Okay," I say, unsure.

"Just getting to know you, that's all," he says.

"Was that the reason for the bizarre, 'Tell me, have you ever been arrested or charged with a crime' question back in the town hall?" I can't help but be highly amused at this man, and I'm not sure why.

"Indeed." He nods and smiles. "Gotta love random questions to strangers, right?" He says the words as though he's been carefully considering them. "This way. Brian is expecting us." He stands back and gestures to me to walk first.

I drape my jacket over the suitcase and pull it along behind me. A black jeep is parked nearby. It beeps and the lights flash on and off, and we settle in. As Tony concentrates on pulling out into the traffic, I steal another look at him. His short hair has speckles of grey. His big, dark brown eyes sit above heavy dark stubble. He's wearing dark jeans, a black T-shirt and workman's boots, those heavy black industry ones. I bet you could drop the heaviest kettlebell on them and he wouldn't feel a thing. His biceps are big, but from manual work. They're not those awful gym biceps. He has dark speckles of hair on his forearms. Manly. Masculine. They are the two words to best describe this Tony Becker.

"Have you been to Cornwall before then?" He makes an effort at conversation.

"Yes." I realise that I'm staring at him, so I look out my window. Small talk has never been one of my strong points. I avoid most situations where I have to engage in it. Another area David and I were so different in. He loved talking to the neighbours for hours. He'd go to put the bin out and be out there for an hour, discussing nothing. It's not that I don't like our neighbours, I do – they are great and I'm blessed to have such good ones even if they are slightly nosey – I just don't have the time to make long-winded small talk and, if I'm truthful to myself, it makes me uncomfortable.

"Right. You like it?" he asks.

"Yeah, I've been here, to St Ives actually. A good few years ago now, but I adored the place. It had a real effect on me, if I'm being really honest," I tell him.

"St Ives can do that all right." He turns and nods in agreement with me. Our eyes meet. He looks down now and fiddles with the radio dial. His forefinger and thumb move the knob around and around until he settles on a song he must like. He turns the volume up high and taps his long fingers on the steering wheel as we drive on. It's a light rock anthem I know and love, so I tap my feet along too. The sun streams in through the window and he suddenly leans across me to the glove box, brushing his hand off my leg. Every sense in my body is heightened by his touch. He flips open the glove box and then pulls out a pair of aviator shades. He turns down the volume as the DJ pipes in at the end of the song.

"Are you married then?" he asks as the DJ drones away. I stare at him. For some reason it's easier to do so now that his eyes are covered.

"That's a very personal question, don't you think?" I say into my own reflection.

He nods in agreement. "Suppose it is, really."

"Are you married?" I ask, although I'd noticed he wasn't wearing a ring in the town hall earlier.

"Indeed I am not. Awful thing, marriage. Horrific." He physically shudders then waves at a car that passes us and toots lightly on the horn. "I mean, why would anyone want to do that to themselves?" His shades glisten into my face.

"Oh, I dunno ... But you really should keep your eyes on the road, Tony ... Lifelong commitment is a huge sign of true love, perhaps?" I offer, unconvinced myself after my shambles of a marriage and Claire's current situation.

"Is it? It is in me arse. Lust! That's what triggers commitment and, as we all know, lust doesn't last." He takes his eyes off the road again, but this time I can't meet his stare.

"It does in a lot of cases, Tony," I tell him.

"Not a lot, Courtney. Lust is new. It's fresh. Lust is something that's so powerful it can't sustain itself. Lust is dangerous and lethal and never-lasting."

102

"Wow ... I'm assuming you have never been married then?" I make a fist and rub an imaginary stain off my passenger window.

"No. Never have, never will."

We drive on in silence. Aromas waft through the window and I think, *Oh, coffee, I need coffee.*

"You wanna see the post office revamp? Check out your new office and living space before we drop into Brian's?"

"Sure. Eh, Tony, any chance I could grab a coffee somewhere before that? I'm gasping." What the hell, I have to ask. Hello, my name is Courtney Downey and I'm a caffeine addict.

"Oh sure, here ..." He suddenly bangs down the indicator with his two fingers. "We're literally passing my house and I've the good stuff. Brian isn't going anywhere this evening," he says, and I nod in agreement. He almost swerves off the main road and I get thrown around the passenger seat as we drive up a long, narrow lane. Branches of trees scrape noisily off the side of the jeep and a fox darts past us. Tony toots the horn again three times.

"That's old Billy the fox. I let him live here rent-free." He laughs and beeps loudly again, sticking his head dangerously far out the window. "Hello, Billy, my old chum, we have a visitor, get the muck off your paws!"

The fox stops in its tracks and looks up at the jeep. I can't help but laugh again. This man is nuts. At the end of the lane, a large house comes into view. It's detached, with a thatched roof. It's uniquely beautiful, all cream brick front and huge bay windows.

"Oh wow, is this your place?" I am gobsmacked.

"Yeah, nice spot, ain't it? I built it myself about eight

years ago. I could never live anywhere but St Ives." He pulls the jeep to a halt as the stony gravel crunches under the tyres.

"Who do you live with?" It's a natural question, as the house is so big.

"With Billy. Don't you ever listen, woman?" He winks at me and the engine dies.

★ ★ ★

You know one of those cups of coffee where every sip is heaven? Strong and piping hot. Caffeine fix. Your blood starts to flow better and your head clears. That's the coffee Tony has just handed me in a chipped yellow mug. Heaven.

His kitchen is huge, and has pale cream walls with granite flooring and a black Aga in the corner. The table sits in the middle of the kitchen, a huge oak one with eight wicker chairs around it. It's kind of indescribable how comfortable I feel at this table. It's littered with various crossword puzzle books, some as thick as *War and Peace*, and a few empty wine bottles. It has a look, this kitchen, of being lived in, but not being loved. I have an unbelievable urge to see what's in the fridge and whip up lunch.

As if he was reading my mind, he says, "No food to offer you, I'm afraid. I never cook in here. I might have a digestive somewhere ..." He pulls out a wicker chair for me to sit in as I shake my head.

"No, this is perfect, thanks a million." I cradle the cup between my hands.

"Great accent, the Irish accent," he says with a smile.

"Tank yew, sur." I mock my own accent and smile at him as he laughs. I am easier in his presence now. Perhaps because it's been so long since I've been alone with a man like this I was a bit knocked off my perch. He is typing a message on his phone, so I sneak another look around. A dartboard and bookshelves crammed with autobiographies are mainly what catch my eye, plus a very large red dog bowl with little black paw prints painted on it. To me, it looks home-made, as though a child might have painted it.

"Lar tells me you might be the one down here next month working in the relocation office for the summer. I come into contact with a lot of people in my other job who are always talking about relocating." He puts the phone down on the pile of crossword books.

"It's a bit of a hard one, I'm afraid ..." Am I imagining it or did he actually pull a face when I said "hard one". His expression is serious again, so I don't know. I narrow my eyes at him in a way that says, "Don't mess with me, Two-Job Tony," before I go on. "I have a daughter you see—"

"Oh right, are you married then? Sorry about all that earlier in the car. Each to their own and all that." He puts his yellow coffee cup to his lips.

"No."

He puts the cup straight back down.

"Well, technically ... yes. I've been separated for well over a year now, but we share custody of our daughter."

"How old is she?" He picks the coffee back up and blows into the mug.

"She turns sixteen next Saturday. Sounds crazy when I say that. Where did those sixteen years go to?" I shake my head and he nods back to me as though in total agreement.

"So I'm presuming she's coming with you? And would I also be right in saying that this is the issue then: that you don't want to take her away from her dad? That's it, isn't it?" he asks, leaning in closer to me again.

I shrug. To be honest, I'd never thought of it that way. It's a bit of a bolt of lightning to my brain. I've never even considered David's feelings in all of this! I haven't even talked to him about it, at all. If Susan says she wants to come, we are doing it. Is that awfully unfair of me?

"I haven't told him yet," I say.

He tilts his head and looks at me questioningly.

"How is that possible? He is her father, right?" His tone has changed slightly.

"Well, yeah, but—"

"Well then, he has a bloody right to know your plans, pet." His tone is now slightly aggressive. Am I actually hearing him correctly? How dare he? I put my cup down carefully on a coaster.

"Yes, thank you, I am aware of that, Tony," I spit back at him.

"Okay…Just seems to me like you might have forgotten his feelings in all of this, that's all."

"Mind your own business," I snap. He jerks his head at me. "Shit … Look, I'm sorry. I think we'd better go now." I push back my chair and stand up, mortified at my outburst.

"I didn't mean to upset you, Courtney Downey." He is out of his chair now and moves the seat further back for me. I walk to the sink, cup in hand.

"You haven't, it's just all still a bit raw, that's all, and

106

please can you stop calling me Courtney Downey? I sound like the accused in a court room or something."

"Okay, Courtney Downey." He is beside me at the sink.

"Seriously?" I hold my eyes open wide and he pokes me in the leg.

"*Ouch!*" I scream.

"Woah, sorry … Jesus, it was a gentle poke!" He looks completely horrified.

"Sorry, I know …" I rub my throbbing thigh. "A guy whacked me there with his briefcase earlier and it's so sore." I feel so stupid now. I just want to get to my hotel.

"Here, sit. Let me put some ice on it for you." He takes the cup from my hand, puts his arm around me and redirects me back to the seat. My tummy is crashing around at his touch.

"No need …" I try to protest, but he's plonked me on the chair and is over at the large fridge-freezer. Returning with a bag of frozen carrots, he kneels by my side.

"Where is it exactly?" he asks, concerned, and I put my hand on the bruise. Gently, he lifts my hand and holds it for a second too long, I think. Lightning bolts run through me at the touch of his fingertips. I pull my hand away.

"If you'd prefer to take your trousers off, you can take my carrots into the bathroom."

I blurt out a laugh now. This is ludicrous. He starts to laugh too.

"No thanks, I'm good. Just let me hold the carrots here for a minute; I'll get ice for it later on in my hotel room. Thanks." I stare up at him, flirting through my eyelashes. He stands up and stretches. Jesus.

"If you're sure."

His body language is jittery now, I notice. He rubs his palms down the sides of his jeans. Lust. It's the four-letter word that's doing a dance through my brain.

Holding the carrots takes me back to reality, and I think about what he has just said. He is right. Of course he is. Could David stop me taking Susan here for the summer? Surely not. Surely he will see what a great opportunity this is for me and to broaden Susan's horizons too? It's only for three months and, of course, he can come and visit as often as he wants. And Mar-nee, if she must.

Suddenly eager to move away from Tony, I pick up the carrots, get up and put them back in the freezer. I see my cup is in the shallow ceramic sink now, so I turn on the tap.

"What an asshole," he says and he looks really cross.

"Who?" I ask, turning back to him.

"That asshole that rammed his suitcase into you! Are you okay? I have some painkillers, if you need any." He looks genuinely angry.

"No, honestly." I turn on the tap to wash the cup, slightly taken aback by his concern.

"Leave that, it's fine," he says. So I do.

We're standing about three feet apart, staring at each other. I look to the right, then I look back, and he's still looking straight at me.

"Right." He shakes his head roughly from side to side, as though trying to get himself out of a daze. "Shall we go?" He grabs his ginormous bunch of keys from the kitchen table. Nodding in agreement, I walk to the door and stand out by the dusty black jeep. The gardens are beautiful. Lots of primroses are in bloom, and they smell divine.

As I move to the car door, I glance across the gardens at a large round rustic table and benches. A gas barbeque square stands beside them. This garden is making me hungry. It's the type of garden that you can effortlessly see hosting a big party: children running around playing hide and seek, adults sipping cold white wine, and the smell of barbecuing sausages filling the summer's air. There is a sense of what this house could be. I strongly feel it.

"Back in the jeep," he says as he beeps the doors open and closes the front door of the house behind him. "We are only ten minutes away from Brian's warehouse," he tells me, and those are the only words we speak for the next ten minutes. He twiddles that damn dial and my head spins about Susan and the possibility of us coming here. More winding roads and small lanes where brambles scratch the paintwork on the jeep. We pull up to a large warehouse.

"Know what you're looking for?" he asks as we get out and stroll up side by side. "I've fitted the kitchen appliances and bathroom fittings, so it's only the furniture for the main room you need to pick out. Brian has it all." Tony puts all his weight behind a green sliding timber door and pulls it back. I see his biceps and I have to look down immediately, pretending to attend to a broken nail.

Brian welcomes me with a big bear hug. He's slim and is wearing beige paint-splattered overalls and a baseball cap. The smell of woodchip is appealing to me and his warehouse has some fantastic pieces. Strolling around his workshop, intrigued by his craftsmanship, I choose a heavy, round beech table and chairs. Then we head into his showroom, where I choose a brown two-seater leather sofa.

"On to the office with us, nearly there," Tony says after we say thank you to Brian. We drive for a few minutes, and just before we hit the main street, Tony signals left and we pull in.

"Off the main street?" I observe rather than ask.

"Yeah, that's the beauty of it: a stone's throw from the main street, and there's parking," he tells me. And he's right. Again. The old post office is a fantastic location. Literally two minutes' walk from outside the town, and its character has been wonderfully preserved.

As we walk he falls into step beside me. "This is it." He opens the glass front door with his jingling bunch of keys and we go inside. A really neat job has been done. There is real brick wall throughout inside. It's a small space, but there is a neatly made desk in the corner where the hatch of a post office might once have been. White shelving hangs from every available wall, and in the centre there is a custom-built table. I can see it's going to be a perfect office space to sell relocations.

"Oh, it's brilliant, Tony, Lar will be delighted. It's a big step for him, I just hope it works out." I run my hands over the marble-topped table.

"Are you kidding me? A relocation business is a no-brainer." He pulls at a stray yellow wire sticking out of a wall.

"Have you seen much of the world?" It's my turn to play question time now, but when I turn to ask him I catch him checking the time on his watch. He pushes his bottom lip out and rubs his stubble.

"Good question. Enough for now. When I retire I want to see more, and I'm planning on retiring at sixty. I bet you want to see upstairs?"

Am I imagining it or does he seems to be rushing me now? Nodding, I follow him to the back of the shop, where there is a small winding wooden staircase with a black steel bannister. Slightly treacherous. Holding the bannister, I go up, making a mental note never to navigate these stairs tipsy. At the top is a glass door. Tony rummages around again on his set of keys, the largest I have ever seen, and eventually finds a small one. He turns it in the lock and the door opens. He leans back on the steel stairwell and I go ahead of him.

As soon as I step in, I adore the space. Totally love it. I get a smell of something new and fresh and free. It's so warm and I look up to see oceans of warm light streaming in through the huge skylight and bouncing off the canary-yellow walls. The empty living space is much larger than I had imagined and I can see it's almost habitable. Dark wooden floors are laid and wires stick out from plug sockets. It has a good-sized kitchen adjoining, all dark-grey sleek presses and modern American-style fridge-freezer. All new fixtures and fittings. Claire's kitchen would be pea green with envy. Basically, apart from personal touches I could add, like soft furnishings to go with my newly acquired table and sofa, it's finished. Strolling across the living room into the spacious master bedroom and en suite, I start to get jitters in my tummy. The little box room is just off the living space, and I realise this apartment is perfect for myself and Susan. When I enter the master bedroom, I am enthralled by the huge bay window that overlooks the ocean. This could be our new home.

"You have done an amazing job." I turn to Tony and see his head almost touches the roof up here.

"It's a great apartment, loads of space up here," he says, and I can tell he's pleased with my compliment. Stuffing his hands deeper into his jeans pockets, he takes it all in. Admires his own work, if you will.

"I absolutely love it." I walk through the space again, trailing my fingers lightly along the walls as I go.

"Hope those hands are clean, Mrs Downey." He grins at me.

"Oops, sorry, Tony!" I step away from the wall and find myself stumbling into him. It's a much flirtier move than I could ever have planned.

Time sort of stands still until he says, "Only messing. Sure, it's your place now, right?" He dangles the big bunch of keys in front of me again. I look out at the ocean, still leaning on him. His big boots seems rooted to the spot.

"I really hope so." I almost whisper the words, and I bob my head from side to side as though I'm thinking about his suggestion, surmising, my head bumping off his shoulder as I go. I'm acutely aware I'm flirting with him, even though it was not premeditated.

Then I realise I'm probably taking up his entire day, so I stand up straight and, faking a stretch, hold my arms high above my head and interlink my fingers. I give a fake yawn. Then I once again tell him what a super job he has done and I snap a few pictures on my iPhone before we make our way back down the winding stairwell. I wonder, will it be me and my Susan or Yvonne Connolly sleeping up there and sitting behind that desk next month?

At the back of the office is a derelict-looking green area. Tony has gone out ahead of me, and when I join him outside he's moved down to the end of the huge long field that the office is built on. Manoeuvring my way over the rough ground in my kitten heels, I guess Tony has all but abandoned me. At the end of the field he stands beside what look like two totally run-down cottages partially joined together. He catches me staring at them before he says, "Come here. My plan is to knock the small one down and use the materials for that to fix up the bigger one. Keep the costs way down." His fingers beckon me to stand beside him.

"You own them?" I'm surprised, and I wobble as I try to regroup.

"I do." He picks up a loose brick and throws it onto a pile of others.

"What are you going to do with them?" I ask.

"Well, I know what I want to do with them, but I don't know yet if I can make it happen, Courtney Downey, do I? You have many questions. I like to see that; I love that. Sweet or sour?" he asks as he crunches his big workman's boots over a pile of cement while slapping dirt from his hands.

"It's hard but, if pushed to the edge of a cliff, I'd say sour. When did you buy them?" I ask.

"Me too … Oh years ago." He picks up various other bricks and stones and separates them into piles. Birds sing and the sun beats down on us. What I wouldn't give to be in a pair of shorts and a T-shirt.

113

"And they are still sitting there?" I put my hand on the bigger cottage. Both have a unique character I can't quite explain. The suns hits one of the broken window and bounces off it. Pebble-dashed in white, they look lonely.

"Sometimes you just have to hold out for when the time is right. It's been a long wait...I'm waiting on some financial backing, if you will." I sense he is embarrassed he's said too much, so I change the subject. Perhaps there is an emotional attachment to the cottages. An ex, maybe?

"The town-hall woman, Marina, I think her name was, wasn't it? She definitely seemed to think the business relocation idea will be a gold mine, and she was incredibly enthusiastic about this location you have; in fact, she referred to it as 'prime'. So you might be sitting on a little business gold mine here too," I say.

"For a second when you said about the late-night licence, I thought she was going to have an issue," he replies.

"I know! Me too!" I say, relieved she didn't.

"Well, in fairness to her, she's brilliant: great woman, great company, and she wants the best for the community, not like that battleaxe Mrs Halpin, who wants to stop the whole of Cornwall expanding at all. That's why I had to get you over today, while she's in with her hip. She hates me." He's picked up a stick now and is bashing both soles of his boots to remove the dry mud.

"You can't hear the traffic from the road here, just the chirping birds, and it's so peaceful," I say when he drops the stick. We both stop in our tracks and just listen. It's a proper summer's day. The light wind blows my hair, which has escaped from the constraints of my bobble, and it's like we are standing in a different world.

"It's funny. I come here almost every day, and for some reason today I can see how perfect this place really is." He inhales deeply.

"It's stunning," I say, and I mean it.

"Yeah. Obviously I've loved this spot for ever, so when Lar told me about looking for a property for the new office, I knew the old post office would be perfect. There is something about this piece of land...You see, it's always been my dream to—"

My phone rings out. Claire's name flashes up at me. The picture I've added to her icon when she calls me is, ironically, her dressed as a very flamboyant Elton John for a fancy-dress party she attended with Martin last year. As I recall now, she had found the party a bit boring and had gone home early, leaving Martin behind.

"Excuse me a minute, I really need to take this," I say hurriedly as I walk away from Tony, towards the dusty jeep. "Hi, how are you?" I breathe down the line.

"Hey, can you talk?" she asks me.

"Of course I can, I've been waiting for you to call me. Go on," I implore.

"Just got the blood work back ..." She stops.

"And?" I clench the fist of my left hand.

She sniffs, but it's a calm sniff. "Well, seems I'm okay, Courtney. God only knows how ...I do have to go in for an internal and she wants to do a smear, but Martin didn't spread any other sexually transmitted disease to me. And both our HIV tests were negative." She snorts out a nervous guffaw.

Leabharlanna Poibli Chathair Bhaile Átha Cliath

Dublin City Public Libraries

"Oh, thank God for that!" I lean against Tony's jeep. A copy of *Cosmopolitan* on the back seat, a pair of red strappy wedges and various donuts for hair buns catch my eye.

"So, what is happening with Martin?" I ask.

"Oh, Courtney, I just can't be married to him any more, I don't think ... My heart is totally broken. I thought we were for life, I really did." I can hear the utter sorrow in my wonderful friend's voice.

"Look, don't make any rash decisions today or tomorrow ... I'll see you Friday night and we can talk it all out. I have to hear what he's had to say for himself, Claire."

"Yeah, okay. I can't think straight. I've cried so much my eyes have an actual infection! Even my own tears are turning on me! On my order he's gone to stay with his perfect mum, who, by the way, told me she always suspected that he was seeing men behind my back. Why, Courtney? Why did he lie to me for so many years?" Her breath goes against the words and she sobs quietly now.

I search for anything to say that might ease her pain. "I wish I knew, I really do, but the only thing I do know is that Martin did love you ... Yes, he led a life that was full of deception, but I know he loved you."

"I just feel like a complete and utter fool. Like everyone has been laughing at me behind my back. I feel like a mug. I go between complete anger, hating his guts, and then I drag the old photo albums out and torture myself looking at all the good times we had, and there were many." She blows her nose loudly now. Tony moves towards me now, looking at his watch.

"Claire, I'm sorry, but I gotta go here," I tell her.

"Sure. Look, I didn't want to keep you, I know you are

116

busy, but I knew you'd be anxious to hear, so that's why I called." She sniffs again.

"Of course!" I stare at the supermodel on the cover of *Cosmopolitan*.

"I'll tell you everything on Friday. Will I book O'Hara's in the back section for eight?" Her voice is so desperately sad that I just want to be beside her, hugging her close.

Tony is nearly on top of me now. "Yeah, eight on Friday is perfect," I say.

"Gotta go," Tony whispers.

"Text you later," I say.

"Love you."

"Love you too," I say as Tony stands right beside me now and gets back into the jeep. I push my phone into my pocket and hop back into the front seat.

"It's getting late. We'd better get you to the hotel. You must be tired and starving," he says. His tone is suddenly less friendly: cooler almost, more professional. He checks his watch again before running his hands through his hair. For a split second I wonder what it might be like to drag my hands through that hair. To lose myself in those lips. To run my hands over his bare chest and scrape my nails down his back. It's been literally years since I've had any type of fantasy about a man. Honestly, I was beginning to think I had become one of those asexual women. I clear my throat.

"Would it be possible to get a look at the tourist office, if it's near? I think it's the top of Street-An-Pol." I chance my arm.

He looks at his watch again. "Sorry, I'm under pressure now, I've to get to my other job ... I've a thing on later. I can spin you past the tourist office, but I'd have to let

117

you make your own way to the hotel." Clipped, short, businesslike. No warmth in that voice any more. Was I imagining there was earlier?

"No, look, it's fine, just drop me to the Carbis Bay hotel, if you're sure you have time. I only wanted to get some updated brochures, but I can order them online," I say, knowing I have all evening to myself and I can stroll down to the tourist office on my own. There is suddenly unease between us, and I have to shake my silly schoolgirl head and cop on to my situation. What am I like? Tony is a busy man with a life; I only met him a few hours ago, for crying out loud. Hormones. PMT must be hailing a cab and coming my way! What was I expecting? For him to ask me out to dinner? Big eejit that I am. Anyway, he's obviously got a girlfriend. Unless I've got him very, very wrong, I can't see manly Tony Becker being a fan of *Cosmo* and high heels. Shaking my head, I gather myself. I'll do all I need to do after I've eaten: he's right, I am ravenous, and I can't wait to call Susan and see how she is getting on. Music fills the silence between us once again on the journey out to the hotel, and when he pulls up this time he doesn't turn off the engine.

"See ya now," is all he says.

"See ya, Tony," I say as I get out. I click the boot open, drag out my suitcase and slam it shut.

Tony quickly drives away, dust rising in his wake.

7

I can't quite explain the smell of St Ives. It's like the sea meets lavender meets coconut oil. It's amazing. Unique. I wish Claire was here with me.

The Carbis Bay spa hotel and estate is stunning. It's situated on the golden sands of Carbis Bay beach and I see a wedding is taking place on it. A groom and his groomsmen hold a beautiful blushing bride across their outstretched arms and the sound of the bride's rapturous laughter floats up to me. All I can recall of my wedding day is that I was ovulating. I hadn't ovulated at all the three months before, so I'd dragged poor David away from our guests twice that day to have sex. I say poor David, but hey, he seemed happy enough. Best day of his life he used to say, repeatedly. I gave him a false sense of what was to come.

Dragging my small case up the cobbled steps of the hotel, I struggle with the pain now in my feet. Eventually kitten heels turn on you too. Purrfect they are not.

Entering via the glass-house conservatory to reception, I can see right through to the Sands restaurant. Some smoked salmon and thinly spread cream cheese drowning in freshly squeezed lemon on thick, nutty brown bread with a bottle of cold white wine is calling my name. If hunger still pushes, a portion of skinny fries. But first I have to get into my room, call Susan, take a lukewarm shower and get out of these crumpled clothes.

The friendly receptionist issues my room card and tells me the floor number and breakfast times. I trudge to the lift, which carries me up to my floor, and to my immense relief I gain entry to my room immediately. David had a habit for years of putting our room key card in the back of his mobile-phone cover, which only served to wipe the card every time. Delighted to see I have a fantastic sea view, I open the window out as far as it will go. Thinking that I must remember to thank Tony for booking such a wonderful room, I let out a huge deep breath.

"That was a rollercoaster of emotions," I say out loud to myself. Even though the sun has long dipped below the horizon, it's still a wonderfully warm evening. Feeling very alive and alert despite such a long day, I can't help but wish Susan was here with me too to see this place. Don't tell me she wouldn't fall in love with it. Down below, couples stroll hand in hand on the beach and around the grounds of the hotel. The wedding party is in full swing. Guys drink from beer bottles, dicky bows now hanging loose and ties long gone. What a wonderful venue to be married in, I think, flopping onto the soft, pristine, white bedcovers. Happily kicking off the kitten heels, I rub my sore feet and bruised thigh. I pull out the phone from the back pocket of my trousers and before I can speed dial Susan, saved in my phone as *Darling Daughter*, I see I have a new text message. Sliding it open, the words jump at me and I can hardly believe what I am reading. I read it again, but my eyes fill up with tears. My breath comes fast and heavy and the tears plop out and roll down my face. I don't think I've ever felt so upset in my entire life. I heave for breath, and then I re-read it again.

Mom, hi. I want to write to you so that you have to listen to me and not interrupt me. I need you to appreciate my wants and feelings. Mom, I want to live with Dad and Mar-nee for the summer holidays. I have talked to them both and they want me here too. I love you, of course I do – but I do not want to go to Cornwall for the summer. I want to work in Mar-nee's shop and learn the trade. She thinks I will make a great beautician. You know I am not academic and this is what I want. Also, as you know, I turn sixteen on Saturday, I know you don't have any plans for me so Dad and Mar-nee are taking me to see the *Titanic* quarters in Belfast. It's really hard for Mar-nee to get a Saturday off so I hope you won't try and say no to our trip.

I really think you should go to Cornwall for the summer, it's a fantastic opportunity for you.

Dad says as soon as you read my text can you call him. I'm sorry, Mom.

Love Susan xoxoxo

My hands are shaking. Do they think I'm stupid? Every word of that was from David's mouth – it had new and chillaxed David written all over it. How dare he? How dare she? How dare they all plot this out behind my back? This is so unfair. I can't stop crying, but I need to, because I can't catch my breath. Walking to the window, I try to control my breathing. I heave. Never have I felt so alone in my entire life. Moving quickly to the bed, I stab in David's number. He answers after the second ring.

"Hi, Courtney." David's voice is clipped, defensive. I just know Susan and Mar-nee are sitting with him. I've never been invited inside their apartment, but in my mind's eye it's what the *Big Brother* house might look like: crazy, Andy Warhol-inspired.

"David, what the hell are you doing?" I pant down the line.

"So you have read Susan's text message then?" He speaks slowly and clearly. Too slowly and too clearly, as though I am some kind of dumb fool.

"Of course I read the text message, David, and she's a fifteen-year-old girl who lives with me!"

"I won't talk to you if you are going to scream and shout—"

"I am *not* screaming and shouting ..." I scream at him, my heart pumping hard in my chest.

"Let's discuss this like adults and all just chillax."

His tone is incredibly patronising. I want to punch him in the face. I punch my leg, right where the guy whacked me with the briefcase. I grit my teeth in pain, but it brings me back to the moment.

"David, firstly I have a surprise party in the local GAA club organised for Susan's birthday night. I've booked a band, invited all her friends—"

"Well, thanks for inviting me and Mar-nee. It seems

you are making quite the habit of hiding things from me."

"It's only for young girls, and I was going to ask you both this week as a matter of fact! I presumed you would take her for dinner or something on Sunday."

"Well, we didn't know that. We asked Sue-Sue a million times what Mom was planning and she said nothing, so we booked for Belfast. It's what she wants to do." He knows how much I hate it when they call her Sue-Sue. It's Mar-nee's pet name for her. I can't even get the words to leave my mouth. I'm gasping like a fish out of water.

"Well, she isn't doing that, David, because I'm throwing her a surprise party."

"I don't think that's what she wants, Courtney."

"David, we need to sit down and talk when I get back tomorrow."

"Indeed we do, because Madam Sue-Sue tells me you want her to go to Cornwall for the summer while you work. Hello? When were you going to ask us? Hardly seems fair or legal for that matter, that you think you can take my child out of the country without my permission." He pauses for too long and I know he's being fed lines. I know him so well I'd bet my life on it. He goes on. "She can stay here with us, near her pals, and get some extra money working part-time in Mar-nee's salon." He's taken on a tone of authority that's new to me.

"David, Susan is only fifteen, I don't think she needs a job! I don't want to discuss this in front of Mar-nee, who I know is sitting on your lap ... Oh God, am I on loudspeaker?" I raise my voice.

"Chillax, will you? I—"

"Stop telling me to chillax! What age are you, you stupid bloody idiot of a man?" I yell.

"Mom! Stop!" I hear Susan's frightened voice. I am right: he does have me on loudspeaker. The surprise party is ruined. I try really hard not to cry again.

"David, I want to talk to you one-on-one tomorrow night. Come to the house, please, at seven o'clock." My voice is steadier now. I know I must calm down.

He takes his time again answering. "No problem, we will be there by nine thirty. Thursday night is late opening in the salon." It's as though Mar-nee is writing down his answers.

"No! Not 'we', just you!" I shout again now. I know I am letting myself down, but I simply can't help it.

He pauses again, then I hear: "We are a package, sweet-heart: we come together or not at all." It is Mar-nee who is speaking now.

Stabbing at the red button, I end the call. Jesus, I need a stiff drink. I throw the phone against the wardrobe. Mercifully it doesn't shatter.

I scream into the soft, thick pillow as I throw myself face down on the big double bed. Why is my life so unfair? As much as I want to text Susan back, I won't. I can't. I am the adult here. This is a situation I need to keep tight control of. I can't conduct our affairs over text messages. This is my child. My baby. I will not lose her.

Rummaging in my bag, I pull out headache tablets for my now throbbing head. I call Claire's phone, but then I hang up immediately. She really has enough on her plate. Getting off the bed, I drop to my knees and open my small suitcase. The beautiful room now seems to be closing in on me. I just have a pair of black jeans and a red denim shirt to wear. My armpits are now drenched in sweat, so I slip off my clothes and head for the shower. As the boiling-hot water washes over me I start to calm down. I find talking to myself helps.

"So, okay, what's the worst that can happen? I make her come to Cornwall and she has a mood on her: it's the same at home. Or I don't come back here and I let Yvonne take the job: we just go on as normal at home. It's only a job, at the end of the day. I will still have my position in Hatch Street." I rub the lemon-scented hotel body wash over me. The thing is, if it was anyone else apart from Yvonne I might not even mind so much. It's not the actual job that draws me. I like my job, but it's not the be-all and end-all. I just loved the idea of change, of a summer in St Ives. I think I need it; I think Susan needs it. A new country, new people, new experiences.

"I don't even know where I stand legally ... We don't have any legal documentation as to how we bring Susan up. Does she have a right to choose where she wants to live? Even if she doesn't, I don't want her to be unhappy living with me," I splutter into the white ceramic tiles as the hot water jets bounce off my face.

Drying off, I turn on the hotel TV and find a radio station to listen to. I happen upon the same station that Tony Becker had on in the car. I like the music it plays: light rock. Slipping into my jeans and shirt, I find the tiny hairdryer in a drawer and blow-dry my hair. The power isn't up to much, but funnily enough the hair-drying relaxes me and the feeling of being clean helps too.

"That's the last time I ever leave Susan with those two!"

I tell myself crossly as I slam the tiny dryer away into the drawer and start on my make-up. Dark kohl eyes, minimal foundation, a bit of pink blush. I unplug my charging phone. Slipping my tired feet back into my black kitten-heeled shoes, I wince a little as I close the door behind me. At the lift, a young couple hold hands and feel obliged to say hello to me. I feel old. I feel old and lonely and washed-up. I feel unloved. We get into the lift together and they plan their evening of romance. Yet, catching my reflection in the mirror, I have to admit that at least I don't look that old and weary. I look fairly okay, to my surprise. I just badly, badly need a massive drink.

The smells emerging from the kitchen are mouth-watering and I wait to be seated at the main door of the beautiful Sands restaurant, but when the maître d' comes over he informs me very apologetically that they don't have a table for at least forty minutes. The wedding that I spotted earlier on the beach is in full flow and some of the reception guests have arrived early to eat before they join the party. He suggests, if I have the time, I take a drink at the bar and he will call me when a table becomes available. I agree and saunter inside. I pull myself up onto a high stool, the barman puts down a pretty doily and some nuts, and I order a large glass of chilled Pinot Grigio. I proceed to knock back the first cold glass of white wine, reckless teenage-drinking style. I'm the girl propping up the hotel bar and I don't care. I'm so upset. Pissed off. That's the only way I can describe it. Pissed right off. Knocking out a text to Claire I simply say, "Thinking of you, pal."

A bubble appears to show she is immediately reading.

A picture of a wine glass half full of red wine and a large bag of cheesy tortilla chips comes back.

"Oh Claire," I type. "Things are really shit right now, but they will get better, I promise." I can't guarantee anything, but I'm her best friend, so I promise. I think of Alice now and how strong she always was for me. I think sadly of how her dementia took hold and how she lost that strength. When I'd take Susan to visit as she got older, Alice was threatened by her: jealous, like a little girl. That was never Alice, the original founder of the term Girl Power! I wish Susan could have met the real Alice.

Suddenly I become very conscious of myself. This is a work thing, I know that, it's the only reason I am sitting here all alone, but I feel like I am being watched. Sitting alone people-watching only reminds me that people are probably looking back at me in pity.

"Ah here, I'm getting out, I'm going out to explore and eat," I whisper like a crazy lady to the empty bottom of my glass, and out the door I go. Immediately I'm hit by the sea air. Cornwall smells as I always remembered it, the salty air and warm breeze. I'm suddenly reminded of Steve, the taxi driver from earlier, and his culinary suggestions. Where was it he said his hard-working brother had a super fish restaurant again? I shut my eyes tight and think. Aha. Meloria's.

"Why not?" I scold myself. "What would Alice say? You are a strong, independent woman: if you want to dine alone, own it!" I take a deep breath and fish my phone out. Opening Google Maps, I type in Meloria's and stroll down to the old fishing village. For whatever reason I get this overwhelming feeling that I belong here, and I'm not sure

127

why. I've only been here once before. I meander leisurely behind an older couple holding hands. The wine is doing its job and relaxing me nicely. The town is bustling, and old and young suck on 99 ice creams, and everyone smiles at me. I glance left and realise I am outside the tourist office. Pit stop! I drop in because I can, because this evening is all mine and mine alone. It's freeing not to be on the clock, or on Susan's back, and not to have to worry about her. I'm ashamed to admit that, but it's true. The tourist office is teeming with interested visitors and I size up possible relocation clients. Armed with various leaflets to read over my wine and dinner, I head for Meloria's.

★ ★ ★

Steve wasn't wrong: the views are out of this world. I ask, proudly channelling my inner Alice, for a table for one, sea view if possible. The waitress, in fairness to her, doesn't bat an eyelid at my request but does seem very frazzled about something else.

"Um ... Hang on ... Um ... Sorry now ... Um ... That's no problem, but I'll need the table back at nine if that's okay? Erm ... Could you just hold on here ... Just one second, sorry!"

I nod and stand back from her desk as she walks rather too briskly, to my mind, towards the open hatch of the kitchen area. A chef is wiping down and delicately squeezing sauces on dishes at the hatch as another waitress moves away. There is something going on, but I'm not sure what. The girl returns.

"Oh look, I'm so sorry. Jessica, one of our chefs, has had

128

a family emergency. Her daughter has a burst appendix and she has to go. In twenty minutes, our boss is bringing some important people, *the* most important ... This is the meeting he's been waiting for ... possible silent partners in for dinner ... This isn't good ... He doesn't deserve this ... He works so hard ... Oh, sorry ..." She fights back tears.

"It's fine, I can eat somewhere else, no worries." I try to move away, but she continues.

"He's been working his ass off! Sorry, pardon my French, but he has, trying to get backing for a new restaurant. It would create lots more jobs, but if we can't even feed them here tonight that's not going to happen, is it? We don't exactly look investment-worthy now, do we?"

"Oh, sorry ..." I offer.

A heavyset man in chef whites and hat approaches. "Daphne, we don't need the drama, thank you, or you upsetting our customers.' He looks at me. "Apologies." He turns to Daphne and wipes sweat from his forehead with the back of his hand. "I need to call him now. I can't do this alone."

"This cannot be happening, Keith." Daphne sniffs and clamps her lips together. A family of four now stands behind me, waiting to be seated. "I'm sorry, I'm afraid we have no tables left this evening ... short-staffed," she tells the family, who mutter annoyances but move away quietly.

"Look, I'll get out of your hair." I fix my bag over my shoulder, knocking a pile of menus down from the desk as I do so.

"Sorry," I mutter and bend down to collect them. I glance at the short menu. Starters are ravioli, pan-fried scallops, king crab salad and bruschetta with sun-dried tomatoes. Mains are Dover sole, Cornish turbot, mushroom curry and seafood linguine. Nothing I couldn't cook and haven't cooked before at home in my crappy little Dun Laoghaire kitchen.

"Are these all the dishes?" I ask, and Daphne nods and takes the menus from me. I stand tall. Keith clocks me, still looking at the one menu I've held onto.

"Don't suppose you can cook fish?" He half laughs. I read the details printed under each item: fennel, crushed potatoes, lovage, sweet-potato fries. All ingredients I cook and make. I nod.

"Huh?" Daphne opens her huge eyes even wider.

"I can help out. I can cook most of these; I grew up watching my granny cook everything, every day – there is one thing I can do really well, and that's cook," I tell an open-mouthed Keith.

"Oh my God, are you actually serious? No ... I mean ... What if ... ?" Daphne looks at her watch.

"Lady, are you serious?" Keith is fanning himself with a menu. "We've prepped all day and evening; I just need someone who can actually cook fish to order!"

"Keith, right?" He nods. "I can cook fish," I say truthfully.

"And you are willing to step in now or are you with someone?" He looks at me.

I glance to my left and say, "Okay if I leave you, Mr Clooney? I'm needed in the kitchen." I air-kiss an imaginary George.

"You are a lifesaver!" Keith grabs my head between his two big, hot hands and kisses my forehead.

"Get me back there, so." I take off my coat and hand it to Daphne along with my bag.

In the kitchen, a tanned guy who I imagine to be the commis chef shakes my hand and looks me up and down.

"You cook fish?" He sharpens his blade, knife off knife, in a heavy Eastern European accent. "My boss, good friend, good man, we need to serve ze fantastic fish meal yesh?" He hands me a blinding-white apron.

"Okay," I say, slightly terrified by him but tying the pristine white apron around my waist all the same. The apron tie string goes around me three times.

Keith quickly takes me through the menu, describing how each dish is put together and how it should be plated. Then he claps his hands and addresses the kitchen brigade.

"Okay, listen up. We have the investors arriving in ten minutes; this service can't go wrong. Courtney is here to help out, she can cook fish to order. Treat her as you would treat Jessica. Now let's go." He claps his hands.

Keith goes through some dockets and then pulls me around the kitchen. He plonks me in front of a station.

"This is Jessica's station. She uses this oil and she makes incredible light fish. It's all yours. I've to finish off table three now they've finished starters. I can do that myself; there's only two of them."

I take stock of the kitchen. Looking around, I see the commis chef prepping the vegetables and making sauces. I look on.

Another waitress approaches the hatch, looking grim, and slams a docket down.

"Okay, this is it! They're here early. No hanging around, this is a business dinner for real!"

"Thanks, Barbara," Keith says as he picks up the docket. "From now on, you're dedicated to the investors. Daphne can take care of the rest of the diners." He shouts out to the kitchen, "Table ten, the big one, is in! Starters in: one ravioli, three pan-fried scallops, two king crab salads – hold the dressing on one ..." He pauses.

"Thank you, Keith!" Everyone shouts, even the little lad washing the dishes, and I jump.

"Thank you, kitchen! Mains are one turbot, three seabass, two seafood linguines and one extra Dover sole for the table to share!" He slaps his hand off an old-fashioned bell.

"Thank you, Keith!" they all shout again and I pathetically trail in at the end.

"Got it! Courtney? You are on the two king crab salads. Jeff, get Courtney the ingredients, and plates." The boy washing dishes jumps up and trots over to my station. "I'll take all the others! Service!" Keith bangs the bell and plates up two incredible-looking Dover Sole dishes. The hairs actually stand up on the back of my neck. I'm wildly excited. I'm intoxicated.

"Come on, Jeff, get me my ingredients!" I shout, and shock myself. "Sorry, Jeff, I don't know where that came from ..." I say.

"Yes, chef!" Jeff runs off and comes back with my ingredients. First I smell the crabmeat, very fresh, and then I prep my starters. I spoon out two nice portions of crabmeat, and cut thick chunks of brown bread and douse them with cream cheese. Jeff throws two side plates in front of me and a huge bowl of mixed salad leaves of every variety.

"Lemons, Jeff!" I shout after him as he runs away

from me again. "And capers ... find me capers." I busy myself making the two starters. I add rocket and lettuce and, spinning around at Jessica's station, I find what I'm looking for: sauces. I gently drizzle balsamic vinegar over the salads as Jeff hands me the lemons and capers. I put them up on the pass the exact same time Keith arrives at the pass with his three plates. We reach for the bell at the same time; Keith gets there first.

"Service!" he shouts and my ear rings. He examines my plates, runs his finger around the edge where a minute splatter of balsamic ran, dips a tiny fork in and tastes some.

"Not bad!" He winks at me. "Not bad at all! Right, Courtney, what do you feel you can handle from mains?"

"I'll take the seafood linguines – it's my speciality at home. I mean, my granny cooked it for me all the time, growing up. Her Seafood Surprise. I'm easy-handed with that dish, made it a million times."

"Great! Jeff! Get beside Courtney again: she shouts for help, you jump, got it? Fresh pasta is in there, garlic and onions on the counter, cream in the fridge."

"Got it, chef!" Jeff stands on top of me.

The bell rings. Keith spins to see Barbara leaning through the hatch, beckoning.

"What's up? All covers are covered right now."

"One crab salad has dressing on," says Barbara. "She's allergic to some dressings apparently, but she saw it was dressed before she tasted it so she's okay, but can we get a fresh one please?"

"Oh shit ... oh shit! Oh Keith, I'm so sorry!" I drop my face into my hands. Who do I think I am? I'm not a bloody chef! Have I lost my mind? I think I've taken Alice's

133

advice – believe in your talent and be ready to seize life's opportunities when they arise – too far on this occasion.

"Not your fault. Mine. I have to check every order that leaves the pass. I forgot about the no-dressing one. Redo it. Then start on the linguines right away."

I busy myself making another one.

"Shit! Shit!" Keith yells as flames reach the ceiling and he runs to a pan on the other side of the kitchen. "Jeff, I told you to turn her!" He grabs the pan and burns his hand and throws it into the sink.

"Two seabass burnt!" he screams into a tea towel.

"Go again!" I yell at him, in an absolute sweat now. "Make them again!" I'm at the pass now and Daphne is still standing there. I hand over the new, dressing-free crab salad, then move along the line and look into each clear box of fish. I have so much to choose from for the linguines. I grab some scallops, mussels, shrimp and crabmeat.

"Come on, Alice, what is that secret ingredient? Let this be the night I nail your perfect Seafood Surprise," I whisper to myself.

"Jeff, when I say 'go', add the pasta to that salted boiling water, okay?" I point to a boiling pot of water already on the go.

I look at Jessica's oils, but I know what I want. "Butter, Jeff!" I call and he comes back running. I melt two table-spoons of it in a large skillet over a medium heat and I add in the shrimp, giving it a few seconds of gentle cooking before I add the scallops and mussels. "Salt and pepper, Jeff!" I yell. I twist in six good sprinkles of each when he hands me the cellars. "Strainer!" I call and he hands me a strainer and I drain off the fish and juices into another free pot. "Garlic and onions, Jeff!" I holler. I add another two tablespoons of butter to my now empty pan, throw the garlic and onion in and give it a minute. "Have we any double cream, Jeff?" I call hopefully.

"Um, dunno, chef? Double cream?" Jeff approaches a frantic-looking Keith.

"Fridge!" Keith screams. "How long have you been here, Jeff? Come on, lad, use your bloody 'ead!"

I throw in the cream and then melt in another two extra tablespoons of butter. I mix until it thickens, then I add the strained seafood back in, along with the crabmeat. I taste. Oh shit, it's a little bit salty. Feck!

"Sour cream, Jeff! I need some sour cream!" I shout. I can't feck this up. Jeff returns with it like my magic Santa and I add a dollop. I taste again. Miraculously it's worked; it's diluted the salty taste.

"Jeff, go! Fresh pasta in!" I turn to Keith. "Five minutes for linguines, chef!"

"Great!" Keith yells back.

Barbara is back. "Starters are finished."

"Empty plates! Bloody marvellous!" Keith shakes his pan and flames rise again. "Heat the plates, Jeff!"

Turning the heat back on, I stir the seafood one last time. I dish my linguine carefully onto the hot plates and get to the pass just ahead of Keith. I bash that bell.

"Service!" I call.

Keith dips a spoon in my sauce, tastes it and smiles. He stabs some fish with his tiny fork. "Perfect," he says, joining his index finger to his thumb and kissing them. "Wow, you are good! I want to meet your granny!"

I blush.

135

"Last sitting: no starters, three seafood linguines, no prawns in one!" Keith calls out.

"Yes, Keith!" we all call out.

"I'm on it, chef!" I add as Keith opens the back door.

"All there is to do now is wait and see." The orders for desserts haven't come through yet, so Keith has a few moments to himself. He stands by my station, not watching over me exactly, but observing. He's more relaxed now. I'm busy, but I can handle it and, what's more, I'm really enjoying it.

"So, your boss, he wants to open another Meloria's, is that it?" I shake my pan. Confident now. All my ingredients to hand.

"Aye, he is very close, but this is the big event we've been waiting for. These guys invest in a lot of Cornwall's top restaurants. I mean, ideally no one wants silent partners like these lot, but…" He shakes his head. "Where did your granny learn to cook like that?"

"She has Italian heritage and her family loved their food. But she's not cooking any more, now. Dementia," I tell him.

"Sorry," Keith says. "But she taught you well. You cook like a pro."

"I don't know that I cook like anything. I mean, I just cook. I learned cos Alice taught me, and I cooked cos I had a family to feed." I don't take my eyes off my pan now.

"You're really great in a kitchen, a natural."

"I just love cooking." I shrug. "I met Steve, the owner's brother today," I tell Keith.

"Ah aye, Steve, he's a good sort. Very different, the pair of them, mind you … Steve's more of a free spirit."

I plate my dishes and bring them to the pass.

"No prawns in one, chef!" I wink at Keith as he tastes. Barbara takes them away and then I start to clear down my area.

"Oh you, no need!" the commis says.

"No, it's okay, I want to." I raise my hand to him and he nods his approval at me, his bottom lip pushed up over his top.

"Federec." He extends his hand.

"Courtney." I wipe mine on my dirty apron and shake before I clean down my area.

"Christ, I hope they're enjoying it," Keith says, then he puts some low music on as we all work.

Daphne and Barbara are back. "They loved it!" says Daphne.

"Let me see? Let me see?" Keith runs to the plates on the trays. "Brilliant!" He claps his hands. "Even the extra Dover sole is gone!"

"They had no time for puddings this time, they said. They want to meet the staff!" Daphne's eyes are wide again.

"No problem. I'll do all the talking … Let's go." Keith pulls off his chef's hat.

"Oh, I can't …" I protest.

"Oh, you can!" he insists. "We need you."

We walk out into the restaurant, empty now apart from the table of six by the window. A candle flickers brightly in the reflection. A tall man in a black suit turns in his seat as we approach, and my heart skips a beat. Surely not?

"Thank you, chefs, floor, service." He clocks me. He is

an expert actor. He doesn't miss a beat as he introduces us to the investors. "This is Keith, Federec, Courtney and Jeff – and you've met Barbara and Daphne."

"Wonderful food ... simply wonderful fish ... Tony has done a fantastic job here keeping Meloria's on the map," says a woman. She is talking to the others at the table more than she is to us.

"Tony Becker, the accidental restaurateur!" another says, and they all laugh a little too hard for my liking.

"Excuse me, please. I'll be back with some brandy." Tony plasters a smile on his face. He looks warm in the sharp, dark suit and tie. We all move away. His hand rests on the small of my back as he whispers into my ear, "What the actual ... ?"

I lean in. "I'll let Keith fill you in. I'd better be off: early flight to catch," I whisper back. I'm sweaty, and I pull the bobble from my ponytail and shake my hair out.

"You look great. Long hair?" Tony whispers.

"Long hair." I confirm, and I run my hands over it as it tumbles over my shoulders. I wind him up. "Incredible things, ponytails."

"I would have sworn you had short hair," he whispers now. He is powerful in this suit, I must say.

"I'm full of surprises today, aren't I?"

As we are talking, we hear seats being pushed back and Tony spins around.

"Brandies? Jim? Pauline? No?"

The lady settling a lopsided wire hat on her head approaches us.

"We are going to call it a night, Tony. We'll be in touch," she informs him.

The others leave without coming over. Tony shakes her hand.

"Thank you, Pauline. I appreciate your time and I look forward to hearing from you ... soon, I hope?" He doesn't let go of her hand. She struggles a little to release it.

"We will meet next week and be back to you then with an answer. Goodnight."

She leaves and Tony pours himself a brandy. "Join me?" he asks. I shake my head.

"I'm just going to use the ladies'," I say, and he points to the sign. Inside the ladies', I check the stalls are all unoccupied and I do my happy dance. I never expected I'd be so completely invigorated and excited. It's thrilling. I am so proud of myself!

When I return, Keith is almost unrecognisable in jeans and T-shirt and is in full flow about me to Tony. Tony is open-mouthed at the tales of our evening in the kitchen.

"Courtney? How?" He holds my hand up in the air now.

"You know each other?" Keith can tell immediately.

"Yes, the necessary day job, the building? I just finished a job for her boss. I met her today for the first time." He releases my hand.

"Woah, that's insane, man!" Keith slowly turns his head. "Like I said, she was awesome."

"Please, let me get you a drink. You saved my bacon and, maybe, my fish restaurant!" Tony asks again.

"It's after ten and I still haven't eaten," I say, my stomach rumbling. "Actually ... I don't really like dining alone, so I'm just going to grab some fish and chips to take away on my stroll home. That way I can lick my vinegary fingers and no one will judge me." I laugh as I move around, looking for my coat and bag.

"Oh come on, are you serious? Step out! Come on, I'm takin' you for some late bar food, my lady. You saved my life tonight." Keith has moved away and he calls out to him. "I'm taking her to the Ploughboy, late pub grubbing, anyone want to join us?" He knocks back the brandy. Mutters of "busy", "tired", "bed calling" float back as Daphne hands me my coat and bag. I thank her, and them all. I feel like I've known them all my life! I'm hugging Jeff as Tony takes my elbow gently, prises me off him and leads me out the door.

Taking a left at the end of the street, we walk along the beautiful coast. The evening air is salty and welcome, and the late heat from earlier is long gone. Music is ringing out from somewhere and we follow the sounds to a small pub at the end of the road. The old oak door takes a hefty pull to open and we go in. It's charming inside, music blaring from a jukebox. The clientele is mainly younger people, but there are a few my age. A waitress with a friendly smile approaches, black and white chequered tea towel over her shoulder, black apron tied around her.

"Hiya, Tony. Can I get you guys the late bar menu or just a drink?" she asks as he leans in. She pecks him on the cheek.

"I'll have a white wine please," I say.

"Thanks, Sandra. We'll have some late menus please, and I'll take a pint of Guinness too."

She jots it all down on her pad. "How was the exam?" She asks him in a soft voice as she moves off, twisting her body back towards him.

"Yeah, it was fine, apparently. Thanks for asking, love."
He pats her arm and she leaves us alone. What exam, I
wonder? I won't ask, as it could be a private examination.

We sit on soft stools at an empty upright barrel and
I watch him remove the suit jacket, open the top two
buttons on the shirt and roll his tie into a ball. A strange
feeling washes over me, through me, around me. My
heart is pounding and my throat is thickening. I can't
be this pathetic, can I? This can't be what I think it is,
surely? Not after all these years of me denying it could
ever exist for me. His white shirt is strained against the
bulge of his forearms and speckles of dark chest hair are
now visible.

"The fish and chips look divine," is all I can say before
Sandra comes back over with our drinks and Tony orders
fish and chips for us both, with extra mushy peas for
himself. Funny, eating is something I love to do but mainly
in the company of Susan and Claire, never with strangers.
But right now, I don't seem to mind at all. I need to just
chill out and enjoy my meal. *Be where you are. Be in the
moment.* I chant Granny Alice's wisdom in my head.

"Aren't you full up?" I ask in shock.

"Oh, I never eat properly at those things. I taste nothing.
I want some salt and comfort food now," he tells me.

"How did it all go?" I ask, intrigued he has yet to
mention it.

He shrugs. "I owe you big time for stepping in there. I
didn't know you were a chef too."

"I'm not! Not at all. Right place, right time, I guess," I
say.

"Oh, come on now…I don't even know what happened

141

to Jessica." He rummages in his back pocket now and removes his phone.

"Her child had a burst appendix." I tell him.

"Oh no? Little Jennifer? Shit." He slides his finger across his phone and his face is illuminated. His ridiculously handsome face. He's nodding as he reads. "Uh huh ... Yeah. Oh poor Jen. I'll pop by and see them tomorrow. Surgery all went well, she says here." He raises his backside and slides the phone back into his back pocket.

"That's good," I say, unable to take my eyes off him.

"So go on, tell me how it transpired that I left you at your hotel a few hours ago to attend one of the most important meetings of my business career this evening and you end up cooking the food I serve the investors."

His eyes are wide as I fill him in on the events. When I'm finished, he stands and high fives me across the barrel.

"So how are things with your daughter? Did you tell her about the big, cool apartment?" he asks me, rolling up his shirtsleeves now.

"No, not yet. Things are a bit ... well ..." I fiddle with the stem on my wine glass.

"Kids can be hard work, right?" he tells me.

"What would you know?" I say, and it comes out way more hostile than I meant it to. Not the way I was planning it to sound at all. He looks at me.

"Well, you'd be surprised ... and hey, I was a kid once myself, ya know."

"Being a mother is very different to being mothered," I tell him, pleased he didn't take offence at my dig at his bachelor lifestyle.

"Ah, mothers, they do it all, eh?" He winks at me.

"What's that supposed to mean?"

Sandra arrives with a full silver tray expertly balanced over her head. The pub is busier now and in the far corner a band is settling in. The guitarist tunes and retunes his guitar.

"Wow, that was fast!" I open my napkin.

"We have a great turnover on our tables here, in and out. Two fish and chips and extra mushy peas for you, Tony." She puts the large cream plates down and I see the crisp white linen napkins are carefully folded around the silver cutlery.

"Can I get you anything else?" she asks with a smile.

"No thank you, this looks delicious," I say.

"Freshly caught this evening." She leans back and grabs the salt and pepper from another table. I squeeze my segment of cut lemon generously over my fish. Tony is already eating his.

"So can you relax now? Did it all go well for you?" I probe now. As I cut through the fish and pop a piece in my mouth, it's so soft and fresh it's mouth-watering, and I groan.

"Em ... oh yeah, I think so. The food was a knockout thanks to you and Keith. Good, isn't it?" he says, his mouth full. Then he's in deep thought. When he speaks again, he says, "I eat here nearly every night. Bit of a busman's holiday eating in Meloria's, ya know. I see too much but I hear too little. The only problem with this place is I'm like a part of the furniture."

"It's cooked to perfection," I say and sip my wine. The wine tastes so much better and less sharp with the food. For the next few moments, we just eat in silence.

"Have you only one child?" he asks, with half a clean plate now in front of him.

"Yeah, just the one daughter. Susan," I say, dipping a chip into the ketchup.

"Do you think in the long term this move will be good for her?" His eyes pierce mine.

"No, Tony, I'm dragging her here to make her miserable!" I try to joke, but again I miss the mark. He doesn't seem to get my humour.

"It's a fair question." He rests his fork on the side of his plate.

I take a long drink and answer honestly. "I'm messing with you, by the way. It's just I think I try too hard to make Susan – who's almost sixteen now, by the way – love me. I'm making her miserable. I need to let her make her own decisions. I can't make her want to come here with me, can I?" As he leans in across the barrel, our faces are only inches apart.

"Probably not," he says.

"I know she loves me, of course she does … It's not that … It's just I think she thinks I smother her," I admit.

"And do you?" he asks carefully.

"I think I must do, Tony. I really don't mean to, though. Her dad, David, he's a fantastic dad but not a great disciplinarian, so that's all down to me."

Tony listens intently and I go on.

"Sometimes I feel like it's good cop, bad cop all the time. Me being the bad one, obviously. Occasionally I just want to be me and not have to be a constant protector, you know? I feel guilty saying the words to you, but they are true. I have lost total sight of who I am. Who is Courtney

Downey? What does she do? Well, she is Susan Downey's mother. She nags and nags and nags. She works hard, yes, to provide for them both, but does she ever get any thanks? No, she does not … not that I want thanks, I just want some respect." I blurt all this out, but finally I've admitted it to myself: I really have no sense of who I am outside being Susan's mother any more.

"When you love someone that intensely it's hard to pull back, so don't beat yourself up about it. If she's anything like her mother I'm sure she's a very smart girl, and she will soon realise all that you do for her."

"It's complicated this parenting lark," I say softly.

"That it is. But if I were you, I would just be there for her. That's your role as her mum. Always be there. I wouldn't get too involved in every area of her life. I wouldn't push her for information or make demands on her time; I'd just listen to her and be there when she needs me. I'd tell her she's my number-one priority and always will be. That's my philosophy on parenting, for what it's worth." Tony looks straight into my eyes and I hold his focus. I wonder how hard that stubble would be against the softness of my skin. I don't know why, but it's like he's lifted a ten-tonne truck off my shoulders.

"I think that's possibly the best advice anyone has ever given me," I gasp in wonder.

"As a rule, I don't give out advice, but if it's helped you, good." He leans in closer to me. I can smell his aftershave, musky and heavy. The dark speckles of hair on his chest dare my eyes to look. He reaches across now and fixes a strand of my hair that has fallen across my eye. I'm like a rabbit in headlights. Struck dumb. It's such an intimate gesture. Smiling at me, he leans back a bit, lifts his pint and nods to my glass. I obey.

"Sorry, I don't mean to bang on about myself."

He grins a lopsided grin and waves the still-raised pint glass at me. "To parenting!" he says now and we clack glasses.

"To parenting." I agree to the one-sided toast and take a big gulp of my wine.

"Where's your ex then? Darren, was it?" he asks.

"David," I correct him. "Shacked up with a younger model," I confess as I regain my senses.

"Sorry." He runs his hand down his stubble all the way to the nape of his neck.

"Oh, don't be. I'm not," I say, and I mean it.

"Well, that's good to hear. But you are happy now?" He rotates his shoulders and sits up straighter.

"I am." I nod my head and curl my hair behind my ears. Then we have these very strange few moments when we say nothing, only look at each other. It's not one bit uncomfortable. In fact, it's totally the opposite. It's incredibly exciting. Our eyes are communicating, but our mouths are silent. It's inexplicable. Almost like we have been here before. But it's more that he's looking at me so intently that I feel completely alive and ... interesting. I haven't felt this way in, well ... ever.

I'm the first to break the intense eye contact as I pick up my fork again and stab at my fish, my appetite more or less curbed. We finish the food and eventually Sandra comes to clear the table and asks if we want dessert. Tony tells her to give us a minute please.

"Herein lies the Ploughboy's downfall: the puddings

are all bought in, all frozen desserts. I can't really recommend any, I'm afraid. The frozen orange sorbet is about the best. I'm a proper currant-cake man myself, or flaky pastry apple pie and ice cream, or a sweet banoffee pie! People who eat regularly in here tend to go home for pudding," he whispers to me.

"My friend Claire makes the best desserts in the world," I say.

He laughs. "She should ask for a job here, so!"

"I'd love her to come see this place ... She's got a lot going on right now." I sigh heavily for my friend.

"Oh, don't sigh like that, Courtney Downey." He leans in closer again. "You are too beautiful to sigh. I have to say I was pretty disappointed when I overheard—"

"Eh, hello?"

We both do a double take at the woman who has dropped her gold glittery mini handbag in the centre of our table.

"Remember me, Big T?" She half laughs, waving her hand in front of Tony's nose.

It takes me a moment and then I realise it is Marina, the woman from the town hall earlier. Tony pales in front of me.

"Oh shit! Marina!" He drops his fork and knife and then his head into his hands. I stare at her.

"We had a late-night drink date, I thought?" she says, clicking her tongue.

"Oh God, we did. I'm so sorry. I apologise, Marina," he gasps.

"No worries, I know business always comes first with you." She glances at our clean plates. "I guess he's not hungry any more! In every sense of that word." She picks up her bag and smiles at me. "Nice to see you again, Courtney. I'm gonna get me a big juicy alcoholic cocktail." Marina laughs, despite the situation she's found herself in.

"Marina, sorry, I can explain…" He stands up, pushing the stool behind him.

"Too late, too late …" She walks away, but only to the bar, raising her hand in the air behind her as she goes.

"Go after her!" I urge him. I'm bright pink with embarrassment for her, and for us. Sandra returns and clears the table.

"All okay here? Can I get you anything else?" she asks.

"Oh, I'm done, thank you," I tell her, pushing the plate away. "Can we get the bill please?"

"You still working away at that, Tony?" She looks concerned.

"Nah, I'm done too, Sandra, thanks." We lift our glasses as she clears the dishes and runs her damp cloth across the barrel. She takes away the dirty plates, then immediately returns and drops the bill onto a small grey plate with two tiny mints and then she leaves.

"No, there's no point going after her. I'm such an idiot, I clean forgot." He facepalms himself.

"I really think you should, Tony." I fish in my purse and leave a fifty-pound note on the table. "That will cover the meal, drinks and a nice tip for Sandra, I think," I say calmly as I gather my bag.

"You don't have to leave!" He looks wounded.

"Oh, but I do," I say, my eyes resting on the huge, bright-blue cocktail that Marina is sucking for dear life through a bendy orange straw at the bar.

"And let me pay the bloody bill, after all you have done for me tonight. At least let me walk you back, please?" We both look over to Marina, who has now plonked her bum on a high stool.

"Absolutely not, Tony, I'm perfectly fine. I want to leave, alone. Thank you, though." I stand firm.

"Ah look, Courtney, this isn't what you think. But it is what you see, so ..." He lifts his shoulders high before dropping them slowly.

"Have a lovely night!" I smile so wide it hurts and I turn and leave the Ploughboy. Outside, I exhale a long breath.

"Well, that was so awkward!" I hiss to myself as I walk back from the old fishing village towards my hotel. Poor Marina, that's just awful on her. I pound the pavement. I'm embarrassed but also hurt, I realise. It was going so well.

"That is so disappointing," I whisper through gritted teeth. It's darkening now and the lights from the boats at sea are twinkling in the dusk. Directions are always something I can just master, so I follow the straight path back from earlier. *Disappointing*. My chosen word rings some bell in my memory. What was he going to say? He was disappointed in what?

"Seriously, Courtney, cop on!" I talk to myself again and then stop in my tracks. A large queue is snaking around the bend for late-night ice creams, and I join on the end. When I reach the front, I buy myself a sinful 99 ice cream smothered in chocolate sauce. Licking as I walk, I then settle on a beachside bench just outside my hotel, watching the boats bobbing in the night air. As I lick like a child, I ponder this crazy evening and Tony Becker. A

149

woman-every-night-of-the-week type of man. Shame. He is pretty magnificent otherwise, but a womaniser I can do without, thank you very much. I shake Tony Becker from my head.

Licking some more and twisting my neck, I catch the melting ice cream as it falls around the top of the cone. He has shown me something incredibly exciting, though: that maybe, just maybe, there is a new man out there for me. But, more than that, much more than that ... holy crap, I loved the buzz of that kitchen! My feet do my happy dance.

"Oh please, Susan, love this place as much as I do," I say to myself as I nibble down the soft cone and cross my legs contentedly.

8

It's back to reality when I open the door to my office and Yvonne follows me straight in.

"Well, how was it? What's the apartment like? Is it huge? Lar says it's big, but you know Lar. What's the new office like? Is there parking? Did you see the builder guy? When will it be ready to open? Town nice? Many shops?" She swirls the hot water and lemon in her glass cup.

I feel different, like the option of the summer in Cornwall now has so much more meaning. Honestly, it feels like it's much more personal to me now. I'm mortified to admit this, but in one of the photos of the new office I snapped Tony is in the background, and I stared at the image the whole flight home like some lovesick teenager. Claire will sort me out. She'll tell me what I already know: that I'm running from reality.

I know Yvonne is talking to me because she is convinced it will be her job there in Cornwall and not mine.

"Looks great," I say. "I've a few pics; I will show you

all when Lar gets in. Tony Becker has done a really terrific job, and yes, I think there is parking all right. Why are you asking that?" I know quite well she is asking for herself. Yvonne is obsessed with free parking.

"It's utterly imperative that people can see a dream and just be able to pull in and go for it. If they are driving by but there is no parking, they will just go on, never stop and never get the chance to relocate." She fishes a slice of lemon out and sucks on it now.

"Right," I say, turning on my iMac and flicking through my post and postcards. But I'm not fully here. I wouldn't call them flashbacks exactly, but I keep seeing Keith wiping his finger along my crab salads, the look of "well, isn't that good" in his eyes, and me banging on that bell and yelling "Service!" I shiver.

"Don't you agree? It's the last day of your incredible holiday and you are driving your rental car back to the Airbnb, then you see our office ... free parking? Pull in. No-brainer. So, do you think you can take the job or not, Courtney?" No beating around the bush for Yvonne.

"I think I most definitely can, Yvonne!" I plaster a horrible, false, creepy smile across my face as hers turns to one of disgust.

"Oh really?" She sits slowly and puts her cup of healthiness down on my desk beside my extra-large black coffee.

"Yeah ... Well, I mean, I have to talk to Lar later and there are still some issues to sort out, but yeah, I think it's on the cards for me." My smile is still plastered on.

"Is Sue-Sue happy with that?"

"Sue-Sue?" I flick my head up and meet her eyes now. She falters. "What?" She swallows hard.

"Why would you call her Sue-Sue?" This doesn't add up.

She struggles to find the words, then pulls a face and says, "I thought that's what you called her." A slight red blush moves up her face.

"No, Yvonne, only Mar-nee and David call her Sue-Sue," I say, deadpan.

She shrugs and stands up. "Don't know where I heard that then." She moves away from my desk.

"Are you by any chance friendly with Mar-nee Maguire, Yvonne? A client of hers, perhaps?" Before the words leave my mouth, I just know the answer.

"I wouldn't say friendly ... but yeah, she does all my waxing, ya know, at her salon."

I stand now. "Anything you might overhear me say in this office about ... about my ex-husband and or my daughter is all totally private. You don't tell Mar-nee all the things I say, do you? Do you discuss my daughter?" My hands are shaking and I'm horrified.

"Not really ... no." She's lying through her teeth.

"Please don't!" I spit the words at her.

"Tonne of stuff to do, see you at the meeting." She takes her leave.

I scratch my head roughly. Of course she does. I bet it wasn't Susan at all who told Mar-nee and David about the proposed move. It was Yvonne. And right now, I'm sure she's going to tell Mar-nee that I have agreed to go. I don't know why I lied to her. I just wanted to rile her. I don't think I can go. But I want to go, I really do. If I can just convince Susan, I know David won't stand in our way.

★ ★ ★

153

When Susan comes home from school she goes straight up to her room. My hands are covered in flour, as I'm making some stuffed mushroom vol-au-vents. I was sure I had puff pastry sheets in the bottom drawer of the fridge, but I don't.

"Hello, love."

I lean back from my floury worktop, wiping my nose with the front of my hand. No answer.

"Susan, love, I'm in the kitchen. Are you hungry, pet?" I call out again.

Again my voice is not acknowledged.

"Lord, grant me patience," I mutter, and get on with the job at hand. For some reason I don't go head-first into a blind panic and dash up the stairs after her, begging her to talk to me, trying to kiss her or hug her and cajole her. Forcing my love on her is something I can't do any more. So I take my time with my puff pastry. Adding fresh lemon juice and real butter, I dribble the cold water in and begin to bind the ingredients together. The rhythm is soothing. Therapeutic. I pop it into the oven when it's ready, then stick the kettle on and pop a teabag into my mug. Upstairs, iPad world is alive and kicking and "Hey guys" fills the broken atmosphere. I should go up just to see if she is hungry, so I force myself. I knock three times on her door. No answer.

"Susan?" I call to her.

The iPad drones lower. "What?" she says.

"Aren't you going to say hello to me, love? I haven't seen you since Wednesday morning." My voice is strict and I'm glad it sounds that way. I've had enough of being treated like shit. I do not deserve it.

She obliges me. "Hello, Mom."

"I just wanted to see if you were hungry?"

No answer.

"Aren't you coming out of your room?" I peel some cracked paint from her door.

"No," she says.

"Fine," I say.

Moving away, I stall, and then I come back to the closed door. I have an obligation as her mother to see her fed, if nothing else.

"I was going to have a late supper of mushroom vol-au-vents, unless you'd like me to prepare something for you before Dad and Mar-nee arrive?"

"No ... That's grand. Mar-nee made me a huge lunch today. I'm still absolutely stuffed."

"What did she make you?" I have to ask.

"We had endurance crackers, salt and vinegar chickpeas and this amazing chocolate chia pudding," she enthuses.

"Okay ... that's good." I don't give her any backchat about how I don't really see the nutrients or the health benefits in crackers and chickpeas for a growing girl. But I'm learning. It's how she eats, and I won't let it become an argument again. At least Mar-nee is feeding her something. I suppose I should be grateful for small mercies.

Turning on my heel, I go. *I love my child. I love my child. I love my child,* I repeat in my head. But right now she has the manners of a wild animal. Billy the fox has better manners. Is this my doing? Have I raised a spoiled brat? Tony Becker's words swim around my head.

"I wouldn't push her for information or makes demands on her time; I'd just listen to her. I'd just be there when she needs me. I'd tell her she's my number-one priority and always will be." Stopping on the third step down, I turn again and head back up. I knock again on the closed bedroom door. The iPad drones down again.

"Yeah?" An impatient tone and a click of her tongue.

"I just want to say that I am here for you, Susan, always. That's never up for negotiation. I love you completely. I will always be here for you. That's all."

Silence. I lean my head against the door and close my eyes. Slowly the American accent on the iPad becomes louder, filling the silence, and she doesn't answer me. However, I feel a bit better. I feel like I can't fight this fight any more. Then suddenly the closed door is opened a fraction and my little girl is standing there in her school uniform.

"Hi, love," I say, relief flooding through my veins as I follow her in and I perch on the side of her double bed.

"Hi, Mom." She twists her dark hair around her index finger. It's hard to fathom how different and innocent she looks in her uniform.

"Dad and Mar-nee will be here at 9.30 tonight. Do you want to talk with us?" I ask her. I look around at her posters of various quotes. She is obsessed with quotes:

The Final Forming of a Person's Character
Lies in Their Own Hands

All Our Dreams Can Come True,
If We Have the Courage to Pursue Them

Never Underestimate the
Importance of Being Yourself

She looks shook up and I immediately want to hug her. But I don't. I give her the space she wants. I remain present, that is all.

"I'm sorry, Mom, I don't want to hurt you. I just don't want to go to Cornwall for the summer," she says quietly.

"I understand that, love," I reply carefully and then I say, "But there is a lot we need to discuss, darling. We can't just say I go and you stay with Dad."

"But why not?" She peeps up at me under her dark lashes.

I know I shouldn't ask her this, but I just have to.

"Would you not miss me, love?"

"Probably ... I dunno ... but Mar-nee said I could FaceTime you every evening."

"You really want to work in a beauty salon?" I ask – not in a judgemental way; I just want to know what she has to say

"I do." She nods eagerly.

"Why?" I ask because I genuinely want to know.

"I love the business, Mom ... the beauty business. I love how the salon smells and the soothing music that's played into the treatment rooms. I love how clients feel about themselves after a massage or a spray tan. It's somewhere that people can feel good about themselves."

I nod and I pull Go-go, her little white bear, onto my lap. I make him cover his eyes with his paws and she laughs. A small laugh.

"Okay ... I get it," I say, and I do. It sounds like a perfectly good career, but I just don't want Mar-nee to force her into it.

"If it's okay with you, Mom, I'd prefer Dad here too

157

when we talk about it. I just…I just feel you don't listen to me…He does…" She bites her perfect lip. It turns white under the pressure.

"But I do listen to you, Susan … I want you to be happy," I tell her, waving Go-go in the air. She snorts. "What?" I say, waving Go-go's paws about now, and I lean across the bed to her and put my hand on her back. Immediately I freeze.

"Are you wearing a bra?" I ask in shock. You see, Susan is extremely flat-chested still. Little buds not yet bloomed. Mainly because her frame is so thin, our doctor said. She will develop in her own time. She pulls away from my touch.

"Stop! So what if I am?" Her defences are up again.

"But…but…I thought we said maybe in the summer we'd look at training bras," I stammer at her.

"I told you, Mom, I'm the only girl in the class who doesn't wear a bra!" She pushes her back up against the headboard.

"You don't have breasts!" I say stupidly.

"Oh I do! I do so have breasts! I am a woman, Mom!" she shouts at me, her eyes blazing.

"That's not what I mean, love…Don't twist my words." I stand up.

"If you must know, Mar-nee took me to be measured and I am a 28AAA – that is my bust size, Mom! She bought me the most beautiful bras. Pink lace and black velvet!"

Spittle flies out of her mouth and lands on my face. I wipe it with the back of my hand. She jumps up now and we stand facing each other. Her eyes are filled with tears. Mine are too. Jesus, how can I stop Mar-nee doing this to me? The timer on the oven shrills out downstairs to tell me the twenty minutes are up.

"Now, if you don't mind, I'd like to get changed and I'd appreciate my privacy!" Instinct makes her cover her breasts with her hands and then she turns her back to me, dropping her hands by her sides. We are so lost.

"Susan, please. I didn't mean that—"

"Just go away, Mom, please ..."

I turn and leave her room, trudging wearily down the stairs again, clasping the bannisters so tightly my hand pains. I'm having déjà vu. I'm rubbish at being a mother. I heard myself in that room: I told her she didn't have breasts. I don't know how to do this any more. It's about time I faced that fact. I'm a failure at this.

Robotically I set the table and put the kettle on to reboil. Putting two large spoonfuls of coffee into a mug, I make a drink for myself. My hands are still shaking. Calming down is an absolute necessity before they arrive. I need to cook. To busy my thoughts, I remove my puff pastry and slice my mushrooms, melting the butter in a pan before I drop them in, then cover and cook them for two minutes. I blend in the flour and milk, and season.

How am I going to get through this? Claire was so bloody right. What a complete and utter fool I was. I should never have avoided the courts, especially now that Susan is almost sixteen. I lay out the good cups and sit at the kitchen table and wait for the doorbell to ring. Can I force her to be with me any more? Is that what this has come to? My biggest and newest question now is galloping around my head: would she be better off with David and Mar-nee?

159

The doorbells rings. Taking a huge, slow breath, I walk down the hall towards it. Opening it, I'm greeted by Mar-nee with David standing behind her. I've never really seen Mar-nee this close up. It's usually in the car or at the ground-floor lift to her apartment.

"Hello Mar-nee, David. Come in, please." I open the door wide and they step in. I can see her taking in the hallway and looking up and down at the pictures of Susan and me and some of David on the walls. She stops at each one and studies them intently. It's like she's not socially aware. That's not something you do in this type of situation.

"Where was this one taken, bunny?" she asks David. It's a picture of me, him and Susan at one of those food festivals in Herbert Park years ago. We are all eating hot dogs. One of those chancers of a photographer took it; he came back twenty minutes later with it printed and framed for us and charged us twenty euros. David told him where to go. I called him back and bought it. I know now, though, David won't have a clue. I stand and wait.

"I haven't got a clue, bunny," he says back to her and heads casually towards his kitchen. She doesn't speak. The smell of her perfume is overpowering. Sweet and sickly.

"We need more pictures up, bunny." She toddles behind him in towering pink heels. If she works all day into late nights in those, she deserves a medal of bravery.

"Susan, love," I call up the stairs. "Dad and Mar-nee are here, pet, can you come down?"

They are both seated at the kitchen table as Susan comes in, dressed now in a green bodycon dress, plastered with make-up and with her hair in a donut. It's like I left her for three years and not one night! The atmosphere is dreadful.

"Ah, stunnin' on ya, Sue-Sue! Didn't I tell ya?" Mar-nee claps her hands in delight. Susan sits.

"Tea or coffee?" I ask impatiently.

"Just water, please, filtered or bottled if you have it," Mar-nee replies.

"Same for me please, Courtney," David says.

"I'll have a green tea, Mom, please." Susan looks at me.

I don't have green tea, but I don't say anything. I get the drinks and put a bottle of still water in front of them all.

"I've made some vegetarian vol-au-vents." I put them on the table but no one reaches for any.

Mar-nee speaks first. "Now, Courtney, we come in peace, chicken." Her bee-stung lips are incredibly heavily glossed and she is wearing her cerise-pink Mar-nee's uniform. Her name is written in big bubble writing over her very large left breast. She is not unlike one of the pink ladies from *Grease*. Frenchy.

"You won't get anything else from me, Mar-nee. I'm here as Susan's mother and I want what's best for her," I steadily inform my husband's girlfriend.

"We all want that." David struggles to open his water and puts it back down.

"Susan, have a vol-au-vent, please?" I ask her.

She leans forward and puts one on one of the small plates I've set out.

"The way it is, chicken, is that Sue-Sue is very comfortable with us. She has new pals in the complex and she loves being in the salon. A brilliant little Shellac nail painter, she is. We love having her and, well, we ... me and bunny ...

161

David … don't think it's very fair, chicken, on Sue-Sue, that you're dragging her over to Cornwall for the summer. We know you have agreed to take the job."

She has to keep her lips slightly parted to avoid them sticking together, I imagine. Reaching for a vol-au-vent now, to give me time to gather some thoughts but also in the hope it will make me appear way more relaxed than I feel, I think of my next line.

"I haven't actually made up my mind about the job yet, Mar-nee," I say calmly and honestly.

"Come on now, we all know you have taken the job in Cornwall for the summer, with a view to relocating there permanently when Sue-Sue finishes school. Your long-term plan is to live there permanently. Don't be telling us little fat fibs, chicken." It's like she's delivered the closing testimony in a High Court trial. She looks chuffed with herself. I rub my fingers into my palms to rid them of excess flaky pastry. How could she possibly know that?

"I'm never living in Cornwall for ever!" Susan exclaims.

"Don't worry, love, I won't allow her to take you!" David pipes in.

"I haven't, Mar-nee …" I say very shakily.

Mar-nee drops her head onto her right shoulder and makes a face at me.

"Oh. But ya have," she drawls, before she adds in a small squeaky voice, "You can't kid a kidder."

"I have not made any such decision."

"Well, one of my clients works very closely with you and she told us that ya most definitely have." Mar-nee rests her case.

162

Of course! That bitch Yvonne Connolly. I knew she had been talking about me.

"Your information is incorrect, Mar-nee, no official decision has been made!" I glare at her.

"I don't believe you." She extends her hands to David and Susan. "*We* don't believe you, Courtney."

Temper explodes in the pit of my stomach, but I keep it there. Breathe. In through the nose, out through the mouth. In through the nose, out through the mouth.

"We are here to discuss only the possibility of me taking the summer job and Susan coming with me for the three months," I manage.

"If you take the job in Cornwall, Susan stays with us. And—"

Mar-nee is interrupted by Susan. "And even if you don't, I want to stay with them for the summer, Mom. I need some space. We need some space ... I don't want to hurt you, but I – I'm begging you let me move in with them for the summer ... when I finish my exams." Susan is standing now. Fingers clasping the corner of the kitchen table. I have a flashback of her around four years old, standing there as the owner of a kitchen in our old game.

David fidgets and tries again to open the bottle of water. Mar-nee puts a protective hand over Susan's. My phone shrills out on the table. I have no intention of answering it, but I take a glance at the caller ID. Then I grab for it immediately.

"Hello?" I say hurriedly.

"Courtney?" a familiar voice asks.

"Yes ... Hajra?"

"Yes. It is with great regret that I call ... I am so sorry,

163

Courtney, dear Alice passed away about five minutes ago."

I hold the phone to my ear. I can't find any words. My heart pounds and my throat dries up. My eyes prickle with tears and I am seeing distorted versions of the three faces starting at me.

"Courtney? Are you there please?" Hajra's voice is soft and kind.

"Thank you … I'm on my way." I sniff and hang up.

"You're leaving?" Mar-nee has stuck her finger into a vol-au-vent on the main plate. She's inspecting the filling on her freakishly long pink nail.

"Get out, Mar-nee," I say quietly.

"Courtney!" David says.

"See? Told you! Told you she'd react like this, Dad, didn't I? What did I say?" Susan shouts like the spoilt teenager I see her to be. "I hate you!" she shouts in my face.

"Pack a bag, Susan … Get your school bag and go with them. Your lunch is in the fridge. David, I will need to see you tomorrow to discuss the arrangements. I will not discuss anything with Mar-nee present. Now, if you will all excuse me, my granny has just died … I need to go and be with her," I tell them all in a quiet, composed voice, despite my head and heart being shattered. All three mouths fall open. I didn't plan for it to be so dramatic, but I just want to be on my own. This argument suddenly seems so silly. Life is just too short. I don't care any more, I really don't. Maybe I really am the worst mother in the world. Like a fighter on the canvas, I want more than anything to get up, but I can't. I know this fight is over.

"Oh no, Mom." Susan steps towards me. "Oh,

Mom ..." She's as confused as I am, although she rarely came up to see her great-granny, if I'm perfectly honest. I never forced her. Maybe that's all my fault too.

"It's okay, Susan, I'm happy for you to stay with Dad for the summer if that's what you really want ... or for as long as you like. I'll be here – here, at home – if you ever need me. I'm not going to Cornwall."

"Sorry for your loss, chicken." Mar-nee says, her eyes darting around.

"What will I do, Dad?" Susan asks him.

"Get your things, pet," David says as he moves towards me. Susan scurries upstairs.

"I'm so very sorry, Courtney." David puts a hand on my shoulder and squeezes it. The human contact is surprisingly appreciated.

9

It was a bright sunny Saturday May morning when I
buried my beloved Granny Alice. I couldn't look at her in
the coffin. I closed my eyes, but Claire led me over and I
put my hand on her chest. I felt her for the very last time.

"Thank you," I'd whispered to her. "Thank you so
much for always loving me. I will miss you so much."

Susan was very quiet and didn't come in to see Alice,
and I, of course, didn't force her.

"I didn't really know her," she had told me as we
dressed in black and waited for the cars to pull up outside.

"She was sick, love, by the time you were old enough
to know her."

Susan had just nodded slowly.

Tom had made all the necessary arrangements and we
spoke little at the Mass. He chose not to have a gathering
for the usual soup and sandwiches after. I'd said goodbye
to him, fully sure I'd never lay eyes on him ever again.

"She left a will, you know, but where it is we don't

know!" he'd told me, white spittle gathering at the sides of his mouth.

"Really?" I'd answered him, surprised.

"Like you didn't know that." He'd raised the left side of his bushy monobrow at me.

"I didn't. She gave me her wedding ring last year … She always told me I could have it." I'd put my hand on it, where I always wear it on a long gold chain around my neck. "I'm sure if anyone can find the will, you can, Tom," I'd said, not altogether unsarcastically.

"You bet yer furry knickers I will. Daft old bat," Tom had said, clapping one hand off the other as though he'd just finished some successful business deal. "Well, I'm gonna start gutting Inchicore next week anyway, so if there's any other old tat you want, you'd better get down there and take it. It's all going in the skip. I see someone already got the good antiques." He'd informed and accused me at the same time. Silly Tom. Little did he know that the weeks before I moved Alice into the nursing home, we had gone through every item she owned. The old sideboard had been emptied out and Alice and I had divvied out all the expensive stuff from the so-called tat. A young boy, Simon, needed treatment in America and his mother was the local nurse, Eileen Kilkenny, who came to dress Alice's ulcer on her leg of a Wednesday. I took it all to an antiques dealer in Capel Street and we got over four thousand euros for it, which we duly gave to Eileen to put towards the treatment. The "tat" I kept preciously in my front room. It was priceless to me. Just like old Alice.

"That's okay, Tom, no thanks." I'd stared at his greedy little beady eyes.

"No ... you got what you wanted already, I'd say, Courtney, what?" He'd smirked at me. "I guess I'll see you in Mr O'Neall's office in the next few weeks for the reading of the will ... when I find it."

Claire and I go for lunch in a fancy little Italian restaurant, Del Caesar's, in town after. It is the first time I've seen Claire since that day at her house. We'd had to cancel our Friday plans. I have no idea what's going on with her when we sit down and I feel dreadful about it.

"You okay?" She leans across the table and takes my hands, which are cold despite the heat outside. I exhale.

"Are *you* okay?" I say straight back. We just look at each other. I am immediately struck by the deep, deep sadness in her green eyes. "All a bit shit at the minute, isn't it?" I half laugh.

She nods like one of those dogs in the back of cars.

"Oh yeah, pretty shitty all round." She draws the words out.

"I'm so sorry, Claire. I haven't been there for you at all."

"Don't be stupid, you've so much going on. I know how deeply you loved Alice. Look, we have all day to catch up. This is our celebration of beautiful Alice. I can't spend another afternoon crying over Martin, I really can't. Today I want to just block it all out. I want to talk about Alice and, knowing her as well as I did, I'm sure she'd want us to eat the best of food and drink copious amounts of good red wine, and that's my plan for you today. First, tell me about Inchicore," she says, her eyes full of tears.

"What do you mean?" I hand her a tissue from my pocket and then break off a piece of bread from the full basket.

"Well, did Alice leave it to Tom then? Is that what that weasel was saying to you?" She dabs her eyes, looking surprised.

"Why would you even ask that?" I pop the bread into my mouth.

"No reason." She sips her water.

"Actually, the will is missing. Tom knows it's in the house, but he has to find it."

"Alice! How dramatic! Love it! Doesn't the solicitor have a copy?"

"Apparently not." I shrug. To be honest, Alice had never mentioned a will to me. I just assumed that all she had would be left to her son, and I totally understood that. "You know, I'm going to have a long, hard think over the weekend, Claire, about my life … I have to finally tell Lar on Monday if I can go to Cornwall or not. My life here is a total mess." I raise my eyebrows.

The waitress comes over and we order a bottle of Merlot and two steaks, medium rare, with all the trimmings. I go for pepper sauce, Claire garlic butter.

"Eh, welcome to the club!" She lifts her water glass. She has lost weight in the short space of a week. She looks so pale and deflated. It's like her fun side has disappeared.

"Please, Claire … I know how hard it is, but what's happening with Martin?" I ask about the big elephant in our conversation when I have tested the wine and nodded for the waitress to fill our glasses. We have both been trying to skirt the topic until we were settled. That's how well we know one another. The time is right to ask.

"It's done. It's over, Courtney. My marriage is finished."

She swallows hard and lifts her glass to her mouth with a slightly shaking hand.

"Oh no, Claire, really?" My mouth falls open. I'm devastated for her, though I didn't expect any other answer really.

"Oh I can't, Courtney...I just can't...It's not like he's telling me it was a one-off affair and he's so sorry and that he will never do it again. It's not like I can scream and shout and smash glasses and try to get over it. He's asking me to accept him for who he is." She shakes her head in confusion. "How can I do that, Courtney?"

"What does that mean exactly?" I ask her, confused. That he just continues to live his life the way he has been? Surely not.

"It means he sat me down and told me how very sorry he was. That his intention was never to hurt me. Martin said he knew when we were teenagers that he liked boys, but he just suppressed it." Her chin wobbles and I reach across for her hand now. She nods and takes a deep breath. "Long story short, a day-long conversation ended with him admitting that he felt freed. He said he felt like a tonne weight had been lifted off his shoulders. I had listened all day to him talking about how sorry he was and all that, so I just stood up and said, 'What happens now, Martin?' and he said, very matter-of-factly, that he wants to continue to have relationships with men, that he wants to live his life as a bisexual man while remaining married to me. He ended by saying he's committed to being faithful to me as his only female lover." She clearly hears how stupid it sounds, because despite the words she half laughs at the absurdity of it all. Dropping my head into my hands, I decide I have no other choice but to be honest with her.

"That's insane ... I'm sorry." I lift my head now and agree with her wholeheartedly that the marriage is over. "How were you during the conversation exactly?" I sit back, ready to listen with as open a mind as I possibly can. Judging has never been a part of my make-up, but fairness always has.

"So we sat in the kitchen up on the high stools at the island. I'd made us tea and double chocolate-biscuit cake. Ready to talk. The night before I had cried myself to sleep but had hoped that he would be dreadfully remorseful and promise not to do it again. Stupid, right? He told me that when he watched *The Sound of Music* as a little boy he knew he felt something different. He fell in love with Captain Von Trapp. But when he saw *Dirty Dancing*, he was besotted with Baby." She takes stock and takes a sip. I sit in silence. "He admitted he asked me on our first date because he wanted to hold my hand. He wanted to prove to himself that he liked girls. I thought he liked me, Courtney." She lets her eyes fill with tears and sniffs.

"He did, Claire," I say softly.

"Not really ... I mean, he was the super-crush of all the girls in my class. No one understood why he liked me. I was so average: slightly overweight, spotty. And I never questioned it. He was gorgeous, popular and sporty. Martin had it all going on. Stupidly, it gave me unbelievable confidence and I thought, 'Well, I must be gorgeous!'" She laughs and runny snot rushes out her nose. She grabs a napkin.

"Don't ..." I try, but she raises her hand to stop me.

171

"Sorry ... So I said, 'Did you ever fancy me, Martin?'" She steadies her chin. "And he said yes, very much so. He insisted that he loved me. He said I made him laugh so much and that I was such a fabulous person, kind, loyal. So I said again, slower this time, 'But did you ever fancy me, Martin?' He couldn't look at me. He just picked at imaginary fluff on his robe and looked to the floor. So I asked him a third time and this time he looked at me and said he was really confused. He said yeah, he fancied me, but that I'd indulged him in his favourite type of movies ... I'm not going into it with you. You think you know all there is about me, but you so don't, Courtney."

I shift uncomfortably but, again, let her talk.

"'So I enabled you, did I?' I asked him, and he said yeah, and that's when he said he presumed I must have known that men turned him on." She throws her hands out into the air and shakes them up and down as though she's trying to dry them. Completely incredulous. "How the hell could he think that? I mean, if two married consenting heterosexual adults are watching an adult movie, you're not guessing it's the fella your husband is being turned on by, are you? Or am I a complete fool?" she asks me.

I won't lie: I am desperately uncomfortable. I'm also very angry with Martin Carney – not because of his sexuality, just because he cheated Claire for so long.

"Take a bloody big drink." I tell her, as I hand her the wine glass. She obliges me. "Look, it's not my world, Claire ... David used to ask me about movies when our sex life dried up, but I said no because—"

"I'm not a bloody pervert, Courtney!" Her green eyes blaze at me now and her face turns a deep red.

172

"I never said that, Claire, and I so don't think that; I'm just trying to understand—"

She slams the wine down now. "What is there to understand? I'll spell it out: Martin married me so he could hide his sexuality, because he wasn't comfortable with it. Adult movies helped him perform in the bedroom. His alias was safe. But I adored him. I'd have done anything to make him love me for ever. But now it's all a great big lie and I just want to cry … then I want to curl up and die." She isn't emotional; she's a matter of fact. "All cried out" I think the term is.

"Stop." That's all I have.

"What have I got? Nothing. No home, no real job, no children." I just know the last thought is the one that must be hurting her the most.

"What you have is me!" I lean in, slightly concerned that the elderly couple at the next table are basically in our conversation. "And what you have is the opportunity to change your life. You are only thirty-eight. Like you keep telling me, the world is your oyster! Practise what you preach, woman!" I bang the table with my fist.

"But I love him, Courtney! I love him … It isn't that simple. I can't just switch off my emotions that easily!" She hits the word "love" hard both times.

"Well, he doesn't love you enough. He can't have loved you enough, because, be it man or woman, he cheated on you, Claire, and he put your health at risk, for crying out loud." I'm sick and tired of people shitting on other people.

"I can't help how I feel. I married him; we had a life, friends, hobbies. He was a good husband!"

"Oh, listen to yourself! Hobbies?" I push my wine glass to one side. "No, he wasn't a good husband. He was a cheat and he lied to you about who he really was. That was so unfair on you. That's the bit that's unforgivable. Don't get me wrong, Martin can't help who he is, but he can't make your life a lie because his is. That's unforgivable," I declare unapologetically.

She takes minutes to answer me now. She is lost in deep thought and I leave her there. I know she will be okay. She's a very strong person.

"I asked him to go to counselling, you know, but he's like a different person now that he isn't living a lie any more. It's like I never really knew who he was. He's asking for a leave of absence from the school for a year. When I said it was over, he informed me without drawing breath that he wanted to travel the world. His eyes lit up. It's why kids were never an option for him, Courtney, I see it all so clearly now...He knew this day would come sooner rather than later. Honestly, I think he was trying to protect me in his own weird way."

"It's kind of unbelievable, isn't it?" I say. "I don't hate Martin, Claire, but he's made a complete cock-up of his life for so many years and taken you along with him."

"You're telling me. Look, I know you are right: I have to move on. I loved him so much and, yes, that's why I agreed to never have children. I loved him that much. That's a lot of love to have for someone. I need you to respect that." She sits up straight, flicking her white linen napkin over her knees, as though all her crying is done.

"I do! Of course I do. Children ... Well, every cloud."

174

I try a joke. Claire and I love a joke in a moment of crisis. We both laugh and then tip glasses.

"I dodged the cock-up joke," I tell her, and she says, "I wondered if you would." We laugh again.

"It's not too late for you to have children, you do know that," I tell her in all seriousness.

"It is. I'm running downhill towards forty, and no way would I be able to afford to support a child. I just have to give myself time to get over all this. To heal."

"And you will: that I promise you."

"Speaking of children...what is going on there?" Claire kindly asks me.

"Oh, today isn't about me and Susan," I tell her.

"It is ... We are shit-sharing today, buddy." She refills the glasses.

"She's moved in with them," I tell her, and the relief is great. I watch Claire's eyes pop out of her head.

"What? Really? Already?" she gasps.

"Yeah. It's what she wants, Claire. She doesn't want to be with me. I just don't get her right now, she's right ... I really have no idea who this young girl is any more. I had to cancel the surprise party I'd organised because she said it sounded like her worst nightmare: that's how well I know my own teenage daughter right now. They went up to Belfast. She is sixteen. I can't make her miserable any more. I have to let her have some freedom." The words pour out of me.

"So you will take the job in Cornwall then?"

"Stop ... I can't bear how much I love that place," I say quietly.

"So take the job!" she says.

"No. I can't. I'm going to give it to yucky Yvonne on a bitter plate," I say, and I pull a sad face.

"What? Why?" Claire slaps her hand off the table.

"I can't not see my daughter for three months, Claire! If she's not living with me I'll have to take her to dinner or to the cinema or just spend time with her. I don't know what I want any more ... I'm thirty-eight years old and all I've ever known for sure was that I wanted to be a mother, and look how that's turned out. Oh, I know I must have issues, of course I do, that's why I wanted to get married and have a family so young. I never had parents and I guess I wanted that norm, even though Alice was both mother and father to me." I lean back as the waitress delivers the food. I thank her and order another bottle of wine. We are getting through it fast. It's most welcome.

"I always thought you'd have more kids, Courtney." Claire peers at me quizzically.

"Just didn't happen," I admit.

"You were so desperate to conceive Susan, so how come you didn't pull out all the stops if it wasn't happening? IVF, that sort of thing ... Intervention ... I mean, so you could have another?" She twists the rock-salt cellar over her meat, scattering it like the first fall of snow.

"Susan was always enough, somehow. Sounds mad now when I say it out loud, but she was. It never happened naturally and, to be honest, the desire wasn't as strong once I had her. I was a mother. I'd achieved my goal, if you will."

"I get it," Claire says, but I don't think she really does. I don't really get it myself. The topic of conversation isn't something I'm sure of, so I change it.

176

"Well, here's to Granny Alice again!" I say, and I fill up our glasses and we toast.

The steaks look incredible, and we add the seasonal vegetables and buttered baby potatoes. I haven't eaten properly in about a week. Hungrily, I cut through the steak with ease and pop a small piece into my mouth. It's delicious. Claire pushes her food around her plate somewhat, I notice.

"So…Martin's going to leave for a year then, is that the plan?" I ask her.

She adds some garlic butter to her steak and shrugs her shoulders. "I guess so … End of the year now. He's working on himself first, he informed me." Claire uses finger quotation marks on the word "himself".

"How will he still pay his half of the mortgage when he's on leave? Is it paid leave?" I ask, assuming her answer will be yes.

"We're selling the house, Courtney," she says matter-of-factly.

"You are? What?" I ask. "Jesus, Claire, this is like an episode of *Dynasty*!" We both burst out laughing despite our current desperate situations.

"When?" I ask. I know how much Claire adores that house in Sandymount.

"After I take the weekend to recover from this well-earned hangover! Monday morning the auctioneer comes and we'll discuss when to put up the For Sale sign. It's all been agreed." She holds her fork aloft, piece of steak attached.

I pour my pepper sauce all over my steak now. "Flipping Nora." I replace the porcelain ramekin beside my plate, my eyes never leaving hers. "How's that going to work? I mean ... what are your plans?" I ask, worried now. Though Claire does make some money with her baking at home for special occasions, it's not that much. Martin's teachering wage and private English grinds made up the big income in their household.

"I have no idea, Courtney, none at all. I mean, I won't even have a job when the house is sold because I bake from home...So I'm not sure where my life is going to go either. I can't stand living in the house with Martin any more, so I gotta rent somewhere now, but I won't have any money until the house is sold, and anyway I can't exactly take over a shared kitchen, can I? While the house is on the market being viewed, I'll be baking like a woman possessed, freezing a gazillion cakes to try to up my income. My plan is to make as many christening cakes and Christmas ones as I can." She doesn't put the steak into her mouth; she rests the fork on the side of the plate and picks up her glass instead, digesting what she has just told me for a minute.

"What does Mrs Carney have to say?" I remember now how she told me that Martin's mother had always known about his sexuality.

"She called me and just said she was sorry. To be honest, probably for the first time since I married her son, she was actually nice to me, Courtney. She said she'd known for years and she had begged him to be honest with me. He'd always denied it."

"That's just mad." I pause. "What is the house worth, by the way?" I ask her. Sandymount is a prime, sought-after location. Even during the recession, property held its value.

"Six hundred thousand euros, we think. We had a Google after the marathon talk. I put the kettle on and he whipped cream for the chocolate-biscuit cake and we acted like it was all very normal," she says.

"Wow...insane...but okay, that's three hundred thousand each."

"But it's only money! I'm totally broken-hearted!" She bites her quivering lip.

"I know that you are. But I will be here for you. We will get you through this, Claire, I promise you that. I mean, you can't stay with him. It's not fair on you. It's not fair of him to even ask you to."

"What's worse is that he's not as bloody unhappy as I am...He says he will miss me, and I know he will, but it's not the same way I will miss him." She gulps.

"We have each other," I say. I've made up my mind I'm going to go on bended knee and ask David if Claire can rent a room off him in Dun Laoghaire for the summer until Susan comes back home. *If Susan ever comes back home...* That little voice inside my head pokes its pitchfork into my thoughts. I look at Claire. She's always been there for me. Her kind green eyes are twinkling again due to the Merlot, I'd say, more than anything. Her red hair is freshly washed and a cream grip holds her fringe off her face. Her freckles peep out cheekily behind her make-up. I love her so much.

"Thanks, Courtney."

"For what?" I say. "I haven't done anything."

"You have: you were honest with me. I needed that. A small part of cowardice in me was saying, 'Tell him that's all right, Claire! Tell him we can stay married, Claire! Stay in your beautiful home, Claire! Who else will ever want you?' I was considering closing my eyes to his extracurricular activities." Claire looks at the steak on her fork and then pops it into her mouth. I'm glad to see her eating properly.

"Isn't it funny how you think your life is going one way and then all of a sudden – BOOM – it's shifted. Just like that, the world is a scary place," I say.

"That it is. I think now – in fact, I *know* now – I want to be more spontaneous, I want to really live." She sits up straight. A light bulb has gone on.

"Me too," I say, and I mean it. "Life is for living."

"Too right. Dublin is too small for me now, Martin's everywhere ... Nowhere's perfect, I guess but—"

I interrupt her. "St Ives, that's perfect! God, what I wouldn't give to live there for the summer."

Claire is silent for a while. Then: "What have we got to lose?" she says.

"Huh?" I say, confused.

"What are we waiting for, Courtney? Where's this sense of adventure we are talking about? We should go to Cornwall! Not for ever – you have Susan to think of, obviously – but what about for this summer? Three months, you and me, babe?" Her eyes light up for the first time all evening.

"Stop, will you? I wish!" I say, my hand over my mouth, squeezing my cheeks together. We stare at one another, telepathically reading one another's innermost thoughts.

"Look, Susan isn't coming home all summer, my husband's bisexual, I've no job, you can't give up this dream summer job to Pole-Up-Her-Hole Yvonne – let's go! I'll get a bar job for the summer, or a job in a kitchen making desserts. Let's pretend we are eighteen all over again! What do you say?" She is highly animated now, but deadly serious.

"Stop ..." I say again, but my mouth is hanging open. Salivating at her insane idea.

"I want to do it! With you! I'll get Martin to lend me some money until the house is sold – I wouldn't ask him for anything, but this is special, and he owes me that much at least. You said that apartment over the office is huge! It's a no-brainer! Ask Lar if I can I live in it with you for the summer. I'll ask him! Lar loves me!" Claire's eyes are bulging.

My mind floods with the image of the sunlight sweeping in through the windows in the apartment in St Ives. The beauty of the coastline. I'm cooking in Meloria's, shaking a pan over a high flame ... and then I see him in my mind's eye. Tony Becker. And I shut my eyes tight. She's right. What have I got to lose? Nothing.

"Damn, gurl! You're right! I'm in! Let's do it! We both need this ... need each other now more than at any other times in our lives," I tell her, feeling rather tipsy and rather alive. Claire stands up from her chair and punches the air repeatedly. The lady half of the old couple beside us claps. We all laugh. Then Claire sits slowly.

"We've got each other." She tests me, with a wicked twinkle suddenly appearing in her eyes. That wicked twinkle I know and love so much. I take the baton.

"Gina dreams of running away ... When she cries in the night, Tommy whispers ..."

She takes the reins. "Baby it's okay ... Someday ..."

And together we sing and fist-pump at the top of our voices while other diners stare in amusement.

"We've gotta hold on to what we've got, it doesn't make a difference if we make it or not, we've got each other and that's a lot ... For love ... we'll give it a shot!"

Then we do what great friends in trouble do best. We make new plans, exciting new plans ... We squeal and laugh and then drink ourselves under the table and hail a cab each home to sleep it all off. For new beginnings are coming our way. We'll give it a shot.

part
2

10

"Can you actually believe we are here!" Claire stands in our apartment in the direct stream of morning light with a huge empty cardboard box in her arms. She's dressed in baggy linen trousers and a big black T-shirt, and is wearing flip-flops.

"No," I say, looking around at how homely the apartment already looks. I adore it. We've brought a lot of stuff from our homes and between us the look is modern and cosy at the same time.

"It's Monday morning: I've to be in the office in an hour. I have to say I'm loving the five-second commute down the stairs and the ten o'clock opening times!" I laugh.

"I'm going to see if there are any jobs in the town this morning," she says. "And I've an appointment at twelve."

I presume it's a doctor's appointment, so I don't ask any questions.

"Come on, we are going out for breakfast to the Porthgwidden Beach Café," she informs me.

"Imagine three whole months to regroup our lives," I say to her. We are both somewhat sad, a bit melancholy, but a small part of us is also extremely excited.

"Fate, Courtney. Alice must have planned this for us. I feel like I've been given a second chance and I ain't wasting it! Now let's go!"

We grab our stuff and make our way out. We stroll in the warmth into the town. It's a busy summer's morning and St Ives is awash with tourists.

"I don't feel at all like a tourist, do you?" I say, linking her arm.

"We're not," Claire replies, her freshly painted ruby-red toenails peeping out as we walk. The birds sing overhead. "God, it's so beautiful here, Courtney. I feel a million miles away from Martin." She inhales the sea air deeply. "Kinda place that makes you want to be fit so you can live for ever." She huffs a little and pants out a laugh. I slow down.

"Won't say I told ya so!" I nudge her and she squeezes me. "Bloody Tom rang me again last night, demanding to know if I knew where the effing will was, and if I did, this wasn't an effing funny game I was playing. He said Alice told him there was a little something for me in it too a few years ago, so it would be in my best interests to tell him all I know. He's so gross!"

"Good for Alice." Claire laughs out loud and looks up to the cloudless blue sky.

"I will have to go back when he finds it, I guess, for the reading," I tell her.

"Well, I'll come back with you if you want. I'd really like to get my mixers, pans and scales over; I feel a bake festival coming on. That kitchen the builder put in is sublime."

We arrive down at Porthgwidden Beach Café and rush for a recently vacated table outside. At the exact same time we both sit down, then slide on our sunglasses.

"Ha ha, what are we like?" Claire giggles as I hand her a menu.

"Pair of middle-aged twins!" I laugh.

"Hey! Less of the middle-aged. Full fry-up has to be done: I've a busy day ahead." Claire doesn't even look at the menu.

"Hear anything from Martin?" I probe gently.

"Not a word." She doesn't look up. "I'm expecting news on the sale of the house, though."

"Think I'll just have a tomato omelette and coffee," I say, changing the subject, and we both sit back, relax and people-watch. I shut my eyes for a moment and feel the heat of the morning Cornwall sun seep into my bones. We did a lot of work in a hurry last week and I'm tired enough. *Early night tonight,* I think, *and no wine!* Since Claire and I arrived in St Ives last week we have been out every night, eating and drinking like we are holiday makers. Emotionally, I'm not too bad. Susan, as I guessed, was thrilled by the news of my three-month departure. She promised she'd try to come visit, but I'm not going to hold my breath. I told her how much I loved her and that I would pay her fare out any time she wanted to see me. My mind wanders to her face, her beautiful face.

"I can see how busy you are, but maybe we can squeeze in that drink soon, Courtney Downey?"

It's like that voice was supposed to be the next thing my ears heard. I can't explain it. It felt natural. I was expecting it. I sit up straight. Slightly spooked. And there he is, standing next to me.

"Sounds great, Tony Becker," I say lazily.

"Hi, I'm Tony." He extends his hand to Claire.

"'Oh right, yeah. Hi, how are you? Fantastic job on the apartment, we love it! It's home already. We've settled in really well." Claire giggles and looks at me, her eyes sparkling. "We've done everything together, Courtney, but it's the first time we've lived together, isn't it?"

"We're getting along just now," I joke. "But let's see how we feel in three months, when the honeymoon period is over!"

We both laugh, but I see Tony staring long and hard at Claire.

"R-r-right…" he stutters. He seems uncomfortable for some reason. I try to bring him into the conversation.

"How's Marina?" I ask.

"W-w-who?" He can't stop looking at Claire.

"Marina, your girlfriend?" I say.

He grabs an empty seat nearby and drags it over noisily.

"Coffee, Marco, please. I don't have a girlfriend … Marina's just a friend. So when did you get over?"

"Last week, mid-week. Claire drove, so we have loads of stuff from home with us," I tell him, smiling at Claire.

"We've been working up a sweat, emptying boxes by day and cosying up in our pyjamas, drinking copious amounts of chilled white wine by night!" Claire adds.

"Right…" He looks like he's just been given some bad news. He sips the coffee.

"But it can't all be fun and games, can it? Now we've got the apartment organised, it's time I got a job. Know of anything going in the hospitality trade, Tony?" Claire asks him.

"No, not really. Summer staff is well in place now."

Now it's my time to stare at him. It's not like him to be so negative.

"Oh well," says Claire, nonplussed. "I'll find something." She is looking hard at him too, now. "You must come to us for dinner. What are you doing Saturday night?"

"Um ... nothing ..." He's still acting strangely.

"Are you sure? You know how you tend to double book yourself, Tony," I joke.

"Funny ha," he says to me. There's an awkward pause, then we make small talk about the weather and the news until our breakfasts arrive.

Claire spears her fried egg with her fork and gooey yellow runs all over her plate. Nonetheless, she stuffs it into her mouth, leaving yolk on her lips.

"I can't take you anywhere, Claire. She's always been a messy eater," I say to Tony.

"You love me really!" says Claire, and she groans with pleasure at her breakfast.

Tony looks pale. "I'll leave you two ladies alone to enjoy." He gets up to go.

"Wait, Tony," I say. "Come on, I was just kidding before. You must come round – how's eight o'clock on Saturday?"

"Go on, Tony," says Claire. "Consider it a thank you for building our dream home."

189

"Are you going to bring a date?" I ask now. If Marina's not his girlfriend, who is? He's definitely a player, I know it. I saw the red wedges and copy of *Cosmo* in the back of his jeep. I'm giving him ample opportunity to tell us who his real girlfriend is.

"Maybe ... um ... I don't know," he says, and he walks away into the crowd.

"That was weird," I say, frowning.

"God, he's divine, Courtney. Funny you kept that part to yourself." She smirks at me, knowingly. Non-pushy.

I don't answer her, but when he rounds the corner out of my eye line, Claire bursts out laughing.

"What's so funny?" I ask.

"Courtney, you're such an innocent. Don't you get why he was all awkward? He thinks we are together! Oh, the irony!" Claire laughs as she hungrily tucks into her fry-up.

11

"Am I getting ready for a date? No, it's not a date, ya big eejit, Courtney! You wish! Well what it then? It's dinner with a man you hardly know." I talk to myself as I towel dry my hair roughly. "A man you've only met three or four times before, and you've acted like a lovesick school girl every time." I hold the towel still over my ear as I chastise myself in my airy bedroom mirror. A mirror he fitted with his own glorious hands. "A man who has a different woman every night!"

I wag my finger at my reflection. I'm already dressed and I now turn on Claire's turbo hairdryer and blast-dry the rest of my hair. It's dinner. End of. Rubbing in some leave-in coconut conditioning spray, I brush it through. Susan has been texting me a bit today, but no actual phone calls yet. I have not heard her lovely voice in over a week. I agreed she could stay with them for the summer, but in August we will sit down again to discuss her living arrangements before school starts up again. *Please let her come back to me then,* I think. I swear to God, if Mar-nee talks her into asking me to leave school before her leaving certificate to work in that salon I will lose my marbles. Standing up now, I turn off the hairdryer and take a good look at myself in the bedroom mirror.

"Not too bad, Courtney." I nod to my reflection. Then I drag at the skirt, pulling it down a little. Is it too short? It wasn't cheap and it looked longer in the dressing room cubicle. The assistant had nodded her approval, but then they nearly all do, don't they? It's a brown suede skirt and I have teamed it with a plain white man's shirt. It is sexy-casual, I think. I'm barefoot now, but I'll slide into a pair of black patent heels when the bell rings. I've a sneaky half glass of white wine on my bedside table and I have light rock on the radio. Heart sing about the rainy night and the man they picked up. Singing along at the top of my voice now, I sip the wine. Susan hated when I sang really loud, as did David. Granted, I haven't the sweetest voice in the world – all right, it's tone-deaf awful – but I love to sing. Right now I give it socks.

"You can imagine his surprise when he saw his own eyes!" I screech out.

When I'm made up with dark smoky eyes and a red lip, I'm feeling pretty confident. Dare I say pathetically excited? The starters have to be made. It's a simple smoked salmon and brown bread with capers and fresh lemon. I've three really good bottles of Sauvignon Blanc chilling. He's going to have to chat to me while I cook the mains. It's my version of Alice's Seafood Surprise. He may have tasted it already the night I cooked at Meloria's, but it's on the menu again because I want it.

192

Jumping as the bell downstairs shrills loudly, I stuff my feet into my high heels by the bedroom door and check my face in the mirror one last time. Carefully holding the rail as I make my way down the steep stairs, I gather myself and open the office door to him. He looks even better than I remembered, standing so tall holding a bottle of wine and huge bouquet of yellow roses, and my heart does this incredibly stupid, almighty flip of a backwards somersault. *Oh for God's sake, woman, cop yourself on.* He goes to kiss me and I go to hug him and we bump heads.

"That's a welcome all right," he laughs, rubbing his head playfully.

"Oh sorry." But I laugh and I instantly feel comfortable.

"For you guys." He hands me the flowers and the wine. He's wearing a black shirt with the top two buttons open, like he read my mind about the effect that had on me the last time, and light denim jeans and black runners. His hair is a little shorter than last time and his amazing dark-brown eyes crinkle at me. The heavy growth of stubble is still there, but I like it. It's so manly. Tony is the polar opposite of David in every way. He really is his own man.

"Can I possibly come in?" he jokes and I mutter my apologies and hold open the door for him. As he walks into my office, a strange feeling comes over me. For the first time, I'm aware of my big empty king-size bed upstairs. And I feel awful, because just for a moment I wish Claire wasn't here right now and it was just me and Tony, alone.

"Are men allowed to comment on how women look these days or not?" he asks as he turns to face me now in the office.

"I think so." I'm unsure myself of how I expect a man

193

to behave. I walk up the stairs and he follows into the kitchen area of the apartment. I'm acutely aware of my short skirt.

"Are they still allowed to pull out a chair?" He rests his arms on the back of a kitchen chair.

"They better be!" I laugh as I sit myself down, taking the weight off my heels and pulling myself in close to the table.

"Well, you look stunning, Courtney … really." He lowers himself onto the seat beside me. "Claire's a lucky lady."

I stifle a laugh. This is too good! I won't put him out of his misery just yet. "Thank you. I did make an effort, I won't lie, so I shall take the compliment. Let me pour you a drink. We're having fish, so is white okay? There are beers in the fridge if you prefer." I get up again and totter to the fridge. These shoes were not a good idea.

"Wine sounds amazing, thank you. I've had a heck of a day," he replies.

I pour us two large glasses and slowly make my way back to the table.

"Where is Claire?" He looks around.

"She's still getting ready, but she says to go ahead and eat."

He nods.

"Fancy the starter?" I ask now.

He jerks his head up. "Only the starter?" He stares at me.

"What?" I ask

"Nothing, I'm only messing with ya." He looks back down, but he's trying not to laugh. His face is quivering.

"Look, I'll dish up the starter, because I'm starving. I worked late." I stand again.

"Sounds so good. I skipped lunch and dinner today," he says now.

I turn and we just look at each other. This is the craziest feeling in the world, but right now all my worries about me being here alone without my teenage daughter have disappeared again.

"Are you usually late, early or right on time?" he muses now out loud.

"I'm always on time," I answer, without looking around, though I still feel his eyes boring into me.

"Hmmm," he says and now I turn.

"I am!"

He nods. "Do you like rainy days or snowy winter days more?" he asks me.

"Rainy," I say, fishing the capers out of the jar with a mini fork. "Snow tends to always disappoint; inevitably it turns to slush."

"Exactly. Now, which is your favourite part of the human face and why?" is his next question. He has his legs out in front of him, crossed and relaxed, taking up half of the floor space in my kitchen.

"Are you actually serious with these random questions?" I stare at him and he's smiling widely.

"I love this shit, don't you? Easy conversation and you find out lots about the other person." His shoulders shrug under the black shirt.

"Okay then ... I suppose the eyes," I answer. I'm only thinking of myself, of my own pleasure, and you know what? It feels bloody great. Liberating. Tony seems to have this effect on me: like I don't have anything to worry about when I'm with him. Who cares if he is the greatest womaniser in the world? I'm not going to think about that any more. I don't want to marry the man, for crying out loud. I want to enjoy the present, live in the moment, and right now I am doing just that. If Tony was a drug, I'd be highly addicted.

Pulling the smoked salmon in tinfoil from the fridge, I begin to prepare the plates. My overwhelming feeling is that he's taking me all in from behind. I squeeze the muscles in my bottom.

"Why?"

"You can tell a lot from people's eyes." I put the smoked salmon on top of the brown bread, but small portions. I don't want to fill up on the starters.

"What colour are my eyes?" he asks, and I turn again, but this time he shuts them tight. I laugh at the expression on his face. I don't have to see them to know the answer.

"Brown," I say. "Mine?"

"Blue," he says and slowly opens one eye and then the other. "Ocean blue. Can I help you there by the way?" He moves on so quickly that I have to skip over the "ocean blue" comment.

"No, I've got it," I say, slicing the lemons.

"Investors declined," he says in a small voice. I spin on my high heels.

"I'm really sorry. Why?" God I hope my food wasn't awful?"

"Only one investor was interested: Pauline. She adored the seafood linguine by the way! The rest cooked me up a big fat no. I'm not the right person for them apparently.

They really are food snobs. They want Michelin stars; I just want good, affordable, fresh food." He raises his shoulders. "It's just so frustrating because Meloria's is so popular, it does really well ... Those cottages would make a fantastic second restaurant, but it's slipping away from me."

"Can't you get other investors?" I ask, setting the starters down on the table and taking my seat.

"Who? Do you have a mill you want to throw in, because if you do, I can promise you a great return on your money!" He laughs.

"What happens now then?"

"The cottages will go up for sale, I imagine. No point in me hanging on to them if I can't develop them."

"Oh." My mouth drops. "So that's where you were going to build the sister restaurant, was it?" It's all crystal clear to me now. That beautiful location.

"Yeah, that was the plan, but hey, it's not to be." He picks up his lemon and drenches his salmon. "It might seem hard to believe, but I'm a very private person." He sucks the lemon from his thumb and takes a bite from the bread.

"As am I," I return.

"Who do you confide in then? Claire?" he asks me now quizzically, as he takes an absolutely huge bite. I know what he's getting at.

"You are full of questions tonight, aren't you?"

"Always," he replies.

"Well, one time it was Susan, believe it or not. Not unsuitable stuff or anything like that, but we talked openly about most things. I really miss that. Nowadays it's probably Claire. Yeah, you're right, she's my best friend ... I tell her everything."

197

"Best friends and lovers. That's … that's wonderful."
He fidgets.

I pause for what seems like an eternity. I eat slowly and take a long sip from my wine.

He looks to me for confirmation just as Claire comes out of her bedroom and into the living space. I can't resist the opportunity to wind him up.

"Hi there." She grins at us.

I really can't help myself. I get up and, with my back to Tony, I wink a few times widely to prepare her for what's coming. Then I take her face in my two hands and kiss her softly on the lips.

"Hey babe," I say, and she knows me well enough to grab what I'm doing immediately.

"Hey you." She pats my bottom softly. "I missed you." She winds her index finger through my hair.

"I missed you too." I peck her a kiss on her nose. "Tony was just asking about us about being best friends and lovers …"

Tony interrupts, "Not in a weird, pervy way! I was just saying, Claire, it's great that you share it … all … I mean." Tony coughs and flushes slightly. I won't leave him to suffer for much longer.

"Have you even been with two women, Tony?" Claire asks in a low, husky tone. Her voice is slightly wobbling – she's biting her cheeks to keep in the laughter.

"Never at the same time, Claire." I think he's on to us.

"There's always a first time for everything." She runs her hand across the table and he sits back, a look of fear now clouding his features.

"We aren't lovers, Tony!" I burst out laughing. "We aren't lovers because neither of us are gay."

"That's my husband's job," Claire adds in for good measure.

He looks confused at Claire's remark, but he has more important things to consider. I see him taking a moment as he digests my words.

"Ya bloody divils!" His eyes light up and I blush terribly.

"Well, I never said we were gay—"

"But ya let me think it! Mixed signals, I was getting..."

"And why would you care?" It's out of my mouth before I can blink. He skips over the question, thankfully.

"But I heard you on the phone that day up at the cottages, saying 'I love you' to someone, and next thing you are taking the job here and here are the two of you together but not your daughter, so I just put two and two together and got—"

His phone rings out on the table and we both glance down. A picture flashes with the name. Phoebe calling. Caller ID shows me the assigned photo flashing is of a beautiful young girl in a black string top.

"I better take this . . ," he says hurriedly and immediately I clam up.

"Of course, go ahead. I'll start the mains," I say as he picks up the phone and slides his index finger across the screen to answer.

"Hello, darling." He smiles as he moves towards the staircase and walks down. Am I absolutely stupid? I can't keep letting this player do this to me. What kind of spell does he have over me when we are together? Whatever it is, I need the antidote! Shaking myself of my stupidity, I begin to make my seafood linguine.

199

When Tony comes back he sits and I finish cooking and serve our food, and we all three of us have a nice relaxed conversation. Tony talks business and Claire and I listen intently. He really is a mine of information on St Ives.

"Would you like to stay on after the summer season?" he asks Claire.

"Well, I don't know to be honest. I've had a really shit time ..." The wine is loosening her tongue and I'm glad: it's healthy for her to talk. "Well, my marriage is over. But it's all good ... It's for the best," she says.

"If you ever do get the investors to open a second place, Tony, Claire's an absolutely incredible baker. I mean, out-of-this-world, *Great British Bake Off*-winner type of talent ..." I enthuse about my friend as I squeeze lemon on my linguine.

"This is exquisite!" He eyeballs me.

"This pasta is to die for!" Claire pretends to cry.

"So do you bake for a living back home?" he asks, his tone and eyes suddenly curious.

"No she doesn't, but I kept telling her she should. She was about to set up a business from home ... before all ... Well, it's a bit private to be honest ..."

"It's okay, Courtney. My husband told me he's bisexual," she says matter-of-factly.

Tony doesn't comment; he stretches his hand across the table and lays it on top of Claire's, smothering her tiny hand. He smiles so kindly that I want to put my arms around him. This is completely ridiculous. My sixteen-year-old daughter can't bear to live with me, I've run away to Cornwall like some J1 Visa teenager for the summer, and I'm fantasising about his man? *Cop yourself on, please,*

Courtney Downey, I think to myself again. I curl my toes up tight in my terribly uncomfortable shoes.

He raises his glass. "To new beginnings!" I'm not sure what that means, but we all toast.

Then Claire brings out her dessert. It's a dark chocolate orange mousse and I slide my spoon through it. Light and fluffy. Tony eats his in seconds.

"Claire, wow. You got serious talent, my girl, that was spectacular."

Claire's green eyes sparkle. "Thanks, T. You're obviously a man of good taste."

"Seriously, you should be a professional. We could do with someone like you in Meloria's. I have a feeling our pastry section is letting us down." Suddenly Tony deflates, somehow, and I just know he's thinking about the investors again.

"No one ordered dessert that night, did they, Tony?" I say gently.

"No ... Pauline said it was because they were full from the amazing starters and mains, but that's just what you say when you don't fancy anything, isn't it? That's what I say when I'm at the Ploughboy, but I thought Meloria's desserts were better than that. We need some of what Claire's got!"

He catches my eye, and I look at him encouragingly. *Go on*, I think. *Are you thinking what I'm thinking?* We both turn and look at Claire at the same time.

"Claire," says Tony, his eyes dancing again. "Fancy coming down to Meloria's to do a bit of consultancy?"

"Consultancy?" she says, puzzled.

"Show Keith where we're going wrong! He could do with some new ideas for puds. You're just the woman for the job. And I'd pay you, of course. Best money I'll ever spend, I reckon!" He slaps his belly.

"Me, getting paid to make desserts? Oh Tony, that's my dream come true!" she gasps, and I see the old Claire sparkle for the first time in weeks. It's about time she got some confidence back, and I'm so grateful to Tony for bringing it out in her.

"Just one question, Claire."

"Yes?" she says.

"Death by chocolate or life by lettuce?"

Without missing a beat, even though she's not familiar with Tony's random questions, she replies, "Tony, Tony, Tony...Do you even have to ask?"

"You're my kind of woman, Claire."

And with that, we all clink glasses.

12

"The office hasn't exactly been mad busy, but people are beginning to hear about us and interest is picking up," I tell Claire as she leans over the counter. The dinner party was two weeks ago and I haven't laid eyes on Tony Becker since. I know he's still chasing the investors, trying to persuade them to change their minds, so I have left him to it. But we are loving our new lives, Claire and I. As time passes, I feel more and more confident and at ease in my own company. Cornwall suits me. I'm beginning to realise that I have to plan for myself too. Plan for my future.

"It will," she answers now, distracted, reading a pamphlet carefully.

"What is that?" I ask, rearranging my desk.

"Nothing," she tells me, and folds it away.

"It was something," I probe. If she didn't want me to know, she wouldn't have been reading it in front of me, I reason.

"Okay," she sighs. "It's about time I told you. Dr Coleman gave it to me."

"Who is Dr Coleman?" I ask, concerned.

"She's my counsellor," she tells me.

"Wow, Claire. That's amazing, and so brave of you."

"Yup. She's amazing. It really works, this shit … Her mother is from the same town in Scotland my dad was born in. Imagine that? Small world. Anyway … we are looking at my … well, my body." She runs her hands up and down her torso.

I see an email enquiry land in my inbox, but I ignore it while I listen to Claire.

"Dr Coleman thinks I'm eating my emotions. In fact, she would go so far as to say I've always known Martin was bi but ate my knowledge away!" She laughs, but it sticks in her throat. "This is a diet sheet and this is a meeting appointment." She pulls an orange card from her pocket. "Otherwise known as my old friend-slash-enemy Weight Watchers, and I go tonight," she declares.

"Good for you! But you never knew Martin was bi. That's nuts," I say, marking the enquiry for tomorrow, as it's five o'clock now and the office is closing. Claire and I are off to Meloria's for our tea.

"Is it? I'm not so sure, Courtney. I was ginger before ginger was in vogue, was always overweight and had pretty bad acne as a teen, but he accepted me immediately for who I was, which was great in one way but not in another, ya know? Like, he never mentioned my weight, not even as a health issue. I'm not blaming him, but I think I knew from our first date that he was just settling for me, and I think that made me eat more, because I desperately wanted him to love me."

204

I just nod. She taps the counter with both hands.

"I knew he needed a certain type of porn to make love to me, and I knew other stuff, which I'm just not comfortable sharing right now. But I did share it with Dr Coleman, and she says I knew ... and I think I did ... Saddo, eh?"

"No. Not at all," I whisper.

"Claire Carney ... sorry, Claire *Campbell*, is going to make some changes. I'm going to fall in love with myself. Ha! How about that? I'm going to give Weight Watchers a real go this time, and I won't ask you to accompany me: this is something I need to do for myself. I'm getting out in that fresh St Ives air and moving my fat chocolate-lovin' ass!" She slaps herself on the backside. "Don't you feel like a different person here, Courtney? I do."

Claire stands aside as a young woman with her baby in a pushchair enters.

"Can I help you?" I ask as she stops in front of the desk.

"Just a few questions really ... I've been staying here the last few weeks, just in an Airbnb, but St Ives ... it's just ideal for me and my Julie. I'm on my own with her, you see, and I've no real family back in London any more. I've a nice home and job, though ... How does one go about this relocating business?"

I smile at her. "I'm Courtney Downey."

"Emma Crowley." She shakes my hand and looks into her pram. "And this is Julie."

"Oh, what a beauty!" Claire is on her knees, peering in at the baby.

"Sit down, Emma, let's see what we can do," I say, glancing at the clock. It's five past five on a glorious hot summer's day, but I think Lar would forgive me for keeping the shop open later than planned.

"Can I lift her out?" Claire asks.

"Oh, of course, she'd be delighted, she's been in there for ages," Emma says, laughing. "There is just so much to see here, isn't there? I could walk for hours."

Claire clicks the strap around Julie and gently lifts the little girl out.

"Hello … hello there, my beauty," Claire goo-goos at the child, but Julie starts to cry gently.

"She's due a feed actually, sorry – I'll come back again." Emma stands, but Claire puts a hand on her shoulder.

"I can do it if you like; I'm just waiting for Courtney to finish up."

Emma nods in agreement and lifts a ready-made bottle from her bag. I smile as Claire settles the child on her lap on the visitors' couch and the baby suckles happily.

After I close the office and arrange to meet Emma for a follow-up, Claire and I set out to Meloria's for dinner.

"Isn't there a feeling of pinching yourself about where we find ourselves, Courtney?" Claire asks me as we weave through the busy streets of St Ives.

"Oh, totally," I say.

"Seconds chances like this don't come around often. I know that," she says.

"No, we are lucky. I wouldn't want to be anywhere else, would you?"

She shakes her head, and we walk towards the front in comfortable silence.

★ ★ ★

"Courtney!" Barbara greets me like an old friend.

I hug her and she hugs me back tightly.

"I saw your name in the book: I've reserved the best window seat for you." She leads us to the table.

Claire and I sit and read the menus. From the corner of my eye, I see Tony in the kitchen talking with Keith. They look deep in conversation. I look away quickly, but not before my heart skips a little beat.

"It all looks amazing," Claire says, "but I'm going to be a dreadful bore and avoid all the carbs and creamy stuff."

"You'll have wine, though?" I ask.

"I'm not dead yet," she spits back.

"Ladies, good evening and welcome to Meloria's." Tony hovers over us now.

Claire warmly greets him. "Beautiful spot."

"Thanks for coming by last week to spruce up our desserts, Claire. You can see if Keith is up to your standards tonight." He pauses and leans in closer. "To be honest, we could do with a dessert chef like you, ya know?"

"You're very welcome, T, and I'm sure Keith will do my banoffee pie justice. And if you're talking about a job, when I'm all fixed up I might chat to you about that." Claire smiles back and it's the first time in weeks I really notice it. It's a real smile. Her eyes are connected to her mouth.

"Can I get you something to drink?" he asks.

"Champagne, Tony," I tell him. "We're celebrating."

"Oh, anything I should know about?" he asks, removing a speck from the white tablecloth.

"Life," I say.

The food is delicious, and though I have a hankering to get back in the kitchen and feel that buzz again, it is a pleasure to sit back, relax and enjoy myself. Claire – only slightly grudgingly – confirms that Keith's banoffee pie is up to scratch.

"Not bad," she says to Tony as he clears the plates away. "That whippersnapper in the kitchen might just make it as a chef one day."

"Oi, I heard that!" Keith shouts through the hatch and Claire throws her head back and laughs.

"Right then, I'm off," she says.

"What? I thought we were making a night of it!" I say.

"I've got a Pilates class in the morning, Courtney."

"Wait then, I'll come home with you," I say, reaching for my still half-full glass to empty it.

"No no, don't rush. Just sit here and enjoy the rest of your champagne. I'm sure somebody will keep you company." She darts her eyes over to the kitchen hatch, where I can see Tony dropping the plates off for Jeff to wash.

"Claire …"

"Bye!" And she's off.

It's a Tuesday evening so the restaurant is quiet, and the only other remaining table is about to leave. I feel awkward here by myself, but why should I? I close my eyes and hear Alice's voice in my head: *Live in the moment.* Perhaps it's the thought of being alone with Tony that's making me nervous.

"Can I get you anything else?"

I jump. Suddenly Tony Becker is right there in front of me, like a dream come to life. "No, I'm fine, Tony. Thank you," I say.

"Your champagne's finished," he says. "Never mind drinking that half-inch that's left in your glass; it's never as good when it's warm and flat. How about another drink?" he says. "On the house? To say thank you for dinner."

"Only if you join me," I say, shocked by my own boldness.

He hesitates. "Oh, all right then. Doesn't look like things are going to pick up now."

"Flatterer," I giggle.

"That's not what I meant—"

"Relax, Tony. I'm just teasing you." Strange how I get so nervous thinking about him, but it feels so comfortable when we're together. "I'll have a glass of Sauvignon Blanc, please."

He brings over a bottle and expertly pops the cork, then pours us both a nice, fresh glass of ice-cold white wine. He sits down opposite me and raises his glass.

"What shall we toast?" he asks.

I think. "To Cornwall," I say.

"To Cornwall."

We clink glasses and look out at the incredible view of the bay: cobalt-blue sea and the setting sun shining on golden sand. It's like paradise.

"So, Courtney, tell me a little more about you. Cooking, you love to do, got it, but what else rocks your boat?"

"What rocks my boat?" I stare at him and guffaw at the saying. But I know what he's asking. "I dunno any more, really, Tony. I've been trying to keep other people happy for so long I'm kinda lost at sea." I take a long slow drink of wine and he does too.

"You love your job, though, right?" he asks me.

"Well…yes and no. I mean, it's a great job and Lar is a great boss, but I'd swap it all to…Oh, I dunno…Open my own little restaurant maybe." I've never admitted this. Even to myself, because I never even knew I wanted that. I'm taken aback.

"Really?" He leans across the table. His face is inches from mine. I have an overwhelming urge to reach out and feel the harshness of the stubble covering half his face.

"Oh look, it's stupid…I love to cook, that's all. It's the one thing that really makes me happy. I always thought… Well, my Granny Alice used to think I'd be great. And when I cooked in your kitchen I felt really alive … I'm embarrassed now!" I drop my head into my hands.

"Don't be …Your food is incredible. I think we might have crossed paths for a reason, Courtney Downey. If I ever get this new restaurant up and running…" He lapses into silence.

After a couple of minutes, I have to say something to break the tension. "You seem quiet," I tell him as I sip my wine.

He nods. "Ah, few things on my mind."

"Anything I can help with?"

"Nah, I got it. Thank you, though."

"Come on," I urge.

His twists the stem of his wine glass round and round in his fingers, and sighs. "So it's …it's stupid. It's this thing I have coming up, black-tie event. I dread these things. Silly, I know – but I really hate them."

Ah, he must be chasing more investors. "Just go. Show up, smile, do what you gotta do, and then slip away."

He nods, taking in all I am saying.

210

"That's not all, though ... This thing ... It's being held by someone that I used to know. In fact, I knew them very well at one point, but ... There are times when we haven't got on. We've argued a lot. And the person I'm bringing to it just doesn't feel that it's going to work out, so she doesn't feel comfortable being there either ..."

My heart plummets. He's bringing a date. I shouldn't have let myself sit down with him, drinking wine, feeling comfortable. Tony might be a player, but I'm not. I knock back my wine and put the glass down on the table, a little harder than I intended. Tony looks startled.

"Look, Tony, my advice still stands. From the sounds of it, you've got to be there because this event is important. No matter what's happened in the past, you've got to be the bigger man. Just suck it up. Show up. Smile. Do what you gotta do. Then slip away if it really becomes unbearable."

"Like you've done by coming to Cornwall?"

I'm surprised into momentary silence. "That's a totally different situation."

"Is it? Back home you've got your husband and his new girlfriend, and your daughter to deal with ..." He frowns. "Is that why you're here, Courtney? Did showing up and smiling get too much? Did you have to slip away?"

I'm suddenly furious. "I did *not* run away."

"That's not what I said—"

But I'm too upset now to listen to any more. Is that what he thinks? That I've run away from my issues, abandoned my daughter? Am I being selfish?

I fire my parting shot. "What I've done, Tony, is the mature thing. I took your advice and gave my daughter

211

space. And if your girlfriend doesn't want to go to this event you're so worried about, maybe she should do the same."

"My girlfriend...?"

But I don't hang around to hear yet another explanation. I'm out of here. Tony Becker can deal with his own problems. Much as I'd like to deny it, I've still got plenty of my own.

13

"Well, lookee here … Good evening." A smartly dressed man leans in beside me at the bar of the Garrack Hotel on Saturday evening, where I had dinner with some possible relocation clients. It didn't go fantastically and it wasn't a great choice of venue, to be honest; I hadn't realised there was a wedding reception taking place in the ballroom. It's noisy, crowded and, I now realise, full of drunks. There is a pungent smell of alcohol from the man's breath. From his pores.

"Hello," I say back politely.

"What's a beautiful woman like you doing all on her lonesome?" American accent. Southern. Creepy.

"Minding my own business," I say in a flat tone. I stare ahead at the polished bottles gleaming at me from behind the bar and don't meet his eyes.

"How sad." He puts his hand on my shoulder and I drop it immediately, allowing his hand to fall away.

"Not really," I say, still not looking at him.

The young barman is hanging over the end of the bar, deep in conversation with a very pretty girl in a tight red dress, a single wedding guest, I'm guessing. He won't look over at me any time soon. He doesn't know I exist. I am all alone.

"Been stood up, I take it?" His hand waves in front of my eyes to try to get my attention. His fingers smell of cheese and onion crisps.

"No, I haven't been stood up," I say, leaning back slightly so his hand doesn't hit my nose, and using the kind of tone one might use when telling someone to fuck off and leave them alone. I don't like him.

"Allow me to buy you a drink. Women really shouldn't drink alone," he offers.

Oh Lord, he probably thinks I'm a hooker. Just when I thought my night couldn't possibly get any worse. Claire might even get a laugh out of this when I tell her.

"Thank you, but I'm just leaving," I tell him politely now. He really is making me uncomfortable and suddenly I feel frighteningly vulnerable.

"Allow me to walk you home then." He comes closer into my space, craning his head around to look at me, and taps his leather wallet off the bar top. I open my purse, lay a tenner on the bar, remove my bag from the back of the high stool and go to stand up.

"Don't leave on my account, lonely lady," he drawls.

I don't really want to leave. I want to have a nice, quiet drink by myself. I want him to leave me alone. Why should I go? I hear Granny Alice's voice in my head: "Stand up for yourself, Courtney!" I glance at him now. His eyes are glazed and his tie is crooked. He's very drunk.

214

"I'd prefer if you left me alone, if you don't mind." I stare hard at him.

"Aren't you already alone? How much more alone can you get?" he continues.

"Please go away or I'm going to call the barman." I raise my voice.

"You more than likely won't get a better offer tonight, sweetheart." His words are cross now and he looks me up and down.

I don't need this hassle. He's beaten me. Again, I go for my bag, but then I hear a voice behind me.

"Did you not hear what she said? Fuck off and leave her alone!" I know who it is immediately.

"And who are you?" my American now non-admirer asks as I turn around.

"I'm a friend of hers," Tony Becker says, dressed in a dark suit and navy tie. I nearly don't recognise him.

"Her 'friend', is it?" The American straightens himself and stands tall.

"Go away, mate." Tony stands up to him. The two men are so close the tips of their dress shoes are almost meeting.

"Or what?" the American childishly replies.

"Do you really want to know the answer to that?" Tony growls in a low voice, and with a snort the American slithers off.

I look at Tony and he looks back at me, nervously.

"I showed up," he says. "And I'm smiling." He grins like a loon, and somehow I forget about how furious I've been. All my anger melts away. I gesture to the free stool beside me and he sits down.

"Allow me to buy you a drink?" I laugh now, relief flooding through me that the American has gone.

"Pint of Guinness, please...lonely lady." He elbows me playfully and pulls himself up.

"Seriously, like I needed that." I wave my money at the engrossed barman and reluctantly he comes over to me. I order another large white wine for me and a pint of Guinness for Tony. "Thanks, Tony." I nod after the insect of man.

"Ah, I'm sure you had his number. He was just starting to piss me off. I hope you didn't mind me stepping in? I was looking for somewhere to hide out for a bit and I overheard."

"Slipping away?"

He nods. "Slipping away. At first I didn't know that it was you. I'm well aware that you can take care of yourself." He turns the glass towards him so that the black Guinness writing is facing him.

"You look very smart, Tony."

He loosens the navy tie. "Thank you. I'm choked here: not really my thing, monkey suits." He shrugs.

"Listen ... I'm sorry, Tony. I flew off the handle the other night. I guess you hit my sore spot when you talked about Susan."

"No worries. I overstepped the mark and it's none of my business. That's what I get for trying out some armchair psychology." He grins ruefully. "You're a great woman, Courtney, and I bet you're a great mam. I'm sure you're doing what's best for everyone."

I blush and can't help smiling at him. He looks so contrite I decide to give him a break. "So, is this the black-tie event you were talking about?" I ask.

216

"You could say that." He puts the pint to his mouth and drinks half in one gulp. "I can't tell you how much I needed that." He wipes his dark stubble and the white froth from the sides of his mouth with the back of his hand. I notice how clean his nails now are. Scrubbed. "What are you doing here, if you don't mind me asking?"

"I had dinner with some prospective clients, but I don't think it's going to go anywhere this time. You win some, you lose some."

"Sorry," he says.

I change the subject. "So why are you looking so smart, Tony? You must be on a date. But where is she then, and why do you look like you are all dressed up with nowhere to go … A row, maybe? Did you forget to pick her up perhaps? Or is Marina waiting in the Ploughboy while you sit here having a drink with me?" I'm tongue-in-cheek, to hide my hurt feelings.

He peers at me. "What makes you always think I have a girlfriend? Or girlfriends?" He looks amused now.

"Well, aside from Marina, you mean? I saw that copy of *Cosmopolitan*, hair donuts and the pretty red wedges in your car. Us women spot these things, ya know." I pause. "And I saw the picture of that pretty young woman on your phone when you were round at our apartment." I stare at the shiny bottles behind the bar as I twist the slim stem of the wine glass around between my finger and thumb on the pretty doily. Lounge music plays around us now. The pianist in the corner must have returned from his break.

"How many have you had?" he asks.

I close my left eye and hold up two fingers, and just

then I see that young girl behind him in a sleek, red, figure-hugging dress. I was joking just now, but he cannot be doing this to me again. She lifts his pint of Guinness and drinks some.

"Hey ... What? Oh come on now!" He takes the glass from her hand gently.

"What? Aren't we celebrating? Isn't this supposed to be a celebration? Didn't you tell me to wear this dress? Didn't you tell me ..."

I have to get out of here, but I'm frozen to the seat.

"Not now, Phoebe." He talks to her like she is interrupting him.

"But—"

"Not. Now." His voice is loud. Oh Lord. Is this how he talks to the women he dates? Is this how he thinks he can treat women? I've gone from being a deserted mother to a hooker at the bar to the other woman. Get me out of here.

"Look, I'm just going to go ..." I say quietly.

"No, you aren't going anywhere ... Phoebe is leaving, aren't you, Phoebe? She is going straight back to her mother's wedding, isn't that right?" He takes her hand now and kisses it. I've seen enough. This girl is only a child, for God's sake!

"I'm so out of here – this is ... this is just too weird for me ..." I jump up to my kitten-heeled feet and back away towards the door. He jumps off the stool and stands in my way.

"Sorry ... Courtney Downey, Phoebe Becker. Courtney, meet my sixteen-year-old daughter and owner of some lovely red strappy wedges that cost me a small fortune. She told me she just couldn't live without them, yet hasn't taken them out of my jeep in about six months." Tony winks at me.

"Your daughter?" I pinch the bridge of my nose. Reversing, I find the seat under me again.

"Yup." He puts a strong arm around her thin frame.

"You never said you had a daughter," I say.

"You never asked." He picks up his pint. "Now, young lady, back to the hotel ballroom, please. I did my bit, so you have to stay." He looks at her and I notice how his dark eyes have lit up.

"I hate him, Dad!" She grinds her teeth.

"He's not that bad, pet, and he loves your mam…Mind those blooming teeth, Phoebe, I've paid a small fortune for them!" She purses her pretty lips together, reminding me so much of Susan that my heart lurches again.

"Speaking of teeth, everyone is laughing at those blinding-white veneers Mam got for the big day!" Phoebe wails at her father.

"I'm sure they aren't laughing, love. Look, she's your mam: be nice to her. Now, I'll come back to the reception in an hour or so, I promise." He looks adoringly at her. This young girl certainly has her daddy in the palm of her hand. Exactly how it should be, I know, and I'm petty to be jealous that my little girl loves her daddy so much. I think, in this moment, if it wasn't for Mar-nee, I'd understand Susan wanting to be with David.

"Who are you anyway?" she demands, turning to face me with a complete Susan look on her face. Oh, I can handle this girl. She's met her match in me this evening.

"Manners, Phoebe, please!" he chastises her.

"Sorry … Who are you anyway please?" She continues to stare hard at me.

"Hiya, Phoebe, it's really lovely to meet you. Your dress is amazing! Lipsy?" I ask, and she narrows her eyes slightly at me before she nods in agreement. I go on. "I'm Courtney from Dublin, just a work colleague of your dad's."

"Oh right." She pulls at the neckline on her dress. "How'd you know it's from Lipsy?" she asks.

"Oh, because I have a sixteen-year-old daughter, Susan, who wanted that dress for a party last year," I inform her.

"I only get dressed up for special occasions. That's why I wanted those shoes, Dad," she says, shooting a glare at him and waggling a red-wedged foot at him. "I'm a jeans and jumper kind of girl usually."

"Want a soda water and lime with us?" I try Susan's tipple of choice on her.

"Oh, my favourite! Can I, Dad?" Her eyes light up.

"No. Back to the wedding with you, please. You know I can't have your mam thinking I dragged you away with me. It's not fair on her. You know how excited she's been about this day for months."

"Years!" she drawls, and throws her eyes up to the ceiling. "Do you have a husband?" She asks, and looks at my left hand.

"I'm separated, Phoebe," I tell her.

"Thank you, Detective Inspector Becker, you may go." Tony gently turns her around to face the door and she takes her leave.

As she shimmers through the open glass doors, she calls back, "Do not be more than an hour, Dad, I mean it! Love you, Big Daddy!" She blows him a kiss. He laughs.

"I can't believe you didn't tell me you had a daughter the same age as mine! She's absolutely beautiful, Tony," I tell him, and I mean it. She really is stunning. A model scout's dream girl.

"That she is." He laughs after her.

"Why didn't you tell me?" I dig him gently in his ribs.

"I was just playing with you. You seemed to think I was some Casanova, a different woman every night, when in reality I haven't … Well … It's been a long time for me." He looks down to the barman. My stomach lurches in excitement, and I'm not sure why.

"Phoebe is a beautiful name. She really reminds me of my Susan."

Tony orders two more drinks.

"So who got married today? Your ex-wife, I take it?" I lick my lips.

"No … I told you before, I don't believe in marriage; therefore I saved myself the torture of ever having an ex-wife." He takes a long drink and replaces the pint square in the centre of the beer mat. He turns it around a few times. His tanned hands rotate it as the world turns.

"Look, I don't mean to pry. You don't have to tell me anything about your private life. I—"

He interrupts me with a deep breath and goes on. "We were never married. Bernie, that's Phoebe's mam, and I met on one of those eighteen-to-thirty holidays in Lanzarote, in an Irish bar no less. Scruffy Murphy's. We had a holiday fling, I suppose you'd call it. No strings attached. We were both young and single … and very burnt!"

I nearly spit out my white wine on that one.

He goes on. "When I got back from the holiday I never really thought much about her, if I'm being brutally honest. She'd given me her address and I'd given her mine; we lived at opposite ends of St Ives. There were no mobile phones or Facebook or any of that stuff in those days. We passed in the street a couple of times but didn't stop to chat. We both knew it was just a holiday romance. As you do, I went to back to work, where I'd just started as an apprentice with me dad on the building sites, and three months later she arrived on my doorstep and told me she was pregnant with my child." He lifts his shoulders and shirt high to his ears and then drops them slowly.

"Shit," I say, dragging my vowels again and rubbing my thumb along my fingernails.

"Correct ... Well, shit or get off the pot, basically."

"Wow, that must have been so tough ... on both of you ..." I acknowledge poor Bernie in all of this. What must it have been like to return from a fun summer holiday only to find out you were expecting a baby with a stranger? My heart went out to her.

"I was only twenty-two years old and she was only nineteen ... I had nothing really to offer her but my total and utter complete support. Takes two to tango and all that. So we tried ... She moved in with me and the folks. While I saved for a house for us, Bernie sat around with me mam all day drinking tea and knitting booties, and when Phoebe was born at sixteen minutes past ten on the night of my twenty-third birthday, it was love at first sight. Hook, line and sinker. I knew there and then I couldn't live without her, not for even one day." He looks back to the door.

"But you never married Bernie?" I am more and more drawn to this man. He's like no one I have ever met before. This feeling is totally discombobulating.

"I never tell people I don't know all my private business. I think, like Phoebe, you have me under your thumb too." Without me probing any further, he goes on. I get the impression he hasn't talked about this in years. "Anyway, where was I ... Oh yeah, so we tried to make a go of it for a while, but we couldn't stand one another! Bernie is very highly strung, has absolutely no listening skills. I'm just the complete opposite, and on this occasion opposites did not attract. I guess the 'Fields of Athenry' was so loud in Scruffy Murphy's we couldn't talk too much, so I never knew!" He laughs, and his handsome face is beautiful. "We were like chalk and cheese. Bernie was a great mam – still is, don't get me wrong, a fabulous mam – but one night we had a big fight over a frozen chicken Kiev if ya don't mind ... and I didn't come home. I stayed at my brother Steve's, and the next morning when I got in, my mother, God rest her soul, told me they were gone. Bernie had packed up all their stuff and taken Phoebe back to live with her parents." He exhales slowly and takes a drink. I don't push for more.

"Basically I followed them, demanded shared custody, which she didn't contest, worked my ass off and saved all the money I could, and started on building my own house nearby. I became a full-time dad, more or less. Because I lived so close by, I could give Bernie a break and take Phoebe overnight. Anyway, we never got back together, but Bernie, in fairness to her was always okay with me being full-time in Phoebe's life – in fact, I'd go so far as to

223

say we more than equally shared out the sleepless nights and teething days." He lifts his thumb and digs it into his chest, raising his eyebrows high at me.

"That's brilliant, Tony. Not many men would do that," I say in awe.

"Oh, I dunno about that. I met a whole lot of men who were doing exactly what I was doing!" He chews his thumbnail, his tanned hand covering his mouth. "I think fathers get very bad press, Courtney. I think family law treats fathers very badly."

"Maybe," I acknowledge. "So she got married today then? Bernie?" I ask.

"Yes, she did. I have to go back there later too. Just for Phoebe, really." He drinks more. Suddenly there is vulnerability about him I haven't seen before. "I gotta go pop my head back in ... but would you ... Well, maybe can you wait and we can have another drink?" he asks sheepishly.

"Marina's not in there waiting for you, is she?" I'm only half joking.

"No! Marina hasn't ever been anything other than a really good friend to me. She's honest and we enjoy each other's company. She jokes that one day I will marry her, but that's all it is, Courtney: a joke." He stands and runs his hand down his shirt.

"I'll wait for you, Tony." I take up my bag. "I have a point to prove to myself more than anything. I should be able to sit alone at any bar in any place in the world and not be intimidated, as should both of our daughters. I hope that asshole comes back, I really do! Now I'm going to use the ladies'." I put a beer mat over our glasses and I walk away, well aware he's watching me.

When I come out of the cubicle, I'm met with a sea of white lace. The bride, Bernie, stands in front of the mirror fixing her veil. Hairpins are scattered all around the sink. A pair of sky-high white stilettos sits on top of the sink area also.

"Have you had a good day?" For some reason I want to know. For some reason, instantly I just like the look of Bernie very much.

"Just the greatest day of my life! Well, apart from the birth of my daughter, obviously." She looks so happy and clutches the lace of the veil lying on her shoulder.

"Need a hand there?" I ask.

"Oh please, would you mind? My bridesmaid is fairly pissed. I warned her, not too much prosecco, but we've had to put her upstairs to lie down for an hour." She squeezes her shoulders up under her ears but laughs warmly.

"No problem." I help pin the delicate lace back into place.

"I know I'm probably a bit old for the veil, but I always wanted to wear one," she tells me. "Are you married?" she asks me now.

"Separated," I say. Like I told her daughter.

"Mr Right is out there for you, you know ... Believe me." She gives me a big glistening smile as she waves her diamond ring at me.

"I guess maybe."

"How old are you?" she asks.

"Thirty-eight!" I tell her.

"Not too bad ... Still an open window to get a ring on it." She giggles, waving her diamond in the air again and pressing her lips to it now.

"You know what, I'm not too pushed on getting married again," I tell her honestly.

"I've never been married before. I wanted to be, but he didn't. He was a quiet one. I think I was too ... alive for him!" She laughs very loudly. It is high-pitched and unique. There is no mistaking Bernie's laugh.

"There you go." I spin her around to look in the mirror.

"Thank you!" She narrows her brown eyes at me questioningly.

"Courtney," I say.

"Courtney! Wow! What a beautiful name. You know, I was going to call my daughter Courtney! I was bit obsessed with *Friends*. Courtney Cox was my favourite as Monica, but Phoebe was more like me in personality, so I called my baby Phoebe. I know her real name was Lisa Kudrow, but my best friend in school was called Lisa and then we fell out big time when I got pregnant on a holiday we went on to Lanzarote – she was pissed off I couldn't go out and party any more. With friends like that ... Right?" She laughs really loudly again and I like it. I like Bernie. She is right. She is very, very alive.

"That's mad," I say in answer to all she has just told me. She climbs into her shoes and suddenly we are eye to eye.

"You are absolutely beautiful, Courtney," Bernie says as she steadies herself.

"God, so are you, Bernie," I say.

"Be happy, love." She winks at me.

"I will, thanks. And you," I tell her as I hold the door open for her. Tony stands in front of us, a glass of champagne in each hand.

226

"I'm guessing one of those isn't for me, Tone?" She laughs again.

He stares at us both.

"We were just getting acquainted, me and Courtney 'ere," she says with a tickle in her voice.

"Is that so, Bernie?" Tony says, handing me a glass.

"That is so, Tone" she says. "Can I get a hug? We haven't had a hug yet today. I'm officially off your back!" There is warmth in her voice that tells me she is very fond of this man. I hold his glass and Bernie steps into his arms. I feel a huge lump in my throat. They were never meant to be, but look what they created. How can any part of Phoebe's existence be wrong?

"Phoebe is a very lucky girl," I tell them as Bernie steps out of the embrace.

"Oh, she is. And this man worships her." She fixes her veil and pats Tony on the back.

"As does this woman," he says, taking the glass back from me.

"Ya know, Tony, obviously we've had our few ups and downs ..."

Tony pretends to choke on his champagne.

"Shut up! Let me go on, will ya? I can never get a word in with you. I don't think I have ever properly said thank you for all you did for us ... I mean, you've been amazing. I know I get on your nerves sometimes, but I don't mean to. I ... I just am who I am, and you are who you are, and sometimes I—"

"There you are!" A small, robust man in a light-blue tuxedo approaches with a skip in his step. "The band are about to play our song, my love." He reaches for Bernie's hand. "Hi, Tony. Thanks so much for coming today," he says.

"Of course, Barry. Congratulations, a beautiful day." Tony extends his hand.

"Oh, don't I know it! Most beautiful day of my life!" Barry says, and kisses Bernie hard on the lips. When they part, he wipes his mouth and continues. "Is there lippy? You can never take the chance: once my father played an entire round of golf with bright-red lips! My aunt Tara had met him in the back car park, that's his sister-in-law by the way, and she'd kissed him hard on the lips ... Maybe you guys could come around to ours one night for a barbie and some beers? I cook a mean steak on the barbie, don't I, Bern? And I do vegetarian too. Are you a veggie?" He looks at me.

"Erm, no," I say and sip my bubbles. These two are a match made in chatty heaven.

"Come on!" He tries to drag Bernie away as the first line of Take That's "A Million Love Songs" belts out.

"Can we have Mr and Mrs Gough to the stage please?" we hear the DJ ask.

Bernie doesn't register.

"Oh! *Oh!* That's me! I'm a *Mrs*!" she screams, and they take off to the ballroom, her hand clutching her veil as she goes.

"Bye, Courtney!" she shouts back over her shoulder of lace.

"Good luck, Bernie," I say as the doors shut.

"Want to sit on the decking?" Tony asks, and I nod and follow him.

"What about our drinks at the bar?" I ask.

"The barman is keeping an eye on them," he reassures me.

We make our way out into the Cornwall night. "Here, you're shivering." He takes off his wedding suit jacket and drapes it around my shoulders. It dwarfs me. "Careful where you walk; these pathways can be a bit dangerous," he says as he takes my hand and leads me down towards the beach.

And then it happens. It happened a bit back in the Ploughboy when he unbuttoned his shirt. That thing people talk about. That bolt of lightning shoots through my entire body. My palms are sweating. I feel like the teenager I never was. All thoughts about Susan, David, Tom and Mar-nee ebb away. I'm completely in the moment and I'm loving it. This man excites and thrills me, I admit it. We walk hand and hand in the darkening night in wondrous silence. Only the crashing waves of the sea in the background. Right in this moment, I don't want to be anywhere else but here or anyone else but me.

"I have something I need to tell you," Tony says.

"What?" I ask as we perch on the sea wall. I can smell his familiar heavy aftershave. He lays his free hand on my leg. So aware am I of his hand on my leg, my right foot immediately goes dead with the shock.

"I ... Well, look, Courtney, I'm not good at dating. I had disastrous relationships when Phoebe was younger, and I just stopped. You see, she will always have to come first for me, and any women I met before just didn't like that. I'm telling you this because ..." He breathes deeply and knocks back the dribble of champagne left in his slim glass, which is dwarfed by his large hand. "Because I really

229

fancy you. I haven't actually fancied anyone in years and it's incredible and I'd like to … to ask you out on a date … but if you were to say yes, I have to be honest with you."

I take my moment. I feel the heat from his hand on my leg. Could what he said be any more perfect?

"Ditto," is all I say.

"Ditto?" He looks at me as though I've lost my mind.

"Ditto," I say again.

I can tell by his expression he is lost.

"You know in *Ghost* when Sam tells Molly 'Ditto'?"

"*Ghost*? Molly? 'Ditto'? Are you drunk?" He makes a face at me.

I laugh. "It's a movie, *Ghost* … When they agree with one another, they say 'Ditto'. I agree. I'd love to see you for a date, or go out for dinner with you, however it's said … But for me, Susan will always come first too. It might not seem like it now that I'm living here without her, but—"

"You are a fantastic mother. It's space she needs and you can acknowledge that. And to be a good mother, you need to be happy yourself."

"You're right," I say, but my voice comes out as a whisper.

"I'm always right." His breath is heavy now and his free hand moves and lifts my chin up so we are staring into each other's eyes.

"This is crazy." I am barely audible. My lips are dry. My heart is racing. I feel unbelievably alive.

"Yeah, that's the right word, Courtney Downey … crazy. I am crazy about you … The second you walked into the foyer of the town hall I felt all kinds of crazy. It's a feeling I haven't had in years…unsettling…The first time I heard your voice on the phone, I felt it. I have had crazy thoughts and dreams about you ever since, and now I find myself here sitting with you in the dark. If that's not crazy, I don't know what is."

He is so close his mouth brushes off mine. It's not a kiss exactly. It's just contact. I can't help myself any longer. I drag him closer and I kiss him like I've never kissed anyone before. It's hard, and the want in me is the definition of crazy.

He pulls back and holds my face in his hand. "Crazy."

"Crazy," I agree, and we fall into one another.

14

One week later and I'm still walking on cloud nine. My phone rings and I answer it.

"How's my girl?" Tony Becker's lilting Cornwall voice asks. It should sound silly and oh-so dated and cheesy, but it doesn't. It sounds bloody wonderful.

"Your girl is doing okay, actually. I'm just leaving the office now," I tell him, closing the laptop and moving to lock the office door.

"I really can't wait to see you tonight. Billy is going out for the night, so we have the place to ourselves," he jokes, but his voice is heavy with desire.

"Me either. But I'm scared too, Tony," I admit. To my lover. To the man I literally cannot keep my hands off. I tremble a little despite the heat.

"Of what?" he asks.

"Oh, I dunno. That this is all so perfect, I guess. Life isn't like this."

"But it is," he says quietly.

"I know, but you know what I mean," I say.

"I just live in the moment, Courtney. I've no intentions of pushing us into anything...Let's take it all day by day." He calms me down instantly.

"Yeah," I say. "Taking our time. That's the most important thing."

"Well, no," he says now.

"It's not?" I say, making my way up the stairs, trying to fold a jumper and hold my phone at the same time.

"You are the most important thing," he tells me.

"I am?" I say quietly.

"Jesus, Courtney, I'm in love ... Probably for the very first time in my entire life and I feel so alive. Every song on the radio reminds me of you...I get butterflies when I hear your voice, and when I am with you I'm truly happy."

"I feel the same," I tell him as I lean back against my bedroom door and chuck the jumper onto the bed. The bed we made love in. The bed that I can't wait to get him into again. We listen to each other breathing for a while. Conversation unnecessary. Then he talks.

"Why does Spiderman not have a cape?" he asks me and I crumple over laughing and fling myself face-down on the bed.

★ ★ ★

As I'm getting ready to head over to Tony's house, Claire comes back in, flushed and breathless.

"That must be some exercise class you've signed up to," I say.

"It's not that, Courtney," she pants. "I've got some news ..."

Alarm bells start ringing. "Oh God, Claire, what is it? Have you had some test results back?"

Her panting turns into heaving laughter. "No! It's not bad news, just the opposite. Our house has sold."

"Claire!" I say.

She starts doing a celebratory dance, clapping her hands and spinning. "Three hundred thousand euros, Courtney!" she cries. And then she stops and looks me in the eye. "And I know exactly what I want to do with it."

★ ★ ★

"We have something to discuss with you," I say.

"Go on?" Tony sits back at his kitchen table. If he was surprised when he found Claire with me at his front door, he did a good job of hiding it.

"Ready for that threesome now, T?" she'd said and laughed.

"Sorry, Claire. I only have eyes for Courtney."

"Oh please ..." She'd rolled her eyes at him as we crossed over the threshold and I led the way to the kitchen. But she'd smiled over her shoulder at me, and I knew she was over the moon for me and Tony.

Now, sitting at the big oak kitchen table, still covered in crossword books, I put my elbows on it and clasp my hands. I get down to business.

"So, Claire's house has been sold and she has come into some money."

"That's great news, Claire. But what does this have to do with me?" His eyes narrow. I can tell he has no idea what I am about to say.

"So...I have talked about it with Courtney, and I would like to sit down and look at figures to invest in your new restaurant!" Claire says, her eyes wide.

His jaw drops. "Oh wow! Oh! Oh, girls, this is incredible! You won't regret it, Claire! I swear, it's a brilliant business opportunity. I have thorough market research, profit projection and a guaranteed return in year one! People will eat here!" He is majorly excited.

"It's so exciting, Tony!" Claire says, her eyes sparkling.

"I was not expecting this." Tony leans back, a delighted look on his face. "Claire, let's meet up with Nathan, my solicitor, and we can go over every aspect of the investment. Like I said, I have it all drawn up. It's a no-brainer: it *will* make you money."

"I haven't told you my conditions yet, though." Claire leans in. I look at her, puzzled.

"What's that?" Tony asks, cautiously raising his chipped yellow mug to his mouth.

"I want a full-time job. I want to make the desserts. I want to be a professional baker!" She punches the air.

Tony swallows slowly and then raises his chipped mug to us. "Deal!" he says, and we all laugh.

"And..." Claire coughs into her hand. "And my other condition is that Courtney becomes a chef in the restaurant too."

"Claire!" I gasp.

"What? You're a brilliant chef, you proved yourself in Meloria's. You can do this. It's a new part of our lives! Time to do what Alice always said and look after your 'you'."

"Oh, I don't know! I mean, I still have to work for Lar—" My phone rings out in my pocket with a text message, interrupting me.

"I think it's a fantastic idea, Claire," Tony says as I slide my finger across the screen. "Keith is going to be head chef, but he'll be delighted to bring you on board, Courtney. He was impressed with you that night at Meloria's, I know that."

It does sound amazing, I won't lie. Me, Courtney Downey: a professional chef!

But before I can answer, my heart sinks. I have a text from *Darling Daughter*.

Hi mom, just wanted 2 txt 2 tell you sum news. I've been spending more and more time at the salon and I have decided that after the summer I won't be returning 2 school. Mar-nee has very kindly offered me a full-time job when I'm trained up. I know this isn't what U wanted but I am doing this 4 me. I need to do this 4 me. I hope you won't be 2 mad. I love you.
Susan xoxoxo

"Courtney … you look like you've been hit by a truck. What's wrong, love?" asks Tony. Claire puts one arm around me and grabs my phone with her free hand to read the message.

"I have … I have to go to back to Dublin … First thing tomorrow," I tell them.

"I'll come with you," says Claire, giving me a squeeze.

"I'm sorry, Tony, but I have to be with Susan right now. This is all David and Mar-nee's doing," I say bitterly. "Susan needs me to talk some sense into her," I say, holding back tears.

I expect him to say I'm overreacting, but he only nods. "Do what you gotta do, Courtney." And he comes over and joins Claire in hugging me. I think about pushing them away, about acting strong, then I sink into them and let them give me their strength. I'm going to need all the help I can get.

15

Standing outside Mar-nee's salon, I feel suddenly sick with nerves. Susan's phone has been turned off since I got here and I know why. She knows I want to talk to her. David said rather nervously this morning that she had gone into the salon with Mar-nee. Work experience and painting the odd set of nails is all well and good, but no way is she leaving school to work there full-time.

The salon is off South Frederick Street, on a corner. It's painted bubblegum pink and the name *Mar-nee's* hangs in small lettering in a pretty daisy-type font above the door. It's much more subtle than I'd imagined. The slat blinds are all down, so I can't see in. Breathing deeply, I fix my bag up on my shoulder, tighten the bobble in my high ponytail and I push open the pink door.

A bell tings. I have to push through a load of pink and white strings now, and when I resurface it's like I'm in paradise. Dipped lighting. Whale music plays lowly and candles burn brightly. Jo Malone. Everywhere. Grapefruit and mango and nectarine filling my nostrils. Pink flamingos and deep-blue waterfalls adorn the walls. I hate to say it, but it's like walking into another world. A very pink world. Picture frames with price lists and special offers are ballet-slipper pink and scattered all over the four walls. Fuchsia lampshades protect low-watt bulbs; cushions are salmon pink. On the floor, a spongy rosewood-pink carpet dissolves under my feet.

"Can I help you?" a young girl asks from behind the desk.

Walking over to her, I ask politely, "Is … is Susan here, please?"

"Sure, she's just in back with a client. Please take a seat and I'll tell her you are here. Can I have your name, please?" The pretty girl's name is embroidered across her pink uniform, but it is crumpled because she's sitting down so I can't read it properly. Could be Tara? Tanya, maybe? Tinkerbell? I don't know. I refocus on what she's just said to me.

"No … Susan Downey, she doesn't work here. She's a kid … She – she lives with Mar-nee?" I stutter a bit. The pain is still physical in my stomach every time I say those words. The girl looks at me as her phone rings out, and she gestures with orange-traffic-cone nails for me to take a seat.

"Good morning, Mar-nee's salon, Tabitha speaking, how can I assist?" she singsongs into the receiver as she frantically types on a hidden keyboard. I'm reminded of airports in old movies when check-in workers typed into the system for any available flights. Sitting into a huge white leather massage chair, it automatically kicks in. I groan as it kneads the tight knots in my back.

"Welcome to Mar-nee's! Here you go: takes the edge off." An older lady also in a pink uniform hands me a pink bubbly drink. "Don't worry, it's all fruit juices, dear." She winks dramatically at me. A long, slow, make-no-mistake-about-it-I-am-winking-at-you wink. "Now then, let's fix you up. Saturday mornings were invented to get those feet up after a long, hard week. Especially for us women. We are the hardest-working species in the world, right, dear?" That wink again, and she holds her finger on a button. The bottom of the chair slides out and she lifts my feet up. I'm horizontal. Vera is her name, I see now. She pops a pink straw into my drink and pats me softly on the head. Taking a sip, I admit that it tastes wonderful and I close my eyes as the whale music washes over me in the massage chair.

"Mom?"

Back to reality. I try to sit up.

"Mom? What are you doing?" I hear the blind panic in Susan's voice. She leans across me and shuts off the chair. At least I think its Susan, because she called me Mom in Susan's voice. My daughter's dark hair is scraped back into a tight bun on top of her head, she is wearing the pink Mar-nee's uniform with her name in the daisy lettering across it, and on her feet are simple white plimsolls. She looks just like one of Mar-nee's employees, but it's her face. I narrow my eyes. She's so completely plastered in make-up and lengthy false eyelashes that I honestly barely recognise her.

"What are *you* doing?" I struggle to find a surface to rest the drink on and she takes it out of my hand.

"Keep your voice down please," she tells me as she turns and puts the drink in a holder. "I'm at work, Mom.

Why are you here? When did you get back?" She takes my arm and moves me to the edge of the salon.

"What do you mean you're at work? Why are you dressed like an employee? I thought you were doing some work experience, that's all. You can't actually work here full-time!" I can't stop staring at her.

"I've been working here since I turned sixteen, Mom. I earn my own money, and I've saved nearly five hundred euros. I'm saving for hair extensions and a limited-edition pink GHD." She looks down to her feet.

"You have amazing hair," I say, for some bizarre reason. She doesn't answer me. "Why didn't you tell me you worked here?" is all I can say.

"Because we knew how you would react. But now I'm sixteen I'm legally allowed to have a job. I love what I do, Mom."

I know my face isn't exactly supportive or proud, and it's not the fact she's working that upsets me: it's the lies they all spin me. I feel cheated, and a fool. I deserve the truth at the very least. David should have told me.

"How do you work with those eyelashes?" I say before my mouth gets approval from my brain. She's like a child of the sixties. A Mary Quant poster. Her eyes roll.

"I'm really busy, Mom. I'm in the middle of a Brazilian."

"You wax now? I thought you could only do nails?" I'm astounded.

"No. Mar-nee taught me how to wax. And if you don't mind, my client is in a compromising position and he's got a wedding to get to—"

"*He?*" I interrupt her with an unexpected shout and I know my eyes are all but popping out of my head.

241

"Shush!" Both Tabitha the receptionist and Susan hiss at me at the same time.

"Yes, Mom, he … Men do get waxed too, you know." She rolls her heavily made-up eyes at me.

My mouth hangs open. I am appalled and mad as hell. "You are only sixteen!" I grit my teeth as Mar-nee appears.

"Do we have a problem here, Courtney?" She's wearing blue surgical gloves, as though she's just delivered a baby cow. "Perhaps we can take this into my office. Tabitha, can you bring Mrs Nicola Pawley a Buck's Fizz and tell her I'll be ten minutes. I've some cooling gel on her now. This way, please."

I follow her out the back into a small office. It's stuffed with supplies of all sorts and a pink laptop sits in the corner. There are two seats. Susan sits, as does Mar-nee. I stand.

"I … I don't think it's appropriate for my sixteen-year-old daughter to wax the penis of a man!" I say.

"Is that so," Mar-nee says.

"That is so!" I reiterate, clenching my teeth together.

"Well actually, Courtney, the penis doesn't grow hairs so much. It's the surrounding area."

"Shut up, Mar-nee, you know what I mean!" I spit at her.

"Oh, Mom, you are so embarrassing … please go." Susan shuts her eyes tight.

"I'm calling your father right now!" I grab in my bag for my phone.

"How very sexist you are, Courtney." Mar-nee tut-tuts.

"This has got nothing to do with being sexist, Mar-nee,

242

this is to do with being totally inappropriate," I hiss again.

"Human bodies are nature, chicken, it's all natural. Why make it out to be something sexual when it's not?"

"Because it's inappropriate!" I shout now.

"Well, I'm sorry you feel that way, but we don't. And could you please respect our place of work and keep your voice down?" Mar-nee asks me quietly.

"I can't believe you, Mar-nee. Why can't you let her be a child? Why are you assisting in her trying to grow up way too fast? It's wrong of you ... very wrong." I open the office door. "I'm calling David." I hit his number on speed dial and it rings. "David!"

I turn my back on them as Mar-nee puts her hand firmly on the small of my back and moves me outside.

"David, did you know Susan is actually working in Mar-nee's, and not only that: she is waxing men's private parts!" I say, walking away from her through the strings and out the main door. Mar-nee shuts the door behind me, and I'm sure I hear her turn the lock.

"I did. They are all just bodies, Courtney, no need to sexualise the treatment ... Just chillax," he tells me.

"That's not what I'm doing ..." Then I stop and turn. Mar-nee has raised the slat blinds and is looking out at me. I raise my middle finger to her and keep walking, heart thumping in my chest. I swallow hard.

"David, I can't believe that you truly think it's okay for Susan to be doing this job," I pant.

"Well, I do," he says.

"How could you?" I have to stop and catch my breath, so I lean against a pillar.

"Just because you seem to think everything to do with

243

the male body is grotesque, doesn't mean other people do!" He raises his voice now.

"That's not true!" I protest. I certainly don't think Tony Becker's body is grotesque. I shiver.

"Well, that's how you made me feel about my body. For years. Look, I've a leaky boiler here and an old-age pensioner who is literally standing over my every move. Susan's saving money. We are teaching her the value of working for your own money – we don't give her pocket money. Mar-nee went to work when she was fifteen, and look what she built up for herself! Her own successful business. Mar-nee is a businesswoman, Courtney, whether you like to admit that or not. Personally, as Susan's father, I truly believe we are setting good moral practices for her. Courtney, we are teaching her how to survive in the real world. We are teaching her how to be independent."

"It's not the fact she has a job ... Don't do this to me, and don't make me feel like I'm totally overreacting!" I squeeze my fist tightly around the phone.

"Well, you are. You really just need to chillax," he tells me quietly.

"David, if you tell me to chillax one more bloody time, I swear to God I will pull every blade of my hair out!" I pinch my cheek. It's childish, I know, but my temper is up.

"Courtney, why don't you want me to be happy? Why are you always causing trouble? It's two zero one seven. We co-parent. It's always going to be tougher. We were brave enough to avoid the courts and Susan more or less rolled with the new way her life was going. Mar-nee loves her. Mar-nee is truly a good person, but you just won't give her a chance," he tells me.

"She makes you look like an idiot, David!" It's all coming out now as I lean against my supportive lamp post on a warm Saturday afternoon. "Mar-nee knows what she's doing with Susan: she's stealing my daughter because she doesn't have one of her own! I'm betting being pregnant wouldn't have suited her, with a growing belly and stretch marks and the occasional unintended wee!" Oh, what am I saying? I grimace at my own words.

David says nothing for a few moments, and just when I'm sure he's hung up, he speaks so quietly that I have to press the phone hard into my ear and put my index finger in the other to hear him properly.

"If you must know, Mar-nee had cervical cancer when she was twenty-five years old and had to have a full hyster-ectomy. Just like you at that age, she desperately wanted children of her own. But she had to just pick herself up and get on with it. You never wanted me, but she does, and I think that's where you hold the biggest grudge!" David's voice rises at the end of the sentence. He is very annoyed now.

"I'm sorry..."

"Oh please, what do you care?"

"I do care about people's lives and feelings, David, you know that...And let's not pretend we never had any good times. We did," I remind him.

"From the day you fell pregnant with Susan, you pushed me out. You didn't want to know any more. I don't really remember any good times, I just remember fighting to keep my place in that family. I remember feeling lonely and isolated and constantly petrified that I'd wake up one morning and you would ask me to leave, or that you would just take my daughter and go. That's what I remember."

"I'd never have left you," I tell him. But I'm not sure that it's true.

"Maybe, maybe not … but I am where I am now, so why can't you just do your own thing and leave us alone?"

"Because you are Susan's father. You need to think about that when you're swanning around Aldi in your three-sizes-too-small jeans!" I'm honest with him now.

"Susan loves me for who I am," he preaches.

"People are laughing at you, David, do you realise that?" I hear how mean I sound, but I'm speaking the truth: they are.

"Who cares? I am who I am," he tells me.

"But that *isn't* you! That's my whole point! Mar-nee changed you! Can you not see that?" I'm exasperated.

"No, Courtney, maybe Mar-nee accepted me," he says slowly.

"What's that supposed to mean?" I say, confused.

"You wanted a suitable husband and father for your baby, you never wanted *me* … In fact, it was you who changed me. You always criticised my clothes in the early days, so much so that I just ended up wearing black all the time so you would shut up. Don't you remember the day we met? At that event you were working at when I was bidding on a pro-golf lesson – which, by the way, you pretended to love. I was wearing my skintight lime-green jeans and black skinny-rib polo neck!"

Flashback. So he was. I just thought it was a golf look. I really don't remember telling him I didn't like it.

"I'd always been flamboyant and carefree, but you knocked it all out of me. I was so miserable in our marriage, and not because you are a bad person ... but because you never loved me," he tells me with a strong voice. Stronger than I've ever known him to be.

"I ... I thought I did."

"You didn't, and I should have gone years ago. It was Mar-nee who told me to talk to you ... to tell you all this ... but I never seemed to be able to do it to you."

"So you just both decided to start an affair." I might as well say it, if he's making himself out to be Mr Hard-Done-By.

"It really was love at first sight, Courtney. It was like we'd known each other all our lives ... But no, you are right: I should have talked to you first and moved out before I started anything with Mar-nee. But you see ... deep down, I knew you didn't really care."

And he was right. I didn't really care. How selfish of me. I look up at the big yellow double-decker bus passing me by. "I'm sorry, David," I say when the thunderous sound from the engine dies away. In its trail is a long rod of smoke and the smell of sulphur.

"Look, it's fine. I have moved on. I'm completely happy. I don't want you to think that Susan living with us is in any way malicious, because I swear on her life it isn't. She's growing up. She's changing. You want her to stay a child for ever," he says.

What's the point? I think now. I can shout and scream till I'm blue in the face, but at the end of the day he's right.

247

I push myself off the lamp post and walk wearily towards my car.

"I'm not back here just to talk to Susan, David. I came to tell her about an opportunity that's come my way. I'd better tell you too. I've been offered a chef job in a restaurant in St Ives. Claire's investing in it."

"Oh, Courtney, that's fantastic!" He exudes happiness for me. Good for him. I have to let go.

"If things work out, I want to stay there after the summer. You're right: Susan has her own life right now. She can come and live with me whenever she wants, but right now, I'm doing this for me." I unlock my car, which is parked on the roadside, and sit into the driver's seat.

"I'm proud of you," he says now in an Oprah-type voice. I find it condescending, though I really don't want to. What is wrong with me? He's being so nice. I start the engine and the phone switches over to the hands-free. Indicating, I pull out into the busy Saturday Dawson Street traffic.

"This couldn't have worked out any better," my ex-husband continues.

"Well, it could have really, David ... My daughter might have wanted to come with me." I stab my foot on the brake as someone cuts in front of me on a speeding, noise-polluting motorbike.

"She doesn't want to leave Dublin. It's not personal, you must see that?"

"I think it is – I think Mar-nee's turned her against me," I reply.

"Oh chillax, don't be a numpty!"

"It's what I think. So I'll talk to Susan myself, if you

248

don't mind, but I wanted to tell you myself. I'll be in touch, obviously."

Tears pierce my eyes as I drive towards Dun Laoghaire. I know he's right, of course. Yes, I have to let go of my old life. Susan will always remain the one true love of my life, but like I told Claire, she needs me to be a role model now. When I talk to her, I want to make it clear that I will always be there for her.

Driving home, I recall the last sixteen years. It all. From the thrilling blue line on the pregnancy test to the overwhelming love and joy in the delivery ward to the first day of primary school. Scenarios play out in my head: the two of us cooking in the kitchen and laughing, all the way up to this present day of her standing, staring at me in her work uniform at Mar-nee's. Then something occurs to me. It strikes me hard and I expend a long, slow breath. Not for one second in those last sixteen years of memories did I see David. He wasn't there. Yet he had been there. I'd ignored him.

I find his number in recently dialled and I call him again.

"Yes, Courtney?" he answers, sounding somewhat despondent that it's me again.

"David, I'm so sorry. For everything. Forgive me. I really am happy that you have found love. You won't get any more hassle from me, I promise you that. You're a good guy, David, and an amazing father. Susan is a very lucky girl." It feels good to say it.

"Thank you. That's so nice," he says.

"I mean it," I say.

"Mar-nee tells me you gave her the finger." There is a light tone to his voice.

"I shall apologise," I say.

"Oh, no need. Mar-nee thought it was hilarious! She said you two have crossed the line and she's not afraid of you any more. You flipping the bird humanised you in her head." He laughs.

"Afraid of me?" I ask. Why on earth would Mar-nee be afraid of me?

"Oh yeah, Mar-nee was terrified of you. You were always so cold and she thinks you look down on her intel-lectually, but she just told me anyone who gives the finger like that is a legend! She's so funny, Mar-nee." He laughs harder now.

"I'm no intellectual, David, you know that!" I tell him as I turn into the driveway. "Oh!" I shout.

"What?" he asks.

"Oh…It's Susan. She's sitting on the wall of the house," I say, amazed.

"Be calm with her!" His anxiety rises, and I smile.

"It's fine, don't worry … You really need to chillax, David." I laugh as I cut the call and kill the engine. I'm so ready for this moment.

16

Susan pushes herself up off the wall as I get out of the car and my phone beeps. I ignore it.

"I don't want to fight, Mom," are the first words from her mouth. "I just need to know what was so important that you had to come to the salon to speak to me. I have to be back at work in half an hour. I've a client booked in."

"Let's make a quick pot of tea then, shall we?" I suggest, and she nods as I open the door. Susan looks on the side table in the hall for post and makes her way down to the kitchen. Following her in, I fill the kettle and we stand.

"Did you want to talk to me about something urgent, Mom?"

"I did, love ... I made a colossal life decision for myself. I'm going to stay on in St Ives after the summer. Claire is staying in Cornwall and investing in a restaurant, and I've been offered a job there. I'm going to be a chef."

"And leave me here?" Her eyes widen in shock.

"Isn't that what you want?" I say calmly.

"Well, yeah, for now … but I might change my mind, Mom, and want to come back here."

"This house will always be your home. It's your Dad's house, love. I'm afraid I won't be living here any more, though. It's time I made a fresh start in my life too." She wants to be a grown-up, and this is the grown-up reality of our situation.

"I know that sounds ridiculous after all the shouting I've done to be taken seriously as an adult. Totally ridiculous. But I just … Well, I … This is our home, Mom."

"I'm guessing Daddy and Mar-nee will move back here, love. They'd be mad not to … So this will always be your home," I reassure her as she sits. I take two cups out and move to the fridge for the milk for me. I remember she's a vegan. I'm not pushing anything on her any more.

"So you're not going back to school," I say as I stare into the fridge. I get the milk and await her answer. None comes, so I turn and look at her. She's looking at me. She shakes her head.

"No. I start work full-time in Mar-nee's in September, Mom. I have two beautician courses I have to complete between now and then. Mar-nee is paying for them. I'm studying nights at the moment."

"I really wanted you to get an education, Susan." I pour the boiling water onto the tea bags. Surprisingly, I'm very calm. I've played out this conversation in my head over and over again since she texted to tell me she wasn't going back to school.

"But I *am* getting an education, Mom – a life education. I'm not good in school, I don't have the aptitude for it. I can't keep up. I hate it … *hated* it."

She hits the "hated" like it's very much in the past tense, and this seems to please her. Squeezing the tea bags, I add milk to mine and put the two cups down on the table. Grabbing a packet of double chocolate digestive biscuits from the press, I tear open the packet and then pause. "Sorry, love, I don't have any vegan biscuits."

"That's okay," she says, and sips her black tea.

"How come I never realised you hated school so much?" I ask her kindly.

"I guess I didn't want to worry you or Dad. There was always something going on between you both … usually a row over Mar-nee. I tried not to add to the pressure. It hasn't been easy on me either."

I nod and dunk a biccie too.

"Mar-nee's so sound, Mom," she tells me now.

"Okay, love," I say.

"The last thing I want to do is hurt you, Mom, and I know I am. It's just I know where I want to be, and it's the salon. The reason I moved in with Dad was all to do with the salon. Mar-nee teaches me things every night. They're both so laid back and I just find my anxiety isn't as bad."

"You haven't got anxiety at fifteen," I tell her with a laugh.

She corrects me first. "I am sixteen," she says. "But I do, Mom. First it was the break-up and Dad having an affair. I thought he loved me so much he'd never leave me. But he did. I detested Mar-nee until I met her. She never pushed me, she just let me and Dad be together when I visited, and when I was ready to talk, she just listened. I was so anxious over school; that's why I Snapchatted all the time, Mom. It's, like, what everyone does, and if you don't, you

253

aren't anyone. Like, I never felt I was pretty enough, so that's why I wore so much make-up – because I had to take at least thirty selfies a day to post! It's different now in the salon because make-up is part of my job. It's hard for you to understand, Mom, but the school world is all about being on your phone, and every time you criticised me for it, you didn't understand how I was just fitting in. Like, if I wasn't on the phone, I was an outsider. How could I go to school when I wasn't up to date with all the latest gossip? It's a full-time job keeping up with social media and I was desperately anxious and unhappy."

I say nothing. I just listen. Maybe this is what I've been doing wrong all these years. Susan looks surprised that I'm not jumping in with my twopence-worth. She tilts her head slightly and continues, but her pace is slower this time, as though she has realised I'm not going to interrupt her and she can finally say what she wants to say.

"Like, I felt you were happy when Dad went, but I was devastated. Even the day he got into the van and he drove away and I was hysterical ... I felt a relief from you. You were glad he was gone, but my world had fallen apart, Mom." She's asking me a question, really, and I have to answer it honestly.

"I was glad the marriage was over, yes."

"For you, maybe. I happened to like our little family." Her pink-glossed lips quiver.

"I'm so sorry, darling," I say.

"I'm not blaming you at all, but I felt different after Dad left. I need you to understand that I changed too. You expected me to be the same little girl, but I wasn't."

"I do understand, love, and I'm so sorry that I couldn't

254

make it work for you, I truly am. More so, I'm sorry I wasn't as present a mother as I gave myself credit for. In reality, I didn't talk to you at all." A huge lump rises in my throat. She had been so unhappy and all I had done was criticise her.

"It's a very different world, Mom, to the one you grew up in. I don't expect you to understand it. I barely do. But all I know is the absolute relief of not having to keep up with my classmates on social media is overwhelming. The bullying that goes on there is horrific ... I don't mean me personally, because I was a sheep ... a follower ...

"But, like, what I think is totes mad is that you think it's some kind of an inappropriate sexual awakening, me waxing a sixty-nine-year-old transgender woman! Well, I can tell you, Mom, you really have no idea what the world is like for teenage girls, what I've been exposed to without looking for it or asking for it ... Guys in class thinking it's okay to send me pictures of their genitalia during school! I never have the phone in my hand any more. I don't bother checking my social media much. Now when I pick up the phone, it's just to call and text. I can be me, and this is the happiest I have ever been. I no longer have that pressure on me to conform to the teenage world, and I love it!"

I'm absolutely shocked. Appalled. I don't know what to say.

"That's heartbreaking, Susan," I finally manage in a deep whisper.

"Look, it's the world now, Mom, it's just a world I don't want to be a part of. I've been acting out a part for the last four years, but, like, I'm okay now, I promise. And, Mom, you did your best. None of this is your fault, okay?" She reaches out and touches my hand.

I nod.

"So what do we do now? When are you leaving?" she asks.

"Well, I was going to suggest we turn the page. A new chapter. I love you so much and I want you to be happy, and if that means leaving school and working in Mar-nee's, I support you all the way. And now you've told me how unhappy you have been, I'll tell the school myself!"

Her mouth drops open a little. "You will?" She's still a child under all that make-up but I have to let her be who she is.

"Absolutely. Will you support me too?" I say.

"Absolutely, Mom!" She laughs and her eyes light up.

"To answer your question, when do I go? As soon as I have everything together."

"I'll miss you, though!" She opens her arms out wide and I move into them. We hold each other.

"I'm two and a half hours away. There will always be a private bank account with flight money there for you, for whenever you want to come and visit me. And if I buy a place eventually, there will always be a room for you filled with posters of the most used proverbs in the whole wide world."

"How exciting for you, Mom," she says, and she checks her watch.

"It is. It's important to be happy with who you are, right?" I say.

"Right." She smiles at me. "I'm sorry, but I've a client booked in for a microdermabrasion now, Mom. It's my

256

first, so Mar-nee's sitting in the treatment room with me. I've been training on the machine on Tabitha a bit, but Mar-nee wants to make sure I'm properly confident to do the treatment on my own. I have to go." She stands up and smooths down her pink uniform.

"Sure, love." I stand.

"Mom...Granny Alice...Why did she never like me?" Her eyes hit the floor.

"She did! Of course she did, Susan!" I'm shocked she would even ask.

"She didn't. She adored you, but she never paid me any attention. She was always so focused on you, and she hated me being with you." She stares at me now, tears prickling her eyes.

"Oh no, please don't think that. She was old, sweetie, and her dementia was incredibly bad ... She could only remember certain things, and I'm guessing most of the time she didn't connect you to me. Does that make any sense?"

Another major failing on my part. I should have explained to Susan properly that in 1998 Alice first started becoming forgetful. It took years for the disease to fully debilitate her and she did become obsessed with me but, selfishly, I liked it. Alice always made me feel like I was the most important person in the room. She adored me.

"I understand ... I guess I was a bit jealous, that's all. I wished she had loved me too." A lone tear escapes.

"I promise you, when you were born Alice worshipped you. I'll have a dig around, I'm sure I must have pictures of her taking care of you. She adored you," I say.

"I'm so sorry she died, Mom," is all she says.

"That's okay, darling. She was ready to go," I tell her truthfully.

"Wait a second. I thought Claire was just taking a long holiday with you. But if she's going to stay in Cornwall, is Martin going to move over there too?" She rinses her cup and leaves it to drip dry.

"No ... Susan, Martin is ... How do I put this? Martin is—"

"Gay?" She raises her perfectly shaped eyebrow at me.

"Well, bisexual, yes." I'm so not comfortable telling her this.

"It's okay, Mom, I get it. I always thought that he wasn't straight ... Poor Claire, though, she is so lovely."

"She'll be all right ... We both will," I say.

I walk her to the door and then I see the yellow Mazda parked across the road.

"I will call you tonight, Mom, if that suits you?" Susan reaches up and kisses me and hugs me warmly. I feel positively elated.

"Suits me wonderfully, darling. Any time that suits you. I'm in all night." I keep walking to the end of the driveway, the gravel crunching under us.

"Okay. Bye, Mom," Susan says, but I keep walking and I take a firm grip of my daughter's hand. Crossing the road, I knock on the window of the yellow Mazda and Mar-nee looks at me. Slowly, she rolls the window down.

"Sorry I gave you the finger. I feel mortified," I tell her. She turns off the radio and looks at me.

"It's okay, I get it," she says, sitting up straight.

"My marriage break-up wasn't your fault, Mar-nee. I was jealous that Susan wanted to spend more time

258

with you than me. I imagine that's not too hard to understand?"

"No." She shakes her greyish-purple hair.

"I was also jealous that you were so outgoing, so flamboyant and independent." Who am I? This feels fantastic.

"I felt silly and overdressed and not very intelligent around you," she gives back.

Susan makes a low, guttural noise. I gesture for her to get into the Mazda and I sink to my hunkers and talk to Mar-nee Maguire face to face.

"I've told David and Susan, and now I want to tell you. I'm leaving. I'm moving to Cornwall. I'm going to sink or swim." I have lowered my voice, as our faces are inches apart.

"I've no doubt you'll swim, Courtney," she tells me as Susan sits beside her and clicks her seatbelt on. "I know this has been really hard on you. All I ever wanted was for the four of us to sit down and talk it out. Susan is a born beautician. Even if we had all insisted she finished school, she'd have gone into the business. She's brilliant at it."

"That's good to hear," I say.

"You're her mother, not me. I wasn't blessed with children, I'm afraid ... I'm her friend. I love her, she's a great young woman, and I worship David. Courtney, he's the best thing that has ever happened to me. I thought I'd be single for ever. No one really understood me, but he does. He's a miracle to me." Mar-nee is clutching the steering wheel and I can see her knuckles are white.

"God, that's lovely," I say, and I immediately see her hands relax. "He deserves it." I smile at her now.

259

"And you deserve to be happy too! Susan adores you, don't, you Sue-Sue?"

Susan nods.

"So maybe we can start again?" Mar-nee licks her huge lips.

"I'd like that very much," I say.

"When do you leave?" she asks.

"I'm going back tomorrow. I've the relocation business to run over there for the summer still, but I will be back wherever I can."

"Well, tell you what: why don't you come in to us for a few treatments: a nice massage, Shellac nails, maybe a facial…all on me?" Mar-nee smiles.

"That sounds really nice," I say. "I have to be honest, your salon was like a little piece of tranquil heaven when I first went in. Before I started shouting my mouth off like an idiot." I throw my hands up in the air.

"Oh, I'll do you, Mom! Can I?" Susan enthuses.

"Great idea, Sue-Sue!" Mar-nee starts the engine and says, "And maybe we can go for a curry after? Maybe I can explain to you just why I refuse to age gracefully and hope you might understand. Mother Nature never blessed me with the features you have. I have to rely on fillers and Botox!"

"Sounds good." I stand up and extend my hand through the window. Mar-nee takes it and we shake. Connection made.

"No giving me the finger now when I drive away, Courtney!" She goes into peals of contagious laughter, her shoulders shaking. I can't help but laugh too.

"No. New me."

I hit the bonnet of the car twice and they drive away.

Just as I'm about to head back inside, my phone rings out. I look at the caller ID and my heart sinks. Tom.

"Courtney, you stupid bitch, you won't get away with this! We found the will. It will be read Monday morning in O'Neall's solicitors on Eden Quay at ten o'clock. I will be contesting!" He hangs up.

"What? Hello? Tom? What?" I ask, suddenly shaking.

I can't believe it. Looks like I'll be hanging around Dun Laoghaire for a little longer than I thought.

17

At five minutes to ten on Monday morning I sit on a low-slung couch outside Mr O'Neall's office as Tom pushes the glass door open. He checks in with the secretary and then stands in front of me.

"Pleased with yourself?" he says with scorn, clicking his long jaw in that way he always does.

"I have no idea what you are banging on about, Tom," I tell him, shaking my head. I really will be happy never to see this asshole again.

"Get her when her head was gone, did ya? Hold the pen for her, did ya?" he sneers.

Mr O'Neall opens his door and calls us in before I can answer. "Tom, Courtney, please come on in." After we sit down and he walks behind his huge desk, covered in thick black and red files, he asks, "Tea or coffee?"

"No," Tom says at the exact same time I say, "Yes please, I'd murder a black coffee."

Mr O'Neall buzzes for one black coffee and a jug of iced water.

"Now then." He opens a large brown envelope that is sitting across the keyboard of his laptop and opens a smart, weirdly trendy glasses case. He unfolds a pair of gold glasses and puts them on, then pulls out a few pages and runs his well-manicured nail down them.

"Okay, let's see what we have here." He hums a happy tune under his breath as he reads. The door opens and the receptionist brings in a cup of black coffee and the jug of water. I thank her and carefully take it. It's a little too full, so I have no choice but to bring it to my mouth and suck some of the hot liquid down. Both men now stare at me.

"Now, this is the final will and testament of Alice Bedford, being of sound mind and body."

Tom grunts at this as Mr O'Neall continues to dance his nail around the page. Then he looks up.

"I'm afraid it's not as you might have expected judging by our phone call yesterday morning, Tom. Like I said, Alice had left a document here, but it was not the official will, which this is. Tom, Alice has left you some money she had from a life-insurance policy, but she has in fact left her house on Emmet Road in Inchicore to you, Courtney." Mr O'Neall looks over his glasses at me.

I spit the coffee right into his face. He jumps up. I grab a tissue from the silver tissue box on his desk.

"This is total bullshit! I'm contesting this shit! How much did she leave me?" Tom roars at the top of his voice.

"Sorry! Sorry!" I say.

"So you should be, you conniving little bitch!" Tom shouts at me, and I stand bolt upright.

263

"Oh, I'm not one bit sorry for you, Tom … I'm not one bit sorry Alice left me the house. In fact, I'm bloody delighted! Over the moon! I need the house: I don't have one and you do!" I dab the tissue on the wet table.

"She can't get away with this!" he tells Mr O'Neall, who is dabbing the stained collar of his shirt. "The ole dear was bat crazy! Couldn't even piss on her own. She wore a nappy, for crying out loud! Are you telling me she was of sound mind!" Tom's face, always red-veined, is even redder.

"I'm afraid it's all above board, Tom, and I can tell you a court battle would be expensive and absolutely useless, as there is also a letter attached dated back to 1996, twenty-one years ago when Alice signed this house over. If you both might be so kind as to sit and have some respect for the reading of the will."

I sit. I don't know how I feel, but I will not be bullied by this asshole.

"Letter dated 14th February 1996. Tom, my reason for this change in my last will and testament in leaving your family home to my granddaughter, Courtney, is this: she deserves it. I love her and she loves me. I can only rest at ease when I know she is fully taken care of. You have a home and a wife and children. I trust you will understand. Courtney is a daughter to me, always has been and always will be. Alice Bedford."

"She always hated me, the stupid old witch," Tom spits now.

"She did not hate you! She never saw you, and don't you dare speak about her like that!" I shout at him.

"Shut your face. Who asked you?" He rises again.

264

"Alice did! She asked me here today to tell me she loved me so much she wanted me to have her home. *Our* home. I'm very proud that I loved her unconditionally. I'm very proud she brought me up, and I'm even prouder that I can stand in front of you now and say goodbye, Tom."

"Fucking joke!" He jumps up and grabs for the handle of the door. "The place is a flea-ridden shithole – good luck doing that up."

"Thank you, Tom, how very kind you are," I say, gathering my bag onto my shoulder.

"I need you to sign some papers, Courtney," Mr O'Neall says. "I'm sorry, Tom."

Tom stands by the door. "So how much did she leave me then? And you said there was another letter."

Mr O'Neall opens another brown envelope. "She left you her life-insurance policy, which is a total twelve hundred euro—"

Tom jumps in. "Sure, I spent nearly a grand burying her!

Mr O'Neall pushes on. "And all that was in her purse: seven euro and nine cents."

Tom has heard enough. He slams the door behind him. Mr O'Neall lets out a long, slow breath.

"Sorry I spat on you," I say.

"Quite all right. I assure you, worse fates have unfolded in this office over the readings of wills."

He pulls a pen from a holder and hands it to me. "Sign here, here, here, here." He flips through pages, marking where I am to sign with a small x, and I sign my name against each one. I'm a house owner. Just like that.

"I really wonder why she never told me?" I ask him.

"Oh, I see this all the time," Mr O'Neall says as he shuffles the pages together and bangs them three times off his desk. "Simple really. A lot of people don't want their loved ones to feel that they owe them. They want to feel that people are surrounding them in their last days, weeks, years even, because they want to, and not because of the fact that they are leaving something to them. Does that makes sense?"

"I wonder what she made of Tom coming to her every day for the last year when she got really ill after not seeing him for years. What didn't she tell him? Alice was smart right to the end. She would have known quite well what Tom was after."

"He was her son, after all. Maybe she just wanted to spend time with him," he suggests softly.

"That's really sad," I say. "I mean, I knew quite well what Tom was up to, but I hoped that Alice wouldn't see through it. But the fact that she had already left her house to me years ago proves to me that she did."

"I shouldn't say this, but in the envelope I gave him with the cheque, there was also a letter marked Private & Confidential for Tom Bedford only. Maybe she explained it to him in that."

"I just hope she made her peace in that letter. He ignored her all his adult life. What kind of a son does that?" I see images of Susan in my head and the hairs on the back of my neck stand up in thanks that we will always be close. "So what happens now?"

"Change the locks, for starters, and get an alarm on," he wisely advises me. "As from ..." He stops, removes his

266

glasses and looks up to the clock on his dark office walls. "As from 10.49 this morning, Tom Bedford is no longer allowed into that house. It's all yours."

I extend my hand and he takes it.

"Oh ... hold on." He pulls a small white folded page from the brown envelope. "I missed this." He opens it up. "For you?" He hands it over the table.

"What is it?" I ask as he rises.

"I'll give you a moment." He smiles kindly and leaves the office.

I unfold it carefully. The paper is so thin. On first glance, it's a load of numbers and letters, then I refocus.

Alice's Secret Seafood Surprise.

"It's your secret recipe, Granny," I sob. My hands shake as I turn the page over.

My darling,
 I know one day this will mean more to you than any house, or any money. This is the secret to your happiness.
 Love you from beyond this life,
 Granny

Bawling and still shaking uncontrollably, I stand up. Mr O'Neall stands at the door and opens it for me.

"Take care, Courtney," he says, and I take my leave.

Outside in the light summer rain, I lean against the railings and write a long text to Claire. I look at it for a moment before I bless myself and press send. The ball is in her court. Then, quickly, I dial Tony's number. He answers on the first ring.

"Hey."

"Hi," I say through heaving breaths.

"Courtney? Are you okay? What's happened, tell me?" His anxiety screams down the line.

"My granny left me her house in her will. I want to sell it. I want to invest in your restaurant," I gasp.

18

Walking back into the house, I have a few surprising hot tears, but I'm happy. Shutting the door behind me and heading up the stairs, this house and this life I have feel like they're not real any more. I know it's time for a new start. The big suitcase is under the bed and I drag it out, then I open the wardrobe and slide back the hangers. I should feel alone and sad, but I don't. The stuff I left behind for when I returned after summer, I am taking back to Cornwall now. Alice's presence surrounds me: I feel her wedding ring around my neck but also, more importantly, her secret recipe in my purse. Susan is happy, and can a mother really ever ask for anything else? David is in love and it's like this episode really is over. The credits are rolling on this chapter of my life.

I remove my phone and look at my messages. There's one from Claire.

Courtney. We'll Give It A Shot. Xxx

The doorbell rings. Guessing it's Claire, I sing at the top of my voice.

"Gina dreams of running away…" I fling open the door and find her standing there beaming. A big brown paper bag in her arms is stuffed with salads and fruit.

"Are you actually serious?" Claire's green eyes light up like a traffic light. But I know immediately it's an amber light, ready to turn green.

"I've never been more serious about anything in my life." I dance in front of her on the spot in my bare feet.

"Oh … oh wow." She runs her hand across her face. "So you have Alice's house to sell, Courtney? I knew it! I knew she wouldn't leave it to that waste of space of a son! Alice was way too smart for him." Claire slaps her hand off her knee.

"So what I'm saying is I want to be an investor too! I will keep up the day job until we're established. We can relocate, Claire. I can relocate! Can you actually imagine it, Claire?" I'm so giddy I'm a little dizzy.

Claire is looking at me as though my head's on fire.

"Eh, aren't you forgetting about someone in all of this, you *Eat, Pray, Love* woman you?" She states the bleeding obvious.

"Susan, yes I know," I say.

"She figuring in your new life plans at all, is she?" Claire raises her eyebrows.

"No," I say and shake my head firmly.

"No?" Claire's expression is dazed and confused.

"No. No in so far as she's not coming with me, yes in so far as I will have a room for her whenever she wants to see me."

"You aren't actually serious, Courtney?"

"Listen to me. If Susan was being treated like this by her own daughter one day, what would I want her to do? What advice would I give her? What advice would Alice have given me right now? *Live your own life.*" The answer reverberated around my head. "I am, Claire, I'm doing this for me … not for you, not for Susan, for *me*, and yes this really is the most selfish thing I have ever done. Despicable, probably. All my life I've wanted to make people happy – Granny, David, Susan – but never really me. Yes, of course having Susan made me happy, but I haven't ever been truly, honestly happy in myself. I want to be. Jesus, you know I'd give anything for Susan to want to come with me, but she doesn't. I think Alice is trying to tell me something. She always stressed the importance of being me. When I'd tell her I was jeered at school because my mother was so old – all the kids thought she was my mother, I didn't want the sympathy of having two dead parents – Alice always told me to just be me. I'm only getting that now, and I'm two years away from forty. I'm only beginning to understand all these years later what that actually meant. I mean, like you literally said – just look at Tom! Alice did everything for him, worked her fingers to the bone for him. He never loved her back and I don't know why. There was no rhyme or reason other than Tom was always a selfish prick. Nature not nurture is what I'm learning the hard way, Claire. Maybe that's the same with Susan: maybe she will never love me in the way I love her. She isn't going back to school – she is going to work full-time in Mar-nee's. She loves it. She is happy! So what do I do, Claire? Do I sit in David's house all alone until they kick me out? Do I hang around Mar-nee's salon day after day, hoping Susan will come for lunch or dinner with me? Gift me with an hour of her time?" My breath goes and I swallow hard, but I'm not going to cry. It's more like a victory speech. I believe in what I'm saying.

"In that case, I think you are dead right," she says, now shaking her overgrown red hair and running her hands through it. "You really are, when I hear it all like that. I think we both need this. You know what, Courtney? I think we both deserve this. Sorry, I just wanted to make sure you had fully thought this through, you know. I think Susan will come to her senses eventually, because you have always been a fantastic mother, but you're right: you've cared for sixteen years every second of every day about that girl's happiness. Did you care for yours?" Her green eyes are sympathetic.

"No." It breaks my heart to answer that way, but it's the truth.

"No," she repeats quietly. "But maybe this is fate. I think what Susan's always needed was for you to take a step back. Maybe, just maybe, Susan needs to figure this relationship between mother and daughter out for herself." Claire nods.

"But can we do this? Can we just invest in a restaurant we know nothing about? Like, neither of us have ever run a business. It's not that simple, Courtney. I'm starting to get nervous about it all now." She looks concerned.

"Don't be! We will go through everything with Tony and the solicitor. It's all meant to be, Claire."

"I'm going to stay at home in Sandymount for another

week, Courtney. Martin has asked me to see his therapist with him and I said yes."

"He doesn't deserve you," I say.

"He needs closure too: his therapist thinks it will be good for him if I could come to a few sessions before he heads away. But I'm ready to do this, if you feel it's right."

"Something deep down inside me tells me this is the right thing to do," I confirm.

"What, like a gut instinct?" she asks.

"Like a really, really strong gut instinct, Claire."

"That's good enough for me. Now can I come in? This lettuce actually weighs a tonne!"

part
3

19

ONE YEAR LATER

The last days of August are blisteringly hot in St Ives. Hottest weather in a decade. I decided to cut my hair into a short bob, as it's easier for cheffing. Funnily enough, nobody mistakes me for Kate Winslet any more – not in any movie. It's a relief. And yes, professional cooking! In the evenings I'm going to be helping out in the kitchen, learning my trade. I can't tell you what a whirlwind the last year has been. Susan and I actually talked properly before I left Dublin for ever. We just cooked some vegan food and watched TV and went for a long walk. I know she was happy for me to go, because the night before I left, she told me so.

"One extra suitcase, Mom? Seriously?" She lay on my bed with cucumber on her eyes when I informed her I was all packed. With two clicks of the case, I'd entered phase two of my life. The house remained as it was. There was nothing in it I wanted to take. Only this person on the bed, who I loved, but she wasn't for the taking.

"Seems so…I mean, I never had a lot of clothes, did I?" I'd folded my red denim shirt in and shut the case.

"No, not really, but that's all right, Mom. Mar-nee has an absolutely ridiculous amount of clothes. Some still have the tags on: have for years! Dad says she could open her own boutique and she said she might one day!" Susan laughed. Her eyes dipped. "I'd like to come for a visit. I have Sundays and Mondays off, so maybe?"

I'd swallowed hard. "I'd love that, and I'll be living to see you, love."

"You're amazing, Mom," she'd said, and I'd looked at her lying on the bed. A beautiful, independent woman.

"You have grown into an amazing young lady, and I couldn't be any prouder of you," I'd said, and really meant it. There were regrets that I hadn't been a better listener. That I'd tried too hard to make her conform to what I thought she should be, instead of growing with her. If I could turn back time, I'd do it all a little differently when the teenage years hit. But hindsight is a fine thing, and I've had to accept where we are now as mother and daughter and embrace this new relationship. She deserves my total respect.

"You know what, Mom, I think I'm going to like being a grown-up." She'd held her index fingers over the cucumber slices and rotated them around her eyes.

"I hope so." Then I'd mouthed silently to her, *I love you so much*. I'd just stood and stared at her and slowly I'd raised my hand to my lips, kissed my fingertips and lightly blown my heart across the bedroom to her.

★ ★ ★

278

When I tell you Claire and I were like two giddy teenagers the night before I left for good, I'm not joking. Martin had been sitting at the island on the high silver outer-space stool when I'd entered their house. It was the first time I had seen him since his hard admission and the marital break-up. Sheepishly, he'd stopped twirling the seat and looked up at me. He'd looked very different. He was the same, obviously, but somehow ... very different.

"Hiya, Courtney," he'd said with an unsure half-smile. To be honest, I'd felt for him.

"Hey, Martin, how are you doing?" I'd replied politely. He was brave; I get that now. I just wish he hadn't suffered all those years either. There were no winners in this case. Only victims.

"Not bad ... Look, I'd love to come out and visit sometime ... when I get back from India. I think this is amazing. Look after her for me, won't you?"

I could tell he'd genuinely meant it. I hadn't felt it was my place to say anything personal to him before. Claire had made her peace with him. Even though she still loved and adored him, she had to accept she wasn't enough for him.

"It would be lovely to see you, and you know I will. Claire's the most amazing woman in the world," I'd told him, smiling warmly to relax him.

Nervously, he'd wrung his hands together. "Well, in fairness we both tried for years to get her to bake more, you more so than me. You were always at her to open up her own bakery. The restaurant will be a huge success with you two at the helm," he'd said as we all stood looking at one another. Then he'd got up and reached his two arms out. Claire moved into them and they'd held each other close before Claire dipped her head and he kissed her forehead gently. Then he'd shuffled off, head down, hands thrust deep down in his pockets. When he'd got to the door, he turned back.

"See you at therapy in the morning." And he'd left. Would he really visit? I'd felt it was probably the very last time I'd ever set my eyes on Martin Carney.

"Do you think he will be happy?" she'd asked me as we moved to the window to watch him. We'd looked on as, obviously still flustered, he'd frantically searched his jeans pocket for his car keys.

"Your top shirt pocket!" She'd pulled the sash window up and called over to him. He delved in and produced the keys and held them up to her.

"This was the moment he always used to look at me and say, 'Claire what would I do without you,'" she'd said softly. "No looking back eh?" she'd added, more to herself than to me. "Do you really think he'll be okay?"

"I think I do, yeah. He's finally at peace with who he is. It's a big bad world out there, but at least he's not living a lie any more," I'd said softly, putting my hand firmly on the small of her back. It was time to move on.

"We weren't a lie, Courtney, were we?" she'd sighed.

"Just a little white one, maybe." I'd narrowed the space between my index finger and thumb and she'd nodded slowly in reluctant agreement. As devastated as she was, she was no longer angry, just sad and a bit scared of the future.

"I've been married for so long … You know what it's like, I don't really know who I am on my own any more." She'd swirled the latte in her hand.

"Oh believe me, I know. I understand that feeling, Claire."

"So would you like to marry again?" She'd looked coyly at me.

"I've no intention of committing by law to anyone other than myself ever again," I'd said.

"So you don't believe in marriage any more?" she'd asked.

I thought for a minute. "I do. It just didn't work for me, so I personally wouldn't do it ever again, but I think it's a beautiful thing when it's right."

Claire nodded in agreement, then said, "You know, let's just see how this Tony Becker thing pans out before you get that particular tattoo, yeah?" She'd smirked.

"What does that mean?" I'd looked at her.

"It means I think you really like this guy, Courtney, and what's more I think he really likes you." She'd smiled warmly at me and crumpled an empty packet of raspberry rice cakes into her pocket. She'd squeezed my hand, resting on my knee now. I'd sipped my tea and chosen my words carefully.

"I do, Claire. I do really like him a lot, I won't lie to you ... but you know what? I've never really been alone, and the last thing I want is to jump into a serious relationship with someone, and I know he feels the same. I want this restaurant to be my main focus. For me, this journey is finally all about me."

That's what I'd told her and I'd meant every word. Never mind the fireworks that went off in my belly every time I saw Tony; there were electrodes of excitement shooting through my entire body when I thought about

281

owning my own restaurant in St Ives with both him and Claire.

"That's us." Claire had knocked back the remainder of her latte as the oven announced the imminent arrival of some magical cake or another. "Okay, well, let's eat this baby!" We'd laughed as Claire grabbed her oven gloves and opened the oven door. I'd inhaled deeply the aromas.

"We need a name for the restaurant by the way! Tony keeps on at me."

"Hmm … Any ideas?" Claire pronged her buns with her baby finger.

"Three-way House?" I'd suggested.

"It's not a brothel we are running, Courtney," she'd said, laughing, as she pulled the wire tray out. They'd looked to me like chocolate-chip muffins, but mini ones. Very unlike Claire. "Tony thinks it should be our two names," Claire told me, putting them onto a large plate.

"When did he say that?" I'd asked.

"Last night on the phone … not a bad idea. Claire and Courtney's Cottage?" she'd suggested.

"Eh, no, what about Courtney and Claire's Cottage!" I'd gently poked her in the ribs.

"What about C&C's Cottage? That way I can imagine the first C is Claire and you can imagine it's Courtney: it's a win–win!" Claire said.

"Deal!" I'd jumped up and kissed her on the cheek.

"Thanks for rescuing me, pal," she'd said.

"Any time," I'd replied.

"Work away." She'd proffered the plate to me.

"What are they?" I'd asked.

"They are tasteless is what I'd say they are." She'd

removed one herself and taken a bite. Her eyes had widened. "Oh, not bad. Not bad at all. It's the Weight Watchers recipe. Very few calories in these babies!"

I'd tried one. "Mmm, delicious," I'd said. "See, if you don't give new things a chance you can just never tell how great they might turn out to be!" I'd winked at her and happily munched away in silence.

★   ★   ★

Back in Cornwall, when I'd arrived at Tony's house one night after work, Claire was there bonding with Billy the fox. We had to sign off on the last of the legal papers as equal partners in the business. His kitchen wall was like an art gallery. Various plans were pinned up and there were Polaroid photos of the site. The dining area would have a big bay window looking onto the sea front, and the kitchen would be open-plan, so the diners could see the chefs at work.

Over the next few months, C&C's Cottage was built thanks to Tony and his team's absolute dedication to our project. Tony added new Polaroids of the restaurant at various stages of development, and the last one was the finished product, with me, Tony and Claire beaming in front of it.

In the meantime, we planned the menu along with Keith. All meat would be local from Ridger Barner, who breeds Jersey cows, pigs and chickens: he does it all. Great fella. Generations of cattle rearing in the family. We use local as much as we can. We have a range of fishermen to choose from that Tony already uses for Meloria's. Apple and pear trees have been planted, so in a few months we can have our own fruit for Claire. There'll be parking for cars behind. Seating-wise, our capacity is twenty-four. We had spent every evening at C&C's Cottage watching the work take shape, taking long walks through the village, sampling menus around other areas and house-hunting.

Every single night, my Susan texted me. Every single night Claire went to a spin class or Zumba or Pilates, and she was looking amazing. More than that, she was happy in herself. Tony and I would spend intimate time together and meet Claire after to discuss our exciting new venture over a cold white wine or a low-calorie hot chocolate. It was a blissful year. Idyllic. Claire was slowly healing day by day and her brilliant therapist in St Ives was really helping her. Although I questioned what kind of mother I was over and over and over, as the days passed I began to get on with it.

And last night, the night before our grand opening, I'd had a very deep and meaningful talk with Tony after Claire went to bed with her bag of peeled almonds and her *Fifty Shades Darker* book.

"Does Billy actually think he's your dog?" I'd asked Tony.

"No, I think he thinks he's my fox, the big eejit," he'd replied, deadpan, using my lingo. "All set for the big opening?" He'd pulled his chair in beside me.

"Obviously!" I'd thrown my hands up in the air.

"Nightcap?" he'd suggested and I'd nodded. He'd poured us two huge brandies and the open window in the apartment welcomed the summer night's breeze.

"There's a sense of achievement about me with this

restaurant I've never had before." He'd sat close, draping his strong arm around me.

"What's that?" I had asked curiously.

"I guess it's like another ... not nest egg, but business opportunity, I guess, that Phoebe can have too."

I'd nodded in full understanding. "Exactly – and for Susan too. I totally get that, Tony."

"So, we are all set to open tomorrow ... Now, the question is, may I have a kiss, Courtney Downey?" His brown eyes gazed at me. I'd leaned across and kissed him hard on the mouth.

"Are you excited to be in the kitchen tomorrow evening as we go live, so to speak? Keith is thrilled to have you with him." He rubbed his hands together in anticipation.

"I'm thrilled you gave him to us and, more so, that he wants to work here. Jessica and Federec are well able to hold their own in Meloria's. I am excited. I'm wildly excited, Tony." I looked into his liquid brown eyes.

"Mmm, me too," he'd murmured as his face moved in closer to mine. I'd put down my glass and run my hands through his cropped hair, then down his stubble. I'd held his face in my hands.

"I think I will just take this day by day ..." I'd pulled him in close and kissed him hard. We're not as passionate as when we first started dating, but it's more meaningful now. It was so lovely, and I wanted to hold on to it for as long as I could.

20

"What do I think I am doing? I can't make all these desserts every night, six nights a week! I'm not a professional baker!" Claire is in panic mode as we sit over breakfast in our restaurant. It's opening day.

"Yes you can!" Tony pours her a large coffee from the pot and I cut her dry toast into two halves.

"No, I can't. Like, tonight I have my banoffee pie, I have lemon cheesecake and chocolate brownies with my home-made vanilla ice cream ... What if they all flop? Like that batch of banoffee you tasted in my house, Courtney, that day before my marriage exploded: you yourself said it was way too sugary!" Claire is dressed in her chef whites, as am I. We look the part anyway.

"Claire, we have put on a stone over the last two weeks in this very kitchen tasting your desserts every night. They are amazing. You are incredibly talented." Tony relaxes her as she spreads half a banana onto her toast.

"Okay, I still need to dress the trestle tables and pick the primroses for later!" I'm trying not to panic.

"Both of you need to calm down," he says, gently rising from his seat and looking out the window. "Who's this then?" he says to himself as he opens the front door of the restaurant. He makes small talk for seconds and returns with the biggest bouquet of red and white roses I have ever seen. "For you." He hands them to me.

"From you?"

"No, I haven't had time to order fresh flowers, I'm afraid, love!" He laughs.

I open the tiny envelope.

To Courtney AKA SuperMam,
    We are so proud of you. The best of luck with C&C's Cottage and we will be over for a taste of Cornwall very soon.
    All our love, Susan, David and Mar-nee xxx

I am truly touched.

"That's so decent of them," Tony says. "I'll sprinkle the petals on our bed sheets later."

"Oh, T. Becker, ya sexy yolk, ya! Go wan, ya good thing!"

Claire moves to him and starts doing what I think is supposed to be twerking, but she looks like she has a bad pain in her stomach. We all laugh heartily.

"I've seen the way that chef Keith looks at me: he's liking the new bod I'm working so hard to achieve!" She blows a kiss towards her tummy area.

"Okay listen up," says Tony, back to business. "Packed

house tonight for opening night, twenty-four covers. Bernie and Barry are coming, Marina and a blind date, Steve and his family ... Menus are printed." Tony slaps one hand off the other. Done and dusted. No turning back now.

"Let's do this, partners!" Claire says but then gulps audibly. Her hands shake.

"You all right?" I turn in my seat and look at her. She's staring out at the beautiful Cornwall coast and looks misty-eyed.

"You know what ..." She inhales deeply and exhales slowly. "I actually think I'm going to be absolutely fine. I've got a second chance. This is my dream ... to bake. Yes, Martin is always in my thoughts and I guess he always will be. But I'll be okay. Hell, I'll be better than okay: I can be anything I want!" She winks at me and we gently fist-bump one another.

"Trestle tables have to be dressed for the outdoor space. I checked the temperature and it's still going to be sixteen degrees at nine o'clock!" Tony says as he indicates towards the garden.

"I'm going to dress them. Claire has to get straight into the kitchen," I say, taking charge.

"Don't forget Sandra is in early too," he tells me.

"I still feel bad for pinching her from the Ploughboy," I say. I do and I don't. She's our front of house, and she also helped us interview and hire all our waiters and waitresses and general kitchen staff. The success of the food in this place rests solely on our shoulders. We walk around the front of the restaurant and once again I marvel at what a job Tony has done. Standing pebble-dashed white with glass all around are the newly transformed cottages, conjoined now by a glass tunnel that diners pass through when being seated at the back of the restaurant. C&C's Cottage Restaurant hangs in dark-red lettering over the front door with white fairy lights running through. It's hard to believe that this is a part of me now. This is my life. It turned on a sixpence. Claire is already chatting with Sandra, who is hauling trestle tables out from the back.

"Here, let me help!" I stop daydreaming and am pulled into work. Opening night starts at seven o'clock, and it will be a glorious, hot late summer's evening. Tony has made an outside dining area like something you might see in St Tropez. It is full of flowers and he has replaced the grass with sand. Tables sink into the two-inch-deep sand, as do the chairs. All around the outdoor area are discreet heat lamps built into the walls for when the evenings are chilly. It's my favourite part of the restaurant.

"I'm going to start my prep." Claire comes back over to me, her red hair neatly tucked into a chef's hat.

"I'm going to dress the tables and then come look at my ingredients. Sandra, has Delia prepped the stocks?" She sees the panic in my eyes and smiles and nods at me reassuringly. Tonight, I have only one of my own dishes printed on the menu: Alice's Seafood Surprise. It was so simple what I was missing – some lemon zest – simple yet unbelievably effective on the taste. I just hope people order it and then like it.

"Ready for duty!" a sweet voice echoes as Phoebe comes out in her black trousers and black T-shirt with discreet *C&C's Cottage* embroidery in the left-hand corner.

"Hi, love!" Tony hugs her.

"Hey, Dad and C!" she says, and I give her a huge hug. "You know, me and Susan had the funniest Skype today. She's impossible to get on the phone, that one, but I got her on her break on the salon laptop. She is so excited to come out and see the place when she can. Who knew beauticians had to take so many courses? Who knows, I told her she might get sick of clipping toenails and come to work here yet. After all, it's our nest egg!" Phoebe giggles.

"What did she say to that?" I ask as I glance up at her from the pale lavender primroses I am hand-picking to sit on the tables.

"She said stranger things could happen. Imagine, I've never had a sibling. I'd love her to come out!" Phoebe grins at me.

"Okay, Phoebe, let's get you inside. There are glasses to be polished," Sandra says.

"Yes, ma'am!" Phoebe clicks her heels and off they go.

I continue to clip the primroses. I'm eerily calm now. Cooking is what I know I can do well. My food is good. It's not crazy ambitious, it's not rocket science: it's good, nourishing, tasty home-made food. I need to learn so much more. One day, when I have the experience, I will tell Lar that Yvonne can come out at last and take over the St Ives branch. I've already confided in him and he totally understands. This place I know holds my future.

"Just going to give the heater holders another lick of yellow paint." Tony pulls a rickety old stepladder behind him. I watch as he goes off and returns with a tin of the bumblebee-yellow paint we had chosen together. He grabs an old paintbrush and climbs up.

He is zero maintenance. Just a fantastic man. I am truly

blessed. We had had the deep-and-meaningful a while ago, and I'd told him a few home truths.

"I don't want to have to answer to anyone any more. I want my life to be my own. If that's incredibly selfish, at least it is the truth," I'd said quietly but firmly.

"Explain that please?" He'd held my hands.

"It's just independence I crave now. Saying when, why and how," I'd told him.

"Oh, kinky," he'd joked, but then his expression had changed. "I dedicated my whole youth ... most of my life, to Phoebe. Don't get me wrong, I wouldn't have had it any other way, but I get exactly what you are saying. It's time to be us now. I don't want ties either, Courtney; I want a lover who I am crazy, head-over-heels for. I want you to love me back."

"I do, but I just want to make sure we are on the same page," I'd told him.

"We are," he'd agreed with a huge smile.

Back in the present moment, at C&C's cottage, I tell him, "Claire saw a little apartment she wants to buy in The Spires, off High Leys." There are speckles of bumblebee yellow on his perspiring forehead in the morning sun.

"Will you move in with her?" he asks, neutrally.

"Ha! Not invited! She wants to be on her own," I say.
He nods.

"And as the sale of Inchicore hasn't left me with much after this investment, it doesn't look like I will be getting on the property ladder any time soon," I say laughing.

"I've a very big house, Courtney. Accommodation won't ever be an issue for you, even when you do come here full-time and leave Lar's business. There is always a room at mine."

We let that information sink in. Despite everything we've said about no strings, not being tied down, there's a moment between us that lingers.

"Why does Superman show off his pants?" he calls down to me with a tone of extreme wonder. Extreme deliberation. After the conversation we have just had, I can't help but burst out laughing at him. A wonderful aroma of sizzling-hot garlic emerges from my kitchen and I can't help but feel that, as random as this particular question is, it is the question I have been waiting for all my life.

This is the moment.

This is the moment I finally know exactly who I am and exactly what I want. Granny Alice is all around me, I feel that for sure. Tony and I both know that life right now is perfect for us, and who knows? Maybe that perfect will last for ever. Maybe it won't. But we both know it's exactly what we want right now. Tony Becker knows the importance of me being me. I inhale deeply and give a little nod to the deep-blue sky. To everyone who is smiling down on me. Part two of Courtney Downey's life starts right here, right now. And when Tony turns his attention back to the job at hand, I do my happy dance.

Leabharlanna Poibli Chathair Bhaile Átha Cliath

Dublin City Public Libraries

Acknowledgements

A huge thank you to all the following without whom I couldn't write a shopping list let alone a book!

Thank you to every one of you who has purchased *The Importance Of Being Me*. I truly appreciate every message I receive from readers and I am still pinching myself that you read my books!

For my husband Kevin and my daughters Grace and Maggie, my true inspirations. I love you all so much.

My Rock Star dad, AKA Robbie Box, keep on rocking! My best pal and No. 1 ally, my Mam, Noeleen Grace. I love you both. For Samantha (you got the dedication!) and Keith my other Rock Star bro: *In Come A Table* has to be the title of your new album btw, you talented brother, you! Niall, Caroline, Ava and Jay and our next generation: Mia, Zoe, Cillian, Olivia, Conor and all my in-laws and extended family!

My other job-making stuff with the lads at Park Pictures, John White, Erik Clancy and that fella Kevin Cassidy, again.

Thanks to Elaine Crowley and all the girls I have the pleasure of chatting with on *The Elaine Show*.

For Emma Hannigan, who inspires me every single day and got me started on this book when I was struggling big-time for inspiration! Thanks Emma! All my fellow writer friends and supporters: Claudia Carroll, Susan Loughnane, Ciara Geraghty, Liz Nugent, Ann O'Loughlin, Carmel Harrington, Cathy Kelly, Margaret Scott, Caroline Finnerty, Claire Allen, Sinead Moriarty, Shirley Benton, Hazel Gaynor, Melissa Hill, Rick O'Shea all at the Rick O'Shea Book Club – a very special thanks to Margaret Bonass Madden for all her support.

Special thanks to Karyn Millar, my amazing editor, who saved me on this edit – thanks so much Karyn for all your hard work! I will never see Cornwall again without thinking of you!

All the fantastic team at Black & White Publishing: Campbell, Ali, Daiden, Thomas, Janne, Chris and Karyn.

Thank to these peeps: Lisa Carey, Marina Rafter, Sarah Flood, Amy Joyce Hastings, Leontia Brophy, Roisin Kearney, Graham Cantwell, Fiona Looney, Barbara Scully, Sonia Harris, Alison Canavan, Maia Dunphy, Eimear Ennis Graham, Marie, David, Paul & Nicola, Kathleen Fogg, Michael, Dominic, Kerry, Michelle and JJ, Denise McCormack, Elaine Hearty, Sorcha Furlong, Claire Moran, Maeve Callan, Steve and Gwen, Sinead Dalton, Tara Durkin, Gail Brady, Michael & Marcelo, Melanie Finn, Suzanne Kane, Angela and Jimmy, Neil, Jenny and welcome Holly Bedford!

For my Margaret Kilroy – because you are with me always.

In loving memory of Barry Grace and Linda Gallagher – gone too soon, forever in my thoughts.